Above Suspicion

Above Suspicion

The Mulgray Twins

ROBERT HALE · LONDON

© Helen and Morna Mulgray 2010
First published in Great Britain 2010

ISBN 978-0-7090-9136-3

Robert Hale Limited
Clerkenwell House
Clerkenwell Green
London EC1R 0HT

www.halebooks.com

2 4 6 8 10 9 7 5 3 1

Typeset in 10/13½pt Sabon
by Derek Doyle & Associates, Shaw Heath
Printed in Great Britain by the MPG Books Group, Bodmin and King's Lynn

For
Mick Stuart
A truly remarkable man and gentleman

ACKNOWLEDGEMENTS

Grateful thanks to all who have helped us in the research for this novel: especially

Mick Stuart of Port Ellen, a fount of knowledge on the animal and bird life of Islay.

Jim McEwan of Bruichladdich who enthusiastically contributed essential ideas and background information for the plot. Any mistakes are ours!

Richard and Ida Killick, and Malcolm Stewart, for providing us with navigation charts for the Firth of Forth, enabling us to plot a satisfactory ending to the novel.

John Davidson for the generous gift of his time to show us round Islay and organising meetings with those who could help our research.

Lynda Tait and Dylan Addison of opticians Dolland & Aitchison, Meadowbank Edinburgh branch, for invaluable help with an essential aspect of the plot.

Sarah McKay, cheerful receptionist at The Vaults who helped us to describe accurately the part of the novel set there.

Donald and Christine Mackinnon, ever helpful in answering our questions about Islay.

Jim and Joan Flett, and John Grant, who introduced us to the delights of the world of whisky at The Vaults.

Grahame McDonald, metal detector man on Portobello beach, who allowed us to experience metal detecting for ourselves.

The 'Para Handy' quartet from the Forth Corinthian Yacht Club for background at Newhaven harbour.

Our thanks as ever to our agent, Frances Hanna, Acacia House Publishing Services Ltd, 82 Chestnut Avenue, Brantford, Ontario for her hard work on our behalf.

Books:

And special thanks to Andy Kelly, who lent us his copy of *Butlers & Household Managers 21st Century Professionals* (Booksurge Publishing, North Charleston) by Steven M. Ferry on whose book DJ Smith relied for her undercover role as butler; and also to the author himself who gave permission for extracts and tips from his book.

Islay by Norman Newton, Pevensey Island Guides, David & Charles Ltd which was invaluable for its coverage of the landscape and history of Islay.

Extract from *The Praise of Islay*, a 19th century translation from the Gaelic by Thomas Pattison.

For those interested in the phenomenon of painting cats, there are amazing works of art in *Why Cats Paint* by Burton Silver and Heather Busch, published by Seven Dials, Orion, London.

CHAPTER ONE

Edinburgh

A man, hooded, dressed in black, materialized out of the early morning mist. Right . . . left . . . right . . . left . . . his metal detector scythed the expanse of deserted beach. Regular as a metronome, the flat plate of the metal detector hoovered in measured sweeps. As the sea fog swirled and eddied over the sands, the figure faded . . . rematerialized . . . faded . . . insubstantial, unearthly, an eerie incarnation of Death. On a chilly, dank, late September day like this, what could he hope to find that made the discomfort worthwhile? I'd take a closer look.

Yesterday the low hills and patchwork fields of Fife had seemed very close, almost swimmable, though in reality they were ten miles away across the blue waters of the Firth of Forth. In the clear air, the island of Inchkeith midway between Fife and Portobello and up to now a misty grey presence, had revealed grassy slopes, a lighthouse and what might have been a harbour wall. Yesterday, on either side of my B&B window the sand had stretched in two tones – pale, almost white above high tide mark, shading to antique gold as it met the incoming tide. In scattered family groups, adults' faces turned to the sun, children dug holes or built castles, enjoying an unexpected return to summer.

'A really warm day brings in the haar, the sea mist,' my landlady had prophesied. And it had, but before that, a low-pressure system had brought gale-force winds and rain overnight. This morning the sand was a greyish-yellow, the beach deserted – what I could see of it, that is, before the mist blotted it up.

By the time I'd shrugged on my jacket and come out of the B&B onto the promenade, the sea fog had closed around him once more. The haar lay in a thick dank shroud over the beach, muffling the *swash* . . . *swash* of the waves, muting the mournful cries of the gulls. Autumn seemed to have given way to winter. At 56°N, Edinburgh is on the same latitude as Labrador, so perhaps I shouldn't be too surprised.

I turned up my collar, suppressed a shiver and headed into the mist, following the line of footprints slowly blurring and losing definition under a thin film of windblown sand. A dark shape loomed ahead, a barnacle-encrusted wooden breakwater colour-washed with emerald weed. Last night's wind and pounding waves had displaced eighteen inches of sand from the base, exposing the bolted struts of the foundation.

Some distance off to the right, along the line of the breakwater, I saw the blurred shape of the man. He was standing quite still, listening intently on his headphones to the signal from the detector plate poised a few inches above the sand.

'Found something interesting?' I called.

He laid down the detector and began scraping gently at the sand with a small pointed spade.

'Something interesting?' I asked again.

He subjected me to a long assessing look, decided that he wasn't dealing with a rival, and waxed eloquent. 'Could be.'

I peered into the shallow depression that he'd made. 'Perhaps it's just an old beer can.'

'Not this time.' He knelt and scrabbled deeper in the sand. 'The length of the signal tells me. This is much smaller. Probably just a coin. Ah—' He picked up something between finger and thumb and held out his hand, palm up. Nestling there was not a coin, but a bullet. Brass-coated, semi-jacketed. Ammunition for a high velocity handgun, such as a Magnum. The rifling marks indicated that it had been fired.

Detector Man didn't look at all excited by the discovery.

That made me curious. 'Ever found anything like—?

He didn't let me finish. 'Oh yes. No value.' He tossed it aside. 'Not like a bunch of car keys or a wedding ring.' He picked up the detector again and moved off along the line of the breakwater.

I followed slowly, pondering on how the bullet had got there.

He stopped again and poked with his spade. 'Got something this time.' He reached for the detector and waved the plate over the disturbed patch of sand.

'Can I listen?'

He handed over the headphones.

In my ears, not a *tick-tick-tick* like a Geiger counter, but an unexpected *squaw squaaw squaaw squaaw squaw*, the sound of a duck with laryngitis.

He took the headphones back and listened. 'Low pitch, so whatever it is, it's not silver. Gold, possibly. A ring or a watch, with a bit of luck.' He dug deeper in the damp sand. Something glinted at the bottom of the mini-excavation. With careful fingers he brushed the sand away from the object to reveal the dial of a watch. 'How about that! A lady's watch, pricey one too.' He cleared more sand away.

It was indeed a lady's watch. The problem was – it came with an attachment. A human arm.

My name is Deborah J. Smith, DJ to friends and colleagues. As an undercover investigator for Her Majesty's Revenue and Customs, I go where I'm sent. International anti-drug agencies had informed HMRC and HM Coastguard that a freighter carrying a huge consignment of drugs was about to arrive and anchor in the busy estuary of the Firth of Forth. Rather than merely intercept drugs, HMRC's objective is always to break up the drug organization behind a shipment. That September I was between operations and since I was familiar with the area from a previous mission, I'd been allocated the surveillance of the stretch of sea from Edinburgh's Leith docks to Gullane Point in East Lothian, looking out for the small fast boat that would slip away from the freighter during the hours of darkness and make landfall somewhere on the Fife or Lothian coast. A boring and run-of-the-mill assignment that couldn't end soon enough for me.

HMRC had booked me into a B&B on Portobello promenade. Situated as it was on the seafront, the B&B afforded an uninterrupted view in both directions along the Fife and Lothian coasts. From dusk to dawn for a week I'd sat at the bay-window of my room and kept watch, tea mug and night binoculars beside me, ready to send an encrypted text message to HQ giving the heading of any unlit vessel. There'd been nothing to report of interest to HMRC.

Boring, boring, boring. The only 'excitement' so far had been the midnight barbecue further along the beach the night I'd arrived. I'd virtuously concentrated on the task in hand and, most of the time, blotted out the dancing figures silhouetted against flickering flames, the strumming of a guitar and the crackle of fireworks.

And last night, there'd been no point in keeping watch. Driven by the north-easterly gale, huge grey rollers pounded in relentless succession up the beach. No small boat would risk such stormy seas. Duty fought with common sense and common sense won. I'd retired to bed. All night long, I was dimly aware of the roar of the waves in competition with the fierce wind howling down the Victorian chimney. My conscience was clear.

I awoke to a pewter-grey sky and a thick, low-lying mist drifting like smoke along the sands. There was no one about on the promenade or the beach. Nobody at all. No cyclists, no dog walkers, no joggers. Nobody. It took more than a little willpower not to return to the cosy duvet.

When I'd booked into the B&B, accompanying me was my drug-detecting Persian cat, Gorgonzola. We're a team, and a successful one, in the war against drugs. HMRC's use of a cat is not as surprising as it may seem – the Russians have used a cat to detect smuggled caviar. I was training sniffer dogs for HMRC when Gorgonzola's sniffing talent came to my notice. She was little more than a kitten then. I'd set a 'search' test for the dogs involving the detection of a small piece of gorgonzola cheese. She found it first, and that's how she got her name. Recognizing the value of a sniffer cat in undercover work, I trained her with the sniffer dogs. Now she and I work undercover together.

I pushed up the window. Cold damp air crept in through the six-inch gap, stirring sniffer-cat Gorgonzola's scruffy coat. With a *miaow* of protest at the sudden draught she leapt from the broad window seat, headed for the bed and tunnelled under the duvet. The tip of her tail twitched once and was still.

'Might as well join you, G,' I muttered.

I'd half-turned away when the movement on the beach caught my eye. There was somebody out there. For a moment the mist thinned. It was the guy with the metal detector. . . . And though I didn't know it at the time, my next mission had begun.

The grim discovery of the body and the police activity that followed were the only other excitements for the rest of the week, giving me plenty of opportunity to ponder the motive of the murderer and why the victim should be buried in that spot. Papers, radio and TV outdid each other with endless on-the-spot reports, interviews with aghast finder of the body, Pete Hudson, and input from anyone who had the slightest connection with Portobello – or, indeed, none at all.

I was not one of those interviewed. When Hudson had discovered the body, I'd vanished into the haar with a shouted, 'You stay here. The police station's just up the road.'

I didn't, of course, pay that promised visit to the police station. As an undercover agent, the last thing I wanted was my face or name sharing the nation's breakfast tables with the cornflakes. Unfortunately, by going to ground in the B&B, I catapulted myself onto next day's front pages. A fact not at all pleasing to HMRC.

BODY FOUND ON PORTOBELLO BEACH
Police Appeal for Woman Witness.

What I hadn't taken into account was the media's thirst for sensation. Every day the tabloids would worry away at the 'mystery' woman angle. The only comfort was the misleading description of myself supplied by Hudson – short brown hair, blue eyes, very tall, about six feet two. Wrong, wrong. He'd got the hair colour right, but that was all. No, that wasn't me, DJ Smith. My eyes are brown and I'm five foot seven.

But what mattered to HMRC was that I, an undercover agent, had drawn attention to myself. Inexcusable in their eyes. A cardinal sin.

'*Under*cover, not *on* the cover, Deborah,' was the gist of the message delivered in that evening's encrypted mobile phone conversation with Gerry Burnside, my head of section. 'It's imperative that your photograph does not appear in any paper. You are under strict orders to keep away from the window.'

'But have I to continue meantime with the night surveillance?'

'Forget the night surveillance, Deborah, someone else will take it on. This is *particularly* important. No matter how tempted you might be to investigate interesting happenings on the beach, there are to be no strolls along the promenade, no going out at all. Is that understood, Deborah?'

After that ticking-off, Gorgonzola's essential coat-grooming session provided the ideal opportunity for a satisfying gripe-and-grumble.

'Totally undeserved, eh, G.' I gently ran the comb through her thick, patchily scruffy coat as she sat on my knees, purring softly.

One ear performed a ninety-degree swivel in my direction.

'How could I *possibly* know there would be a body buried near the breakwater? Or that the storm would bring it close to the surface?'

I interpreted the twitch of her ear as signalling complete agreement.

'And it isn't as if I hung around waiting for the press and TV cameras to arrive. I vanished into the mist. So what more could I do, G?'

She scratched at her ear with her paw indicating that she wasn't able to think of anything either.

The injustice of it all. Ordered to stay inside the B&B. Confined to Barracks. Grounded. I was still smarting about it when, a couple of hours later, I received another phone call from Gerry.

'Something important has come up. I'm setting up an operation centre in Edinburgh, and as of now, you're on a new assignment. Expect a Special Delivery postal packet. Read, digest, memorize.' He rang off.

Was this new assignment a promotion, a demotion, or just a sideways shuffle?

I was about to find out. The next morning just as I was tucking into my full Scottish breakfast, Hilda Galbraith came across to my table.

'This came for you with the post.' She placed a book-sized packet beside the teapot.

Eyeing the package warily, I continued with my breakfast. 'Digest and memorize', Burnside had said. I poured milk on the porridge. Special Delivery meant there must be some urgency, but I knew better than to open it here. It certainly wouldn't be holiday reading to help pass the long boring hours. This innocent-looking package spelt t-r-o-u-b-l-e, I just knew it. I was aware of its baleful presence all through breakfast while I was spooning up the porridge, buttering the toast, spreading the marmalade.

As I sipped my tea, I flicked through the morning newspaper. The body on the beach story still featured, though relegated to a small paragraph on the sixth page.

Finally, opening the packet could be put off no longer. I folded the newspaper and headed for my room, ready to read and digest the info Burnside had sent me.

When I'd gone down to breakfast, sunlight had been streaming through the bedroom window. Now the room was dull and cheerless, the sun fighting to penetrate a layer of thick cloud, fading the colour of sand and sea with an over-wash of grey, darkening the breakwater posts into black skeletal vertebrae.

'It's not the best of days to go out for a stroll along the promenade,' I consoled myself, trying to make the best of 'no strolls along the promenade, no going out at all.'

As if to taunt me with a freedom I didn't have, Gorgonzola cast me a
'*I'm* going out, anyway' look, limboed under the sash of the open
window and jumped down onto the flat roof of the dining-room
extension from where a lilac tree gave easy access to the small front lawn.

No mountaineering would be needed on the return journey – a
plaintive *miaow* or two at the kitchen door would ensure entrance and a
saucer of food. The owner of a nearby B&B where G and I had stayed
on a previous undercover mission had told the Galbraiths that
Gorgonzola was a rare Artist Cat. Ever since then they had lived in hope
that G would pause on her way upstairs and reward them with one of her
cat paintings. With this in mind, Tom Galbraith had cleared wall space
next to the fridge, taped a large sheet of cartridge paper above the
skirting and beneath it placed an inviting row of foil takeaway trays with
a different colour of acrylic paint in each. I didn't have the heart to tell
him that G turned artist only when deeply upset by a traumatic event in
her little world. On our previous visit, my hospitalization and consequent
sudden absence had produced two fine abstracts, sold on eBay by the
B&B owner for a substantial sum.

I tore open the packet, slid out the book and stared at it in
bewilderment. *Butlers & Household Managers* by Steven M. Ferry,
subtitle *21st Century Professionals*. With some trepidation I turned to the
contents page: *Butler Etiquette; Looking after Guests; The 21st Century
Butler, Butler as Valet*. Three sections had been highlighted in yellow:
Chapter Seven, *Valet – The Gentleman's Gentleman*, a line had been
drawn through the last two words and replaced with *Gentlewoman's
Gentlewoman*; Chapter Fourteen, *For the Beginning Butler*, including
Interview and *Where to Start once you Arrive on Duty*; Chapter Nine, *The
Orchestration of Fine Eating Experiences*, giving detailed instructions of
a butler's duties while serving meals, from breakfast in bed to dinner in
the evening.

With a sigh, I flipped through the pages. Presumably there was going
to be an interview, so I'd start there. Dress smartly . . . arrive early
enough to spruce yourself up so that clothes and shoes are immaculate
. . . address your employer as 'sir' or 'madam'. All obvious, nothing
unexpected.

The pitfalls of any interview – the answers to tricky questions, such as
references and reasons for leaving one's last employer, would be covered

in the department's briefing. I began to feel more confident.

Not for long. Confidence took a knock with the section on the nightmare employer – the bully, the outwardly respectable involved in some illegal activity, the mentally unhinged. Since HMRC was involved, it was very likely that my employer would be someone who was a combination of all three.

I sat down heavily on the bed. Putting two and two together made a dispiriting four. I'd adopted many undercover roles, but this was the first time I'd felt a surge of apprehension, panic might not be too strong a word.

CHAPTER TWO

'As you will have already gathered from my instruction to keep a very low profile indeed, Deborah, there's something much more important come up than night surveillance.' Gerry handed me a briefing file. 'A man responsible for scores of murders to protect his narcotic empire has slipped into the UK. Present whereabouts unknown.'

Slowly he doodled a zero on the notepad beside the desk telephone. When I'd worked with him in Tenerife on my last undercover assignment, the way he had mistreated his spectacles, swinging them lazily in one hand or chewing an earpiece had been an invaluable clue to his mood. Now that the long-suffering spectacles had been consigned to the recycle bin in favour of contact lenses, a doodle pad seemed to be the current aid to getting his thoughts in order. To gauge his mood now, it would be a matter of deciphering, decoding, reading the doodle runes.

His pen crossed out the zero. 'The name's Louis Moran. We're confident we'll be able to catch up with him soon via his last known girlfriend, whose whereabouts we do know from a confirmed sighting of her in Edinburgh.'

I opened the file he'd passed me. The eyes of a beautiful woman stared up at me. Long jet-black hair tumbled past her shoulders. The full, almost pouting, lower lip hinted at foot-stamping tantrums and a stormy personality behind the smiling face.

'Gabrielle Robillard. We've been keeping her under surveillance. She rented a house on the outskirts of Edinburgh. Not just any house, you understand, a large house set in its own extensive grounds with security gates etc. We waited for Moran to make an appearance. Just a matter of time, we thought. But—' He sighed. 'You women are fickle. After less than a month, the place was up for rent again.'

'You mean she ditched her boyfriend? Was that wise with Moran's reputation?' A thought occurred to me. 'That body on the beach, it wasn't *her*, was it?'

He stared at me, not bothering to reply. Facetious remarks were not worthy of comment. Point made, he continued, 'We know where Robillard is – and it's not in the Edinburgh mortuary. Forget the body on the beach. That's not yet been identified, but it's a much older woman, aged about forty. Her watch may give us a lead – it's expensive and of an unusual design. All we know at present is that the cause of death was a gunshot wound to the back of the head.'

I couldn't resist making a clever deduction from no apparent evidence. 'The make of gun was a Magnum, I'd say.' *That* should restore my standing with Gerry.

The casual doodling came to an abrupt halt. Too late I realized that I'd made a big mistake, shot myself in the foot.

'Is this just an assumption, Deborah? Or do you have something to tell me?' Gerry's tone made it clear that I'd be wise to get down on my knees and confess all. *Now.*

'Well . . . er. . . .' Too late to cover up now. That first find with the metal detector had completely slipped my mind when writing my report. My only excuse was that unearthing the arm had been a bit of a shock and my priority at the time had been to fade into the background. 'The watch wasn't the first thing Hudson found. . . .'

'It was. . . ?' He paused, waiting for me to continue.

'A bullet,' I muttered.

His voice was misleadingly calm. 'And would you care to divulge where it is now?'

I'll draw a veil over the scene that followed.

When he was sure that I was suitably contrite and had seen the error of my ways, he directed my attention back to the briefing file.

'In case it has escaped your deficient memory, I said a few minutes ago that Robillard had a sudden change of mind. Yes?'

I nodded, perhaps a shade too vigorously.

'No need to overdo it, Deborah.'

'Sorry,' I muttered, reddening.

'As I was about to say, she's elsewhere in Scotland, seems to have given up all idea of renting another property and is now the guest of a certain Sir Thomas Cameron-Blaik, a very wealthy businessman who specializes in whisky futures and owns a small distillery, the Sròn Dubh.' He sketched a set of traffic lights. 'Where she is, Moran won't be very far away, and this is where you and the cat come in. He won't just be there on holiday, he'll be finalizing another drugs operation. All the cat has to do is tell you where the consignment's being held; all you have to do is perform the duties of a butler and report back.' He added a fringe of rays round the bottom lamp. 'Simple really. It's the green light for Operation Scotch Mist.'

One thing it wouldn't be was 'simple'. An undercover mission never was, never would be. Keeping that job wasn't going to be easy.

'He's hired me as a butler for this property?' Previous undercover roles had not required such specialized knowledge. Detailed briefing had been enough. I scowled. 'I have the option of refusing a mission. . . .'

'But you never *have*, Deborah. So that's all right, then?'

'However,' I said slowly, 'I think that this time. . . .'

His pen hesitated for a mere fraction of a second, an indication that I'd rattled him. 'Reasons, Deborah?'

I played what I considered to be my trump card. 'I presume I've been chosen for the mission because it involves a role for Gorgonzola?'

'Hmmm.'

I took that to mean yes. 'Well, have you considered *how* I am going to smuggle her into a house, no matter how spacious, and keep her hidden?' I sat back, confident I'd served an ace. That confidence was misplaced.

'Mustn't make assumptions, Deborah.' An oval doodle morphed into skull and crossbones. 'The dictionary definition of "property" is "a piece of real estate, either building or land", and in this case it's a Victorian hunting lodge, Scotch Baronial style, complete with crow-stepped gables, corbels, turrets – the lot. Plus extensive grounds, including a converted gardener's cottage, ideal for butler and *cat*.'

I was snookered. And he knew it.

The skull acquired a set of triumphantly grinning teeth. 'Louis Moran is in the business of drugs and money laundering. If Gabrielle Robillard has chosen to stay at a remote 'holiday' hideaway, that's another indication that Moran will be around. Her destination fits perfectly with this criminal profile report.' He consulted a paper on his desk. 'When planning new ventures, Moran will likely seek out a tourist area, somewhere just busy enough for him not to be noticed, yet not so isolated that he is conspicuous. . . . So that can only mean that he's got a new project in mind, and Sir Thomas's whisky business may well be the target. I'm sending you and that cat of yours to find out. So while you've been swanning around at the seaside enjoying the bracing sea air, we've been busy setting up a butler CV for you, backed up by the highest references.'

I noted the lightest of emphasis on 'we've', but didn't rise to the bait.

'Now if you care to turn to the next page, you'll see the property in question.'

The building was certainly impressive. I was puzzled. 'But won't somebody with a house like this have a butler already?'

'Because of the Robillard connection, we have made some investigations into Sir Thomas's background. He has several other homes around the world – in the USA, South Africa and New Zealand. He visits each property once a year, hiring in staff from an agency.'

'And the hired butler has left suddenly?'

Occasionally, if an undercover agent adopts someone's identity, that individual would be sent on a cruise, or flight to the other side of the world, kept safely out of the way.

Gerry's expression was deadpan. I knew I wasn't going to get any more out of him and turned back to the file. 'So I'm to take up residence in the gardener's cottage as butler. . . .'

'I appreciate your enthusiasm, Deborah. I know you're anxious to try out those butlering skills you've been swotting up. You'll have the chance in three days' time.'

I studied the photo of Gabrielle Robillard. She ticked all the wrong boxes – a natural bully, spoilt as hell, and probably involved in her boyfriend's illegal drug activity – a nightmare guest for a butler to deal with.

'In the meantime, can't have you sitting around doing nothing at the tax-payers' expense.' He slipped a card across the desk. 'This will make you a member of the Scotch Malt Whisky Society and gain you entry to The Vaults, the Society's place in Edinburgh. Sir Thomas Cameron-Blaik is a well-known figure there. You might be able to pick up on rumours that have been circulating about his investment in whisky futures.'

No point in asking Gerry what those rumours were. I was to bring no assumptions with me to The Vaults. My mind was to be a *tabula rasa*, a blank disk on which to record my impressions.

He put the finishing touches to another sinister doodle. 'And by the way, here's your air ticket.' He slid a long brown envelope across the desk.

An air ticket? I'd been expecting to travel by rail to a hunting lodge in the Scottish Highlands, somewhere near the Queen's estate at Balmoral, for example. The department were notably penny-pinching when it came to travel expenses, any expenses if it came to that. So why were they going to send me by air?

'Balmoral, is it?' I said, eyeing the envelope.

'A bit more remote.'

'Remote as in John o' Groats? Hunting, fishing and shooting in the steps of the Queen Mother at the Castle of Mey?'

'Nope. You're going over the sea. Here's a clue.' He hummed the first few bars of *The Road to the Isles*.

I sighed in exasperation. Why did he have this obsession with 'exercising the brain' as he liked to call it. *Your* brain, not his. 'That clue of yours could mean *any* of the Scottish islands of the west coast.' I inserted my finger under the flap of the gummed envelope and tore it open. 'It's Skye, isn't it? That's where Gorgonzola and I will be heading?'

It wasn't. We were to fly to Islay, the most southerly of the islands making up the Inner Hebrides.

'A bit remote for a society girl like Gabrielle, isn't it?' I couldn't see a cocktail party socialite like her trudging over the heather after deer, or standing in the rain to watch a golden eagle soar the thermals, allowing smudged mascara to ruin her perfect make-up. No. The nearest she'd get to that scenario would be a Barbour coat, man's tweed cap, fashion trousers – and venison on the plate.

'Assumptions again, Deborah. From the Scottish mainland, Islay's only half an hour by plane, under three hours by ferry *and* about twenty miles from Ireland, so it's not remote at all. However, the property where she'll be staying, the little hideaway our lady has headed for, is indeed secluded: tucked away on the south-east coast, ramblers and the inquisitive discouraged by *Danger, Trespassers will be Prosecuted* notices – not correct under current legislation, but effective enough to put off most people. Why has she chosen to go to this place, *Allt an Damh*, The Stream of the Stag? That's what we are sending you to find out.'

A giant question mark doodle sprouted two stalked eyes and an ear.

I stood up. 'Perhaps she wants to shoot her own deerskin coat.'

There was no answering smile. 'A warning, Deborah. Moran is utterly ruthless when anyone threatens his interests, or if he thinks his true identity has been discovered. For that reason, as soon as he joins

21

Robillard there, you have strict instructions to make some excuse to leave the estate and send us a coded signal from the nearest telephone box.'

'Telephone?' I said. 'But surely—'

'You won't have with you mobile, laptop, or any other gizmo that might suggest ability for secret communication. Anything like that found in your possession will flag up a danger signal to someone as twitchy as Moran. Once you've sent that signal, I want you to remain in hiding on the island till you can board a plane or ferry.'

'Understood,' I said.

But it is one thing to lose yourself among the crowds of a big city, quite another to lie low on a sparsely populated island of only 3,000 inhabitants where few roads and vast empty tracts of treeless countryside make it easy for the hunter to track his prey.

It was nearly dark by the time I got back to the B&B. I stood by the window looking out across the sea to the Fife coast. In that magical half-light when it's neither day nor night, sky and sea merged, a luminous soft blue. The tide had receded beyond the end of the breakwater, leaving a wide expanse of wet sand gleaming like molten silver. Pools reflected in mirror image the red shirt of a boy running beside the sea. Peaceful. Uncomplicated. Uncorrupted. A very different world from that of Gabrielle Robillard and Louis Moran, a world I would enter in three short days.

Mindful of the cost to the taxpayer, I travelled by bus to the Leith district of Edinburgh. The Vaults turned out to be a very old four-storey building of hand-hewn grey stone set in a courtyard surrounded by a high wall. I climbed the flight of stone steps to the entrance porch. I'd been expecting cellars lined with barrels, cheerless, gloomy and dark, so the welcoming members' room came as a complete surprise. Subdued lighting, dark-red wallpaper, brass chandeliers, small table lamps on partitions between the scattering of tables, and comfortable brown leather sofas set invitingly on either side of two roaring fires, all combined to give it the cosy hushed ambience of a gentleman's club. One corner of the high-ceilinged room was taken up by a curved bar, the mirror wall at the back shelved with three tiers of seemingly identical green bottles.

I was tempted to sink into one of the sofas and drowse the afternoon away reading a newspaper, glass of whisky in hand, but I was here to engage in conversation, to eavesdrop, to bring up the topic of Sir Thomas

Cameron-Blaik and his investment in whisky futures. Looking round, I realized that the odds of finding someone who knew of Cameron-Blaik were not high. Apart from the barman and myself, there were only four other people in the room.

I leant on the bar, reading through the entertaining titles and notes of available whiskies. At the same time I covertly studied the other members. Who would be most likely to provide the information I required? Probably the white-haired man nodding over his newspaper beside the fire, empty whisky glass on the low table in front of him, or the woman by the window pouring herself a cup of filter coffee from the heated jug. I'd certainly get short shrift if I disturbed the two engrossed chess players at the little inlaid table near the sofas.

'Yes, madam?' The barman gave a final polish to a glass. 'What can I get you?'

'An Islay whisky, I think. What do you have?'

He flicked through the tasting notes and pointed to a page.

Since I knew nothing whatever about whisky, I chose an interesting name. '*Siren in a Wet Suit*,' I said.

He reached for one of the green bottles on the shelf. 'Cask 29, that's Laphroaig distillery.'

Reflected in the mirror behind the bar I could see the woman at the coffee machine was studying the books lined up on the window ledge.

I drifted over, glass of whisky in hand. 'I'm thinking of investing in a cask of whisky, Islay whisky, to be exact. Would any of these books be useful?'

'Whisky futures? Can't help you, I'm afraid. The person to ask is Alistair over there.' She nodded in the direction of the man dozing on the sofa. 'He's one of our oldest members. He'll know about futures, or point you in the direction of someone who does.'

I settled myself on the opposite sofa and stretched out my legs to nudge his foot. His head came up.

'Sorry,' I said. 'Hope I didn't disturb you.'

He smiled. 'Not at all. New member, are you? Haven't seen you around before, have I?'

'No, I've just joined. I'm hoping to invest in a cask or two, combine business with pleasure, you might say.'

'Whisky futures?' He nodded. 'I know a bit about that, but Cameron-Blaik's the man to ask. He's been doing well in that line recently, they say.'

I took a sip of whisky.

He smiled. 'Have you tried *Viking Warrior*? The smoke's very pronounced.' He toyed meaningfully with his empty glass.

'Can I get you one?'

We savoured our drams and watched the flames flickering over the coals while he told me how money could be made from investing in whisky.

'. . . but as I said, Cameron-Blaik's the man to get hold of.' He finished the whisky and folded the newspaper. 'He's made a packet recently. He needed to. Sròn Dubh, the small distillery he inherited from his father has been losing money for some time. Rumours were that it was about to be mothballed.'

'Sounds like the man I need to talk to. Does he come here regularly?'

'At least once a week, but come to think of it, I haven't seen him recently.' He pursed his lips in thought. 'Last time was a couple of weeks ago when he hired the private room to entertain a few guests. They had a drink in here first. One was a very pretty young lady, foreign by the sound of it.' He winked. 'She and Sir Thomas were very attentive to each other. Don't know what his wife would say if she heard about it.'

'So she wasn't there, then?'

He gave a man-of-the-world shrug. 'We all need our bit of freedom in a marriage, know what I mean? And besides, Lady Amelia's not a whisky drinker. She often doesn't go with him on his visits to Islay. She's got her own interests and her own circle of friends.'

On the bus back to Portobello I thought about what I'd learned. Was it significant that Cameron-Blaik had recently found an answer to his financial difficulties? And could that young attractive woman at his private party have been Gabrielle Robillard?

CHAPTER THREE

The tiny plane circled, lining up for landing. Beneath the wing, beads of white houses were strung out along an aquamarine bay fringed with white sand and green fields, a tourist poster come to life. A sideways lurch, then with a thump we were down, rushing along the runway, engines screaming in reverse thrust. Islay airport's terminal building was a low white shed topped by a mini control tower. On a pole in front, the blue and white flag of Scotland fluttered a welcome in the stiff breeze.

While I had been enjoying marvellous views of green islands and blue inlets, Gorgonzola had travelled in the hold in a regulation small-animal box. I knew that she would be in a foul mood. And I couldn't really blame her: to the constriction of the hated cat carrier had been added the indignity of treatment as a piece of luggage. To arrive with a cat would have blown my role as a butler, so I swapped the regulation air travel box for a wicker basket that could have held anything, and headed for the pre-booked rental car that was waiting for me just outside the airport building. Watched by furious copper eyes glaring through one of the handholes, I heaved the basket onto the front passenger seat and secured it with the seatbelt. *Tshssh. Thwack.* A large furry paw battered the lid's securing strap.

This temper tantrum of G's was an ideal opportunity to practise the butler techniques I'd been studying on the journey. From the driver's seat I reached over and delved in my bag for the butler manual and turned to chapter three, *Sticky Wickets: Tricky Situations That Can Occur.*

'Listen to this, G. *Guests can often be prima donnas requiring kid-glove treatment.*' I fixed her with a stern look. 'A prima donna is an extremely sensitive, vain, or temperamental person. That's you.'

Tshssh. Her eyes narrowed to slits. *Thwack.* With an ominous splintering *cra-ack* three razor-sharp claws penetrated the wickerwork.

Hmm. Not quite the response I was looking for. Where had I gone wrong? *A good butler is never confrontational or judgemental.* Oops, I'd just managed to score not one, but two own-goals. A change of tactics was obviously needed. I consulted the book again. *Put all parties as much at ease as the situation will allow.*

I poked a finger through the hand hole and tickled her behind an ear. 'There, there, don't fret,' I soothed. 'In another half-hour madam will be in residence.' Only a small white lie. The journey would take double that time, but what the head doesn't know, the heart can't grieve over.

Claws withdrew through the wicker, a low grumble signified partial appeasement. Deciding that I could count this as a success, I studied the map of Islay and was intrigued to find a Low Road and a High Road running parallel to each other. I took the Low Road, otherwise known as the A846.

'You'll take the High Road and I'll take the Low Road. . . .' Humming the refrain of *The Bonnie Banks of Loch Lomond*, I drove in the direction of Port Ellen. The unfenced road ran straight as an arrow across flat peaty moorland towards a swell of low hills on the horizon. In the next three miles I saw only brown sedge grasses, occasional clumps of straggly bushes, a handful of farmhouses and a couple of cars.

Port Ellen was one of the two ferry ports of the island. I'd expected an urban scene of wharfs and quays, and was surprised to find the ferry terminal was a simple metal pier on a small peninsula jutting into a pretty bay edged with white sand. The square white tower of a lighthouse was perched on the western point. Cottages and lighthouse, fields, sea and sky – white, emerald green and blue, the colours of Islay.

I was tempted to linger, but a meaningful *miaow* from the passenger seat reminded me that G expected freedom in another twenty minutes. Egged on by impatient grumbles from the substitute cat carrier, I sped past the picturesque pagoda-shaped chimneys of the three famous distilleries of Laphroaig, Lagavulin and Ardbeg with no time for more than a sideways glance.

The road soon deteriorated to a rough track. After another few miles I rounded a bend. Ahead were metal gates set into stone pillars and a wooden sign, freshly painted. My destination.

Allt an Damh.
Strictly Private. Positively NO Admittance.
Trespassers will be prosecuted.

Now I had a problem. I'd been briefed about the gates and intercom, but not about the shiny CCTV camera mounted on a pole inside the gates. My original plan had been to smuggle Gorgonzola into my living quarters in the gardener's cottage, and after that if anyone spotted her, I had a cover story ready – that I'd given sanctuary to a feral cat (Gorgonzola is a red Persian but has a disreputably scruffy coat). 'In my considerable experience of country estates,' I'd say, 'a cat is essential. Danger of vermin, you know.'

The CCTV camera was angled to give a picture of everything passing through the gates. It would pick up my innocent-looking basket on the passenger seat, but I wasn't going to take the risk of questions being asked.

'There's a little difficulty, G,' I muttered. 'This is where you go under cover, a bit earlier than I intended. Can't take any chances.'

Reaching over to my jacket on the back seat, I dropped it over the wicker basket, ignoring her astonished squeak.

'Duty, G,' I hissed, confident that her training would ensure no further protest.

The intercom was strategically positioned to compel driver or passenger to leave the car to state their business. I got out and stated mine. 'Elizabeth Dorward, engaged as butler.'

Someone was listening. *Click.* The gates swung silently open. I eased the car over a series of speed regulating humps. With the barest whisper of sound the gates swung shut behind me, and wheels scrunching on gravel, I drove slowly up a tree-lined avenue. Some rich estate owner a generation or two ago must have planted these beech trees to emulate the lifestyle of the great houses of the mainland. As I drove through the green tunnel, sunlight slanting through interlaced branches flickered on the windscreen. The shadows of the trunks, elongated prison bars, reminded me how difficult it would be to make my escape from here if things went wrong.

My first sighting of *Allt an Damh* was through the trees, sunlight sparkling on glass, a corbelled roof and the Scottish Saltire hanging limply from a flagpole. A right-hand sweep of the drive brought me out onto a wide gravel turning-circle in front of the house.

'Quite a building, eh, G?'

The original grey-stone Scottish fortified keep, or tower house, had been added to and 'improved' during the centuries, culminating in a Victorian mock-medieval fantasy. The two wings, set at right-angles to the central block, were topped by crow-stepped gables and conical turrets sprouted at every angle of the building. Impressive double-height windows with stone mullions marked the public rooms on the ground floor, and a pillared entrance porch sheltered arriving guests from the elements.

I'd have to leave Gorgonzola in the car while I met with my new employer. Eyes would be watching so I couldn't even release her from the basket. As there was no way of telling how long it would be before I returned, the best I could do was to park in the shade of the building and let in as much air as possible by fully lowering the windows on the side away from the house. A casual rearrangement of my jacket on top of the basket to maximize airflow, a whispered warning, 'Still on duty, G,' and I strode across the gravel with what I hoped was appropriate butler gravitas.

The front door opened and a rather anxious-looking young man wearing thick black-framed spectacles hurried down the short flight of steps.

'Ms Dorward, you're a woman!' A nervous twist of his fingers. 'We were expecting a man.'

'Yes?' My surprise was genuine. Gerry *had* pointed out to me that I shouldn't make assumptions, but I had thought that the staff hiring agency would have informed Sir Thomas that the replacement butler was female.

I recovered quickly. 'I was not aware that this would be a problem.' My tone was frosty.

'Er . . . no, no.' Distractedly, the young man ran a hand through his hair. 'Not at all. Sir Thomas is out by the river this afternoon. I'll inform him when he returns.' He held out a hand and offered a decidedly limp handshake. 'Welcome to *Allt an Damh*. It translates as the Stream of the Stag, you know. I'm John Waddington, secretary to Sir Thomas Cameron-Blaik. Er . . . er . . . you will wish to settle in, of course, before I take you round the house and introduce you to the staff. Your accommodation is in the gardener's cottage.' Then presumably struck by the thought that I might envisage a rundown outbuilding and depart forthwith, he added hastily, 'Refurbished to the highest standards, of course.'

I nodded graciously, signifying that was only to be expected.

'If you drive through there,' he indicated an archway on the left, 'you'll find the cottage next to the stable block. Come over at five o'clock and I'll show you round, and afterwards Sir Thomas will see you and er . . . er . . . acquaint you with your . . . er . . . duties.' As I drove off, I glanced in the rear view mirror. He was standing at the foot of the steps staring after me.

The most striking feature of the gardener's cottage, a nondescript slate-roofed building, was an exceptionally tall chimney topped by a lazily turning wind cowl. In Edwardian times a rhododendron shrubbery had been planted to conceal the low building from the gaze of the gentry in the main house. Amid the dark green leaves, next year's lighter green buds were already thrusting through the seed heads of the spent flowers. Now over-grown to the height of small trees, the shrubbery was doing an even better job than before.

Safely inside the cottage, I deposited the wicker basket on a chair and undid the straps.

'Those bushes are an ideal hunting ground for cats, G,' I said cheerfully. 'You'll just love—'

I was speaking to empty air. She'd shot out of the half-open door and vanished into the bushes. I wasn't worried. Shrubbery for snacks, cottage for meals. I knew she'd be back.

The original two rooms of the cottage had been knocked into a studio apartment. At one end, semi-hidden behind a shelved room divider, was the sleeping area with bed and small wardrobe; the rest of the space was furnished as a modern bachelor pad with table, chairs, sofa and a wall-hung flat screen TV. A recessed area at one end had been fitted out with cooking facilities: worktop, electric kettle and microwave with two hotplates on top. An indication, I hoped, that my main meals would be taken in the house with the rest of the staff. A curtain on the back wall concealed a door and, behind that, a small extension with shower and lavatory, a great improvement on the chamber pot under the bed that would have been the lot of an Edwardian gardener.

The fittings and furniture were indeed of good quality. But why had someone gone to the expense of providing separate accommodation when there must be a large number of rooms available in the main house?

Surely it would be more convenient for Sir Thomas and his guests for me to be on hand at all hours?

From the shrubbery a loud *flutterflap* of wings and the harsh *craa craa* of an alarmed bird indicated that Gorgonzola was in hunting mode. I stuck my head out of the doorway in time to see a pheasant batter into the wall of leaves and perch precariously on a high branch. Of G herself there was no sign.

The shrubbery would provide ideal cover for feline coming and goings – and for me too, as there was little chance of being spotted from the big house. But that worked two ways: except for its chimneys, the big house and the coming and goings of its occupants were hidden from *me*.

I carried the two suitcases into the sleeping area. One contained two weeks' supply of food tins – tuna, sardines, mackerel, all marketed for humans rather than cats, a very necessary precaution in case someone snooped in my cupboards. G would have to go without the costly gourmet brands of cat food that she expected as a reward for duty done. If I were to ask in Port Ellen for that kind of thing, the news would fly round Islay at twice the speed of sound that Sir Thomas had sent his butler to buy a five-star meal for a cat. If it came to the crunch, G would have to make do with a catch-it-yourself dinner of salmon in the river or pheasant on the branch.

I changed into butler uniform of striped trousers (feminine cut), black jacket, white blouse and black cravat. And after a quick revision of the butler's manual, at five o'clock walked over to the main house to present myself to Sir Thomas Cameron-Blaik.

I paused on the front steps, as if to admire the coat of arms carved into the stone above the front door. A sideways tilt of the head enabled me to glance along the façade of the building. Unobtrusively sited under the bracket of one of the floodlights illuminating the walls at night was a camera to monitor the approach of visitors. Something I'd have to bear in mind. Where there was one camera, there would be others.

The entrance porch was furnished with a cast-iron stand for umbrellas and Wellington boots. Above it on a line of brass hooks were two dark-green waxed-jackets and a tweedy feminine number more suited to a fashion shoot than the rigours of the Scottish moors.

The inner door's leaded stained-glass did a good job of obscuring the hall from view. On Islay, I'd heard, few people lock their doors, but this door was locked and an intercom had been installed beside the brass bell button. CCTV camera, intercom – were these security precautions that a rich businessman might think necessary to bring with him to his Scottish holiday home? Or did it indicate something to hide? I was sure that was the case. HMRC were convinced that Gabrielle Robillard wasn't here on a get-away-from-it-all, relaxing holiday, so where did Sir Thomas Cameron-Blaik fit in? That's what G and I were here to find out.

I pressed the bell and spoke into the intercom. 'Butler for five o'clock appointment with Mr Waddington.'

From a window in the turret above, a man's voice shouted, 'You *bloody* fool, Waddington. Can't you do *anything* right? That butler fellow wasn't to see me for another hour.'

'Yes, I wasn't forgetting that, Sir Thomas, but I was intending to show Dorward the—'

Another enraged bellow cut him short. 'Just keep him away from the back of the house. One more mistake like this and you're out. *Out*, do you hear?' A door slammed.

This had obviously not been an opportune moment for Waddington to bring up the gender of the butler. When Sir Thomas discovered that I was definitely *not* a fellow, his short temper would spell trouble for me too. My position here hung on a knife-edge. My mission could be terminated before it had begun.

I was about to ring again when I saw movement through the stained-glass panel. A key turned twice in the lock and a somewhat flustered Waddington flung open the door, his flushed cheeks a sign of the furious dressing-down he had just received.

'I must apologize for the delay, Ms Dorward. I was just going over an important matter with Sir Thomas.'

He ushered me into the entrance hall, an impressive space of oak panelling, maroon flock wallpaper and heavy gilt-framed pictures. A fine example of a grandfather clock stood at the foot of the ornately balustraded dark wood staircase that wound its way to the upper floors. In a splendid piece of one-upmanship, a magnificently antlered stag's head gazed down glassy-eyed from its vantage point above an ornate antique mirror.

I thought about what I'd overheard. If Sir Thomas wanted me kept away from the back of the house, I'd make things difficult for Waddington in the hope I'd learn something.

'I think I would like to start the tour of the house in the kitchen, Mr

Waddington, if you please. This way, is it?' I advanced purposefully towards a door set beneath the staircase.

'Yes, of course you must see the kitchen.' He glanced at his watch. 'But this is just the wrong moment, I'm afraid. You see, chef is preparing Sir Thomas's evening meal and he flies off the handle if there are *any* interruptions. I wouldn't like you to get off on the wrong foot with him, old chap . . . er . . . I mean. . . .' The flush darkened. He whipped out the handkerchief from his top pocket, took off his glasses and subjected them to an agitated polishing.

His quick thinking impressed me. Appearances were deceptive. The owlishly bespectacled Waddington was not the callow, guileless young man he seemed. Something else I would have to bear in mind.

'So we'll start with the billiard room, Sir Thomas's pride and joy.' He opened a door to the right of the staircase. Keeping to Cameron-Blaik's instructions, Waddington took me into a room with the windows looking safely onto the wide expanse of gravel at the front of the house. A covered billiard table with green-shaded pendant lights dominated the room. The walls were lined with shelves of leather-bound books of the type that might have been bought by the yard rather than collected over the generations. He indicated the impressive row of bottles behind the bar in the corner of the room. 'Sir Thomas comes here most evenings after dinner, and I expect he'll want you to man the— er . . . serve the drinks. The cues, chalk and balls are kept in this wall cupboard and. . . .'

But I wasn't really listening. My attention had been caught by the sound of a vehicle approaching at speed up the drive.

'. . . and your duties will' – Waddington broke off and dashed over to tug the heavy velvet curtains across the windows, plunging the room into darkness – 'will be to draw the curtains and switch on the lights over the billiard table so that the room has . . . has. . . .'

I groped my way towards the door and swept my hand over the top row of switches. Bright light coned down on the billiard table from the three green shades, leaving the rest of the room in shadow.

'A cosy feel?' I said helpfully.

'Exactly.' He advanced into the circle of light, and making no reference to his sudden lunge for the curtains, continued smoothly, 'Now let me show you how Sir Thomas likes the billiard cover folded.'

I produced a notebook from my pocket and made the relevant notes, but my mind was busy. There had been some miscalculation over the timing of the arrival of the vehicle and he'd attempted to cover up its arrival by that sudden pulling of the curtains. His quick thinking had prevented me from seeing it, but I had heard the engine with its distinctive screech. And anything I wasn't meant to see was certainly worth investigating. What was the time? Looking at my watch might rouse his suspicions, but above the bar was a large wall clock, such as found in station waiting rooms and classrooms of the past. Even in the gloom I could make out the position of the large black hands on the white face. Five-fifteen. If it was only a van making a delivery to the kitchen, what was there to hide?

When we left the billiard room, I was permitted a quick glance into the adjacent drawing room with its comfortable sofas covered in red-and-green tartan tweed, and then steered quickly up the stairs. Confident that he'd done all that was necessary to conceal from me whatever it was that was going on, Waddington paused at the half-landing to expound upon the Victorian stained-glass window composed of small panes of clouded glass with a border of red and green. Beneath a ribbon bearing a Gaelic motto, a hand-painted oval panel depicted a stag standing in a stream flowing through a heather moor.

'The motto is that of Clan Cameron. *Aonaibh Ri Chiele.*' He pronounced the strange words confidently. 'In English it would be *Unite.*'

I decided to test him out. 'Aah, you speak Gaelic?' I chose the 'Ah' in preference to 'Oh', thereby implying that I myself spoke the language; 'Oh', would have expressed admiration, suggesting that I was one to whom Gaelic was a closed book.

He hesitated, tossing a mental coin, torn between the one-upmanship of being able to speak a difficult language when I did not, and the humiliation of being found out, if I did indeed have knowledge of Gaelic. I gazed at him expectantly, amusement at his dilemma carefully concealed. His hesitation had already told me the answer.

Like a practiced chess player, he considered the options open to him and played a winning move. 'Well, just a little.' Whatever my knowledge of the language, this reply would not catch him out. John Waddington would be a dangerous opponent if he was one of Moran's men. He was definitely not to be underestimated.

'Now, up here are the bedrooms and bathrooms and Sir Thomas's study.'

He'd turned to lead the way up the remaining stairs, when from the rear of the house came the rising whine of an accelerating engine, increasing as it passed the side of the house, fading as it sped down the drive. The design on the window glass obscured any view of the outside, but I didn't need to see the vehicle to know that it was definitely the one I'd heard previously – that screech was quite distinctive.

I was interested to see how Waddington would handle this. Would he pass it off casually with a throwaway comment such as, 'Time John Thomson got that engine of his seen to', or 'That'll be the fish delivery van, always in a rush?'

He did neither. He didn't make any reference to it at all, thus playing it down, reducing it to an everyday happening not worth remarking upon.

At the top of the stairs he paused. 'Some visitors find the décor here rather unusual, not to say unnerving.'

The gilt-framed varnish-dark pictures beloved of the Victorian era, featuring misty heather-clad mountains and a Stag at Bay, had been mothballed to the attic in favour of a surreal display of Victorian kitsch: a row of ten stags' heads burst out on each side of the wall as if intent on locking antlers in mortal combat across the narrow corridor.

'I see what you mean,' I said, somewhat unsettled by all those glassy eyes gazing down on me. 'Victorian overkill.'

Waddington had walked ahead and was waiting for me at a doorway further along.

'The door on the left is the bedroom of Sir Thomas and Lady Cameron-Blaik. However, Lady Amelia has important social engagements in Edinburgh and won't be joining us in the near future. And this,' he opened the door, 'is their bathroom. In the circumstances, you will not be attending to his personal needs, but he will expect you to run his morning and evening bath and ensure that he has warm towels and anything else he requires.'

I wrote, *Sir Thomas – warm towels* in the notebook.

'And that is the bedroom of Miss Robillard, one of Sir Thomas's houseguests. She has her own bathroom,' he indicated a door, 'and will require the same service.'

I pencilled in, *Miss Robillard – warm towels.*

We moved back along the corridor to the top of the stairs.

I pointed to the two doors on the far side of the staircase. 'And these rooms are guest bedrooms too?'

'No, these are the rooms that Sir Thomas and I use as our offices.'
Unexpressed was a definite Keep Out.

One of the office doors was suddenly flung open. 'Gabrielle, are you
remembering that we—'

A man with thick dark hair greying at the temples was standing there.
He had an indefinable air of steel about him, a man of authority.

When he saw me, his eyes narrowed. 'Who the hell is this,
Waddington? What did I tell you about letting strangers into the house?'
He didn't wait for Waddington to reply. 'Well, who the hell *are* you, and
what are you doing in my house?' Fierce blue eyes glared at me from
under bushy eyebrows.

I inclined my head in a professionally deferential nod. 'Elizabeth
Dorward, replacement butler, sir.'

'A *female* butler. Never heard of *that*.' A snort of derision. 'Why would
I want a female butler? Get out before I throw you out.' This last was
delivered in a hectoring bellow.

It would not only be futile to argue my case to try to change his mind,
it would be completely out of keeping with my role as butler. That was
that, then. Operation Scotch Mist down the drain.

'I'm sorry you feel like that, sir.' I drew myself up and with a stiff little
bow, turned to go.

Behind me I heard the squeak of hinges as one of the bedroom doors
opened. A woman's voice, softly husky, sultry, said, 'What eez 'appening?'

Gabrielle Robillard. I didn't look round.

Sir Thomas continued as if she hadn't spoken. 'And stay with her,
Waddington, until she leaves the estate.' The words hung in the air as I
walked towards the stairs.

As we reached the half-landing I heard the quick *tap tap tap* of heels
on the thin carpet, followed by Gabrielle's 'Who eez the woman,
Thomas?'

'A female butler, would you believe! Never heard such nonsense!'
Another snort of derision. 'The agency mentioned that it might be
difficult to find a replacement for Paterson at such short notice, but a
woman's of no use to me, no damn use at all.'

'Oh, but Thomas. . . .'

We'd reached the bottom of the stairs and my attention was on
Waddington who was muttering apologetically, 'I'm afraid I'll have to ask
you to pack and leave within the hour. You'll find a hotel at Port Ellen,

Bridgend or Bowmore. One of them should be able to accommodate you.'

What was foremost in my mind, however, was the thought that I'd have to make sure that Gorgonzola left with me. And that meant tracking her down. At this moment she might be dozing on my bed in the gardener's cottage, but she could equally well be roaming the extensive shrubbery, savouring its delights. And, I realized with some dismay, *that* was exactly where she would be. I hadn't opened a tin for her before coming over here – that had been a misjudgement on my part. She'd be on the search for a self-service meal, and till hunger was satisfied, she'd be deaf to any whispered calls of mine. Yet I couldn't leave her here at *Allt an Damh*. It might mean me having to sneak back to get her. And that could make matters worse. That the operation had failed through no fault of mine, was disaster enough, but if I was caught by one of their security devices, that would alert Sir Thomas and frighten off Robillard – and with her would go Moran. He'd vanish into thin air again. And this time it *would* be my fault.

Waddington had unlocked the front door and was holding it open for me. 'I'm sorry, Ms Dorward. When he has a strong view about something, Sir Thomas doesn't change his mind.'

But he did. And it was thanks to Gabrielle Robillard. Gerry, it seemed, hadn't been so far off the mark in his decision to send a lady butler.

With a shout from above of, '*Attendez, attendez*! Wait . . . wait!' she came rushing down the stairs two at a time in her stocking feet, having divested herself of her spiky-heeled shoes in the interest of speed and safety.

She pushed past Waddington and grabbed my arm. 'Thomas does not want you as the butler, but *I* want you.' She shook back her long hair and clapped her hands with excitement. 'You are the birthday present from 'im.'

Mission saved by the bell(e), as it were. And no need to worry now about the consequence of failure to winkle G out of the shrubbery.

Relief gave way to apprehension as I registered the gleam of possession in Gabrielle's eyes and the implication of her words, 'You are the birthday present.' A personal slave was what she had in mind.

'So – Dorward eez the name? – you are ready to receive the instructions?'

I produced my notebook. 'Of course, madam.'

She gazed thoughtfully up at the stag's head above the antique mirror. 'I'll 'ave breakfast served in the bed at nine hours – *le chef* knows what I like – and with eet the morning newspaper.'

I poised my pen over the notebook. 'Madam wishes the newspaper ironed?' Seeing her puzzled frown, I added, 'I recommend it, as otherwise there is the possibility that the newsprint will stain your fingers or the sheets.' This gem of information, newly culled from the butler's manual, I delivered with an air of authority.

That went down well. Her purr of, '*Mais oui*, yes, you are right,' bore an uncanny resemblance to G's purr of satisfaction when I dished out a particularly choice morsel as a reward.

'And shall we say nine-thirty for the bath, madam?'

This time I was treated to a pout of displeasure. '*Non*, Dorward, too early. Eet makes the breakfast too *much* rushed. Nine-forty-five, *peut-être*, for the bath. Two 'andfuls of the so expensive bath crystals, Dorward. Do not forget. Now, my clothes—'

'*Gerrrawt!*' The angry shout came from somewhere in the rear of the house. It was followed by a string of blood-curling oaths and the *clatter claaang* of a metal object hitting a solid obstacle.

Waddington frowned. 'Something's upset Chef. I'll see what's up. Liaising with him is part of your household duties, so you'd better come too, Dorward. If you'll excuse us, Ms Robillard. . . .'

I noted with some satisfaction my loss of title, denoting loss of status. In his eyes, as well as in Sir Thomas and Gabrielle's, I was now ranked as a humble minion, part of the background scene. Underestimation lowers the guard.

He slammed shut the outer door, turned the key in the lock and made a dash for the door under the stairs. I followed close on his heels, pretending I hadn't heard Gabrielle's wail of, 'Wait, Dorward, wait. I 'ave not finished. . . .'

Waddington paused outside the closed door at the end of a long stone-flagged corridor. No longer muffled by distance, the particularly inventive swearing on the other side spoke of a culinary catastrophe of epic proportions. *Thud.* A door panel shuddered under the impact of something solid.

'This could be tricky, Dorward.' He turned the handle and eased the door open.

Thunk. A large kitchen knife hung quivering in the wood of the frame, its point inches from his hand.

'*Shit*. Bloody prima donna.' He slammed the door shut.

I gazed thoughtfully at the closed door. Danger was coming from some unexpected quarters on this operation. 'Er . . . is Chef often like this?'

'Fortunately, no.' Waddington banged on the door. 'Burns, calm down, man.'

His answer was another *clang* from within and a cry of, 'Get you next time, you bugger-r-r!'

Waddington muttered a few oaths of his own, mild in comparison with those emanating from the kitchen, took a deep breath, squared his shoulders and again grasped the door handle.

'Perhaps we could make an entry through the back door,' I ventured, not particularly relishing being the target of another knife-throwing episode.

'Good thinking, Dorward. He'll not be expecting that. We'll go out the front door and round the side of the house.'

The entrance hall was deserted, Gabrielle having vanished upstairs, no doubt to spend a delicious hour compiling a long list of duties to occupy my day. As we turned the corner of the house, Waddington put a cautionary finger to his lips and pointed to the kitchen window that had been pushed up several inches to aid ventilation.

'Keep off the gravel,' he hissed. 'He'll hear us coming.'

We crept over the herb bed to peer into the kitchen. A stocky man in chef's whites was standing with his back to us. With a 'Stay still, you filthy br-rute,' he hurled a large copper saucepan at something hidden by the bulk of the island unit.

'Surely he's not found a *rat* in the kitchen!' Frowning, Waddington shielded his eyes from the reflections in the glass and stared at that corner of the room. He seemed more shocked by that possibility than by his narrow escape from the flying kitchen knife.

'Quick, before he picks up something else to throw at us.' I rushed to the kitchen door and flung it open.

Burns whirled round. The dark hair curling in tendrils round his ears writhed like unruly Medusa locks. At that very instant there was a blur of movement from under a trolley of stainless steel bowls and colanders as Gorgonzola darted out, shot between my legs and went to ground in the kitchen garden among the yellowing haulms of the vegetable patch. Clamped in her jaws was a succulent piece of cooked poultry.

Chef's brows drew down in a menacing scowl. '*Shit, shit, shit.* That guinea fowl is half of tonight's dinner-r! And you've let the sodding mog escape!'

I ducked as a china mug came hurtling towards my head.

'Do you have many of these feral cats around here?' I said, and made a strategic withdrawal of my own.

CHAPTER FOUR

Gorgonzola knew better than to come back to the cottage immediately, but I was waiting for her when she jumped up on the windowsill and peered cautiously through the glass. I went to the door and held it open. She sidled in and twined round my legs, purring ingratiatingly.

'You know perfectly well you've been very bad,' I scolded. 'Not only *stealing*' – I glared at her sternly – 'but in the process nearly getting yourself *killed* by that maniac of a chef. Killed, do you hear? Killed.' Saying the word brought home to me the narrow escape she'd had. I scooped her up and rubbed my cheek against her fur.

Mi-a-ow. Mournful copper eyes gazed at me, agreeing that she had indeed been very silly. She licked my ear as a reassurance that she would never, *ever*, do it again.

Lies, all lies. 'Fib,' I murmured. 'Some temptations are just too strong, eh, G?'

She purred assent. A cat had to do what a cat had to do.

'After all, it was really my fault, wasn't it? I should have left out some food for you, shouldn't I?'

A louder purr signified total agreement but magnanimous forgiveness. She struggled out of my arms to leap lightly to the ground and stood looking up at me, running a moist pink tongue meaningfully over her lips. Emotional blackmail.

I gave in to it. Before I went across to the house to preside over Sir Thomas's dinner, I dished out the expected gourmet meal to G to ensure she succumbed to an after-dinner nap. And just in case that plan misfired, before I left for my duties in the main house, I took the extra precaution of closing all the windows and locking the door, confident that there would be no raid on the kitchen during dinner tonight.

Waddington had told me that the staff included a maid and that she would prepare the dining room ready for me to put the finishing touches. I found the log fire lit, the tablecloth on the table and Sir Thomas's choice of wines lined up on the sideboard. Donning the requisite pair of white gloves, I set out cutlery, plates, glasses and napkins, finishing off with the precision placement of a silver candelabra on the stiffly starched white damask tablecloth.

I couldn't afford to get anything wrong. From what I'd seen of him, Sir Thomas was an exacting employer. With that prejudice of his against women butlers, no breach of butler etiquette would be overlooked. I stood back to survey my handiwork. Was the cutlery in perfect alignment and a thumbnail distance from the edge of the table? I stepped forward and tweaked a knife fractionally closer. A brisk stab at the logs with the poker had the flames leaping up the chimney. Then dimming the lights to create a cosy ambience, I took up position by the sideboard.

Dinner was scheduled for seven o'clock, but how would Gorgonzola's raid on the kitchen have affected Chef's timing? Or had he been forced to change the menu? When I came over to the house, I hadn't visited the kitchen to enquire about this matter, considering it more prudent not to renew Chef's acquaintance while his temperature might still be on the boil.

While I waited for the message that Chef was ready, I had the chance to do a bit of thinking. Gerry had been convinced that Moran would join Gabrielle very shortly. In the file he'd passed to me was a rare photo of Louis Moran captured on a hidden camera in South America. Of necessity it had been taken at a considerable distance and in dim light: the image was fuzzy and of poor quality, but it was the best we had. It showed a long face, thin lips, dark brown hair and a drastically receding hairline. The high-domed forehead was distinctive. I'd memorized that face, but was this just one of the many disguises that had kept him one step ahead of the forces of law and order? The only fact beyond dispute was that his eyes were brown.

But it didn't matter if he'd changed his appearance. Gabrielle was not one for subtlety. I was confident that a change in her behaviour would signal his arrival as clearly as a gundog points a gamebird. After Gerry's warning I wasn't looking forward to the moment I would come face to face with him. I'd have to be very careful. . . .

The intercom on the sideboard buzzed. A male voice, very Scottish with its rolled 'r', announced, 'Dinner-r's r-ready.'

'Thank you, Chef.' I flicked off the switch and proceeded to the hall to perform my J. Arthur Rank act on the gong.

Bonngg . . . nngg . . . nngg The oak panelling acted as a sounding board, lengthening the deep note and sending it drifting up the staircase and along the bedroom corridor above. The first to answer the summons was Waddington in dinner jacket and bow tie.

'Evening, Dorward. Nasty business, that feral cat. Gin trap or snare, that's what we need. I'll have a word with Callum, the gamekeeper on the neighbouring estate.'

With an effort I kept my expression neutral. 'Oh, we'll *never* see it again,' I said. 'Chef's volley of missiles will have scared it off for good. I'm sure of that.'

He walked over to the mirror and studied his reflection. 'Best to make assurance doubly sure, as Shakespeare said.' A twitch of the bow tie, an unnecessary smoothing down of hair. 'I'll see to it tomorrow.'

Sir Thomas, resplendent in jacket and cravat, sporran and red and green kilt (presumably the Cameron tartan) appeared at the top of the staircase. When he reached the bottom, I announced gravely, 'Dinner is about to be served, Sir Thomas.'

The briefest of nods acknowledged my presence. He turned away and called up the stairs, '*Do* hurry up, Gabrielle,' then paced up and down the hall glancing irritably at his watch every few seconds. As he passed by me for the third time he said abruptly, 'Where was your last position, Dorward?'

Gerry Burnside was always meticulous in setting up a cast-iron CV for his operatives, so I was prepared for this question and confident that all would be in order if Sir Thomas decided to check.

With a respectful half-bow, I said, 'With the Honourable George and Lady Fotheringham in Sussex, Sir Thomas. Due to Lady Fotheringham's delicate state of health, they have taken up residence in a warmer climate.'

All true. I hadn't been their butler, of course, but someone by the name of Elizabeth Dorward had been employed by the Fotheringhams and when her employment with them ended, had signed up with the hiring agency. Courtesy of HMRC, the real Elizabeth Dorward would now be enjoying a holiday in the sun on the other side of the world, safely out of reach.

'Hmm.' For a moment the fierce eyes stared at me, weighing me up, then he snapped, 'Sound that bloody gong again.'

Bonngg . . . nngg . . . nngg. A door opened in the corridor above and closed. We heard the unhurried *tap tap tap* of Gabrielle's heels and she appeared at the top of the stairs in an expensive-looking red evening dress.

'*Voilà, chéri*, 'ere I am.'

He looked pointedly at his watch, 'Better late than never, I suppose.'

Behind me as I led the way to the dining room, I heard angry whisperings and a sharp, muttered '. . . not in front of the staff. . . .'

The maid brought in the salvers for each course and placed them on the sideboard for me to serve, each time scuttling out again as if scared that she might bring herself to Sir Thomas's attention.

I served the soup and stood back unobtrusively against the wall, gazing straight ahead as if seeing and hearing nothing. I put to the back of my mind my worries over the danger to G of gin traps and snares, all the more difficult as there was nothing of interest for HMRC in Sir Thomas and Gabrielle's conversation. Waddington, in keeping with his status as superior servant, spoke only when addressed directly.

When it came to the meat course, I saw that Chef had been forced to replace the missing guinea fowl with chicken. He'd bear me a grudge for allowing the 'feral' cat to escape. When I ate tonight with the rest of the staff, I'd have to do my best to win him over. It would be disastrous if he took against me, watching my every move and reporting back to Sir Thomas.

I pushed that worry, too, to the back of my mind and resumed eavesdropping on the dinner conversation between Sir Thomas and Gabrielle, hoping that she would drop a hint as to where Moran might be, or when he might arrive at *Allt an Damh*. But, of course, she didn't, just prattled on about the shopping she'd done in Edinburgh.

I moved forward from my unobtrusive position at the back of the room to serve the raspberry charlotte dessert. As I placed his plate before him, Sir Thomas broke off his conversation with Gabrielle.

'By the way, Dorward, there'll be another house guest coming tomorrow, so we'll need an extra place setting for dinner.'

'Very good, sir,' I said. And indeed it was. This could be what HMRC had been waiting for, the chance to pin down Moran to a definite location. Perhaps I was about to meet him at last.

I must have absorbed something from all those hours I'd spent studying the butler manual because the meal finished without any of my actions provoking an outburst of temper from Sir Thomas.

There was an outburst later, however, in the billiard room where Gabrielle and Sir Thomas were relaxing in armchairs in front of the log fire while I served coffee. It came without warning but it wasn't directed at me.

'I'll have a dram of the Bruichladdich 15 Year Old, Dorward.' He lit a cigar and blew out a cloud of smoke, watching it drift lazily to the ceiling.

I put the drink on the table beside him and turned to Gabrielle. 'And can I bring you one, madam?'

'Well . . . only if there eez a. . . .' She drummed her fingers thoughtfully on the leather of the chair. 'What was the whisky we 'ad in *Edimbourg*, Thomas?'

'No idea.' The irritation in his voice should have warned her not to persist.

'Of course you 'ave, Thomas. Remember, the one we 'ad in the . . . The Vaults. That was the name of the place, *non*?'

He downed his dram in one, set the glass down sharply and snapped, 'It was from a Bruichladdich cask. Like *this* one. Pour one for her, Dorward.' He gestured brusquely towards the row of bottles on the sideboard. 'And another for me, and then you can go. Just make sure that the heating is on in the bedrooms.'

As I closed the door, I heard Gabrielle protesting, '*Non*, Thomas, this eez not the same at all. Don't you remember, when we were in The Vaults we—'

'*Good God*, woman! How often do I have to say it?'

I went off to check the bedrooms. Even Sir Thomas's guests, it seemed, weren't safe from being the target of his fiery temper.

Duties completed, I made my way to the kitchen, expecting to find Chef there with my evening meal. On the way I rehearsed how I would introduce, or rather reintroduce, myself to him. I was looking forward to sharing Sir Thomas's menu once that rather tricky moment had passed. I wasn't fussy whether it was the sea bass or the chicken and avocado salad. And for dessert I'd have a slice of the raspberry charlotte.

The kitchen door at the end of the stone-flagged corridor was closed. This presented a bit of a problem. Now I was unable to gauge Chef's mood from the sounds within – be it cheerful whistling, humming, or indeed, a string of muttered oaths. I took a deep breath and eased the door open. What kind of reception was I about to receive?

None, no reception at all. The kitchen was in darkness, the only sound the *humm swish* of a dishwasher. I felt for the light switch. On my left was a range-cooker, a double sink and a large American-style fridge; on my right, a large Dutch cupboard-dresser, the plates, cups and saucers protected from dust by small-paned glass doors. Alongside it, stacked with stainless steel bowls and colanders, stood the trolley from behind which Gorgonzola had made the lightning dash to the door with her prize.

The kitchen worktops were bare, cleared of all bowls, knives and spoons. Perhaps there'd be a chicken breast in the fridge – cooked, of course, for like Gorgonzola, I drew the line at eating raw poultry. Alas, the fridge was locked, as was a door marked 'Pantry'. Chef had taken his revenge.

Pangs of hunger struck home. In the expectation that I would be tucking into a late meal with the rest of the staff, I'd had only a cup of tea and some biscuits before I'd come over to the main house. Gerry had warned me about making assumptions but I'd made the same mistake again.

I went round the kitchen on the forage, pulling open cupboards. No luck. There was nothing for it but to head back to the cottage and demolish a packet of biscuits and a tin of G's salmon.

CHAPTER FIVE

Next morning, before going over to the house for the staff breakfast at 7.30, I sat down with the butler manual and a cup of tea. I looked across to where Gorgonzola was curled up on the duvet, peacefully sleeping off the stolen feast.

'Prima donnas, you and Chef both,' I said loudly.

She opened one eye and yawned an am-I-bothered? yawn.

Nibbling the last of my biscuits, I thumbed through the pages to the section *The Kitchen Under the Chef*. I ran my eye down the page: *knock before entering . . . address the chef by his title . . . give him the final say in his domain.* In my encounter with him yesterday evening I had done none of these things. My score on a butler rating scale would be zero out of three.

'And it's all *your* fault, G,' I growled.

A faint but unmistakably dismissive snore rose from the heap of red fur on the bed. The fact that she hadn't gone out on her customary dawn patrol was another indication that, unlike me, she wasn't suffering any pangs of hunger. Nor any pangs of remorse, it was clear. I locked the door on G's unrepentant recumbent form and set off on my charm offensive.

Waddington had instructed me always to enter and leave the house by the kitchen, presumably by order of the security-conscious Sir Thomas. The irresistible aroma of brewing coffee and freshly baked bread wafted through the half-open door, evidence that Chef was on duty. This time I'd get a meal. I *scrunch scrunched* my way across the gravel and tapped lightly on the door.

'May I come in, Chef Burns? It's Elizabeth Dorward, the new butler.'

The approach to the chef recommended in the butler manual went down well. His grunt of 'Come in' was a decided improvement on yesterday's bellows of rage and hurled mug.

As I pushed open the door, he turned round from the range-cooker, spatula in hand. The shadow stubble on his chin and upper lip invested him with a villainous look only slightly less menacing than before.

His, 'Oh, it's you', was followed by an equally ungracious, 'I suppose you'll want eggs and bacon? Or is it to be porridge?'

'I'll have both, chef. I'm absolutely starving.' Hunger and the sight of food had driven out of my mind the manual's advice not to challenge the cook in his domain. Too late, I realized he might very well take the remark as a pointed reference to last night's bare kitchen and a complaint that he should have had a meal ready for me.

He renewed hostilities, his tone brusque. 'You can have one or the other. So what's it to be?'

'Well, er. . . .' I endeavoured to weigh the filling quality of porridge against my preference for eggs and bacon.

'Porridge it is, then.'

'That's fine,' I said diplomatically, sitting down at the kitchen table.

He ladled out a bowl and thumped it down in front of me. As I poured milk on my porridge, I heard a *crunch crunch* of gravel outside and the fair-haired girl who had brought in the salvers at dinner last night appeared in the doorway.

She flung herself down on the chair opposite me. 'Hi ya, I'm Ann-Marie.' She cast a quick glance over at Chef who was busying himself at the range-cooker and lowered her voice. 'He's still in a bad mood after all that stramash over the feral cat in the kitchen. It takes him some time to calm down after going ballistic like that. Even took it out on me last night, so I left him to it and went back to the staff quarters as soon as I'd scoffed my meal.' She eyed me as I hungrily spooned up the porridge. 'He knew you wouldn't be able to come to the kitchen till Sir T had finished with you' – she winked and raised her voice – 'so he should have left something out for you last night.'

I made a final scrape with my spoon round my empty bowl. I was still hungry. I leant across the table and mouthed, 'Do you think I dare do an Oliver Twist act and ask for more?'

'Better not risk it. I don't know who's worse when it comes to temper, Roddy there' – she rolled her eyes in the direction of Chef Burns – 'or Sir T. And, a week ago, *Miss* Gabrielle arrived with tons of luggage, throwing her weight about and treating people like slaves. I can tell you this: I've only been here a couple of weeks, and I won't be staying much longer. Sir T's been blowing up over nothing, over flipping bloody all. I bet that's the reason the last lot all left so suddenly.'

That *was* interesting, but before I could enquire further, Burns came over with two plates of bacon and eggs and placed one in front of each of us with a grunted, 'Here you are.' I was being offered an apology, and I smiled my thanks.

Ann-Marie seemed as hungry as I was, so we ate in silence and it was only when we had finished and were chatting over mugs of tea that I had the chance to steer the conversation once more round to that abrupt departure of all Sir Thomas's agency staff.

'So you've been here a fortnight? And Chef ... er ... Roddy, the same? Only the two of you?'

She nodded. 'Yup. The agency phoned me in a bit of a panic wanting someone who could start right away, and I needed the cash.'

'So Sir Thomas has had to manage these last two weeks without a butler?'

A shrug. 'He's just had to do without till you came. And he'll have to do without me too if he shouts at me again. I worked here for a week last year, standing in for a maid who was ill. He never shouted at me once then. If I'd known he was going to be like this, I wouldn't have come back. Don't know what's got into him.' She pushed back her chair and stood up. 'Gotta go. I've to make sure there's a roaring fire in the breakfast room and the table's laid, or that'll give him another excuse to bawl me out. Not that he needs one. . . .' The corridor door banged behind her.

I sat for a minute or two thinking about what she'd said. It might be worth investigating why all the staff had left at the same time – and so suddenly. There might be nothing to it, nothing to it at all.

On the other hand ... since last year Sir Thomas had become noticeably bad-tempered. In undercover work it is dangerous to discount or disregard *anything*, no matter how unimportant or insignificant it might seem. I would have been inclined to put the bad temper down to financial, or even health, worries, if it hadn't been for Gabrielle's presence here and her connection with Louis Moran.

As soon as I was free today, I'd get in touch with Gerry. The cottage had no external line to the outside world – even if it had, I couldn't have used it to contact him as anyone from the big house could have been listening in. I'd phone from Bowmore, the biggest town on the island, and far enough away from *Allt an Damh* for me to pass unnoticed, just one among the many visitors to Islay.

The *beep beep beep* of a timer interrupted my thoughts. I turned round to see Burns pulling a steaming pan off the heat.

'That's the Robillard woman's tray ready.' He spooned an egg into an eggcup. 'If I were you, I'd get a move on. You don't want to get on the wrong side of that one.'

I scraped back my chair and leapt up from the table. 'She wants her newspaper ironed. Where—?'

Burns scowled. 'No time for nonsense like that. I don't cook eggs to perfection for them to get cold and be r-ru-ined.'

The rolled 'r', it seemed, was a storm warning, a useful barometer to the state of his temper. I snatched up the tray and beat a hasty retreat.

As I hurried through the entrance hall to the stairs, Ann-Marie came out of the breakfast room wiping her hands on a cloth.

I paused, one foot on the bottom step. 'Have the newspapers arrived yet? Miss Gabrielle wants one with her breakfast tray.'

She glanced quickly round, and seeing that the coast was clear, gave a snort of derision. 'Well, milady will need to have her breakfast at ten o'clock, then. The ferry doesn't get in with the papers till well after nine – that's if it's not delayed.'

Under the glassy stare of the rows of stags' heads I carried the tray along the upper corridor to Gabrielle's room and tapped lightly on the door. 'Breakfast, Ms Robillard.'

At the muffled, '*Entrez*, Dorward,' I balanced the tray and turned the handle.

Like a Hollywood-starlet, Gabrielle was reclining against three overstuffed pillows in the large double bed, a modernized version of a four-poster with white and gold silk canopy and matching coverlet. I put the tray down on the bedside table and moved over to the window to pull back the curtains.

She stretched out a languid arm and picked up the alarm clock. 'You are two minutes late, Dorward. Punctuality eez *most* important, *n'est-ce pas*, you understand?'

I murmured an insincere, apologetic, 'I'm very sorry, madam.' She certainly hadn't considered punctuality important last night when she'd kept Sir Thomas waiting for his dinner.

I'd got off to a bad start. Though I doubted if it would ever be possible to satisfy Gabrielle Robillard. I'd be subject to this tyrannical whimsy again when it came to preparing her bath. I made the required grovelling responses to her other demands and when eventually dismissed, went off to see to Sir Thomas's warm towels. At least I didn't have to bring *him* breakfast in bed.

At eleven o'clock I returned to the cottage, satisfied that now Chef and I were on speaking terms, I'd have access to the house in my off-duty hours. I'd made some progress this morning.

While performing my duties I'd been pondering the significance of Gabrielle Robillard being a guest of Sir Thomas. It was surely a sign that *Allt an Damh* featured in Moran's plans. And the only reason a drug baron would be interested in a small landowner on a sparsely populated Scottish island was its proximity both to Ireland and the west cost of Scotland. Ireland had become an important link in the international drug smuggling routes from South America and West Africa to Britain and Europe. Islay with its coastline of caves and secluded inlets would be just the kind of place Moran would choose for a venture.

Who was the guest due to arrive tomorrow? Moran, or someone connected with his organization? If I could find out when Sir Thomas and his guests would be away from *Allt an Damh*, I'd sneak Gorgonzola into the house for a sniff around on the chance that she might discover a sample shipment or some other evidence that drugs had been handled.

'Pretty satisfactory, DJ,' I said to myself, humming a little tune as I put my key in the cottage door. 'And it's another eight hours before I have to put up with that prima donna Robillard again.' I'd forgotten about the prima donna waiting for me in the gardener's cottage.

'*Miaowgrrr.*' The half-mew half growl from behind the door as I turned the key, left me in no doubt as to the mood G was in. On leaving this morning, I hadn't filled up her bowl. I'd reasoned that she wouldn't be hungry, would still be dozing and digesting when I got back, but after sleeping off last night's stolen meal, and ready for breakfast, she must have gone to her bowl and found it empty. Cats like to snack little and often. In view of the near crisis caused by my failure to feed her when we arrived yesterday afternoon, I should have known better.

I eased the door open, blocking the widening gap with my leg to forestall a rush to the happy hunting ground of the shrubbery, or worse still, Chef's kitchen. I peered through the narrow gap to find that I needn't have bothered with these precautions. Gorgonzola was nowhere in sight. I stepped quickly in and closed the door behind me.

G too had been assessing the situation. The slowly opening door had indicated that strategy number one, the surprise rush, was unlikely to be successful. She had abandoned it in favour of strategy number two, emotional blackmail. In the kitchen recess a prostrate furry body lay on the worktop beside the empty bowl I'd put aside for her food. From her came the faintest of mews, piteous, heart-rending. It was the mew of a cat so weakened by starvation that it couldn't lift its head.

'Well done, G, I'll nominate you for an Oscar.' I picked up the bowl and opened a tin of salmon from the supply in the cupboard. When I turned round, she was sitting behind me, tail curled round paws, bright-eyed and drooling.

I held up the tin. 'This is salmon, salmon for humans, not your usual gourmet cat food, but it's no good complaining. Your raid on the kitchen has scuppered any chance of passing you off as a feral cat recruited to help with the vermin problem.'

I emptied the salmon into a bowl and started breaking it up with a fork. 'You realize, don't you, that this is a reward for restraining yourself from shredding the curtains and scratching the furniture? It is *not*, I repeat, *not* a sign that I approve of your raid on Chef's kitchen.'

As I watched her eat, I realized I'd taken a risk this morning by leaving her here, an error I couldn't afford to repeat. If somebody had come to search the cottage, they'd have found her. It would be safer to allow G to roam loose.

But first I'd have to convince Waddington that there was no need for snares and gin traps. Seeing G playing dead had given me an idea of how to torpedo his plan. I'd tell him that while walking somewhere in the grounds – somewhere, of course, I wouldn't be able to find again – I'd come across the remains of the 'feral' cat.

I lightly cupped my hands round her face. 'It all depends on you not being seen. Not being seen, do you understand? You must not go *anywhere* near the big house.'

She stared at me, copper eyes wide, then gently extracted her head from between my hands, and plunged it once again into the bowl.

I put my plan into action right away in the hope that I would be in time to forestall Waddington getting in touch with the gamekeeper of the neighbouring estate. Things didn't turn out quite as planned.

I picked up the phone to the big house and when he answered said, 'I was wondering if Sir Thomas or Ms Robillard has mail they would like posted in Bowmore, since I'm going to drive there to have a look round and have lunch.'

This was met with a curt, '*I* handle all aspects of Sir Thomas's correspondence, Dorward. And Ms Robillard does not send or receive mail.'

I didn't view this as a setback. It was only what I had expected. Now was the time for the casual mention of my 'discovery' of the dead feral cat.

'Excellent news, Dorward.' Just as I was breathing a silent sigh of relief, he added, 'But as Shakespeare said, "Let's make assurance doubly sure", eh? There could be a whole family of the brutes out there. Breed like rabbits, I believe. I'll get Ramsay to lay out a few traps near the house tomorrow.'

There was nothing I could do about it. G was still in deadly danger. But she would be safe enough today, so I let her out into the shrubbery and set off towards Bowmore.

As the gates swung slowly closed behind me, the first raindrops spattered the windscreen, a bit disappointing after yesterday's sun. Gone were the brilliant blues and greens of sea, sky and grass, and in their place, low grey clouds pressing down on hills and fields. Gone, the calm waters of the large bay where seals had basked on the little islets. Gone, the two swans gliding across waters smooth as glass. Now a stiff breeze was whipping the pewter surface into angry little waves. Buffeted by the wind, a kestrel hovered, side-slipped and sank behind one of the large stony outcrops bordering the road. Disappointing too for a tourist planning a day on the white sand beaches or photographing otters frisking in the shallow waters, but weather was of little concern in my plans for the day.

As I drove along the narrow single-track road, I was taking note of my surroundings. Gerry's instructions had been that I was to leave *Allt an Damh* when I was sure I'd identified Moran. The best time to slip away would be during the day, as if I was making a normal trip to town. With luck, several hours might pass before my disappearance was noticed, and that would give me time to catch the ferry or the plane. But I had to cater for the worst-case scenario – escape through the grounds to lie low somewhere with shelter in the surrounding fields and woods. I hoped it wouldn't come to that. Islay didn't seem to have much in the way of woods, only scattered clumps of scrubby bushes and the occasional shelter-belt of trees round a big house.

By the time I'd driven as far as Ardbeg, the first of the three distilleries on the south-east coast on my way to Port Ellen, the lack of hiding places was more than a little worrying: experience had taught me that if something can happen, it will.

I drew up at the red telephone box near the entrance to the Ardbeg distillery. Even on a grey day in the rain, the white distillery buildings with the pagoda-topped chimneys had a magical quality. Between the buildings, I glimpsed a pier, and seagulls wheeling over a turbulent sea. I let down the window and sat for a few minutes taking deep breaths of the salty air. Then caution prevailed. I couldn't risk being seen at a telephone box so close to *Allt an Damh*. I drove on.

No ferry was pulled up at the pier as I passed through Port Ellen, a reminder that I'd have to memorize the ferry timetable as an escape option. The Low Road to Bowmore stretched into the rain-swept distance, on both sides of the road only peat moor and juniper bushes bowed by the prevailing winds from the Atlantic. White dots of sheep scattered across the short grass of the fields like litter left behind after an outdoor ceilidh.

At Bowmore's Tourist Information I collected a handful of leaflets, as any visitor would, useful cover for my visit here. Even in the rain it was an attractive little town, houses washed in white, grey or beige, windows and door-frames outlined in a contrasting colour. The oddly-shaped eighteenth century Round Church and the distillery might be worth a visit, but first I had to make that phone call. I stepped outside and headed for the public telephone straight across from the Tourist Office.

In these modern phone boxes there are no small panes and glazing bars to partially obscure the occupant from passers-by, so I propped up the map I'd picked up in the Tourist Office to give the impression that I was phoning one of the businesses featured round the map's border.

I dialled the number of Gerry's office on the secure line, gave the password and while waiting to be put through, kept an eye on what was going on outside. Nothing out of the ordinary . . . a small group was gathered outside the entrance to Bowmore distillery, and in the harbour a white boat was mooring at the wooden pontoon.

Gerry came on the line. 'Progress, Deborah?' Straight to the point as usual, no time for pleasantries.

As a precaution against anyone out there reading my lips, I turned away from the street. I never take chances. 'I've something to report re my employer' – I told him what Ann-Marie had said – 'and I think these recent displays of bad temper are significant.'

No comment from him, only a brisk, 'Anything to add to that?'

I had been expecting more, on the lines of, 'Interesting, Deborah. That's certainly worth noting.'

'Well,' I said, somewhat put out, '*all* the staff left suddenly, and at the same time.'

A non-committal grunt was followed by silence.

I frowned at my reflection in the glass side of the telephone box. 'There's something you haven't told me, isn't there, Gerry?'

No reply. I didn't even try to keep the irritation out of my voice. 'You knew about the staff already, didn't you?'

'Not till after you'd gone off to Islay,' he soothed.

Gerry going out of his way to placate me could mean only one thing: he knew something I wouldn't want to hear.

I watched a man wander along the pavement in my direction. He stopped a couple of yards away at the bus shelter to study the timetables.

It's always safe to be suspicious. I raised my voice so that it would carry to listening ears. 'So you have Hebridean Glass workshops . . . Can you tell me when they are held?' The man moved closer and hovered as if waiting for the phone. I held up five fingers, signifying how long I was going to be, then resumed my imaginary conversation. 'Yes, that would suit me fine. What exactly do you teach in the workshops?'

The man moved away.

'OK, Gerry, I can talk now. You're hiding something, aren't you?'

The pause before he spoke, confirmed it, but all he said was, 'You mustn't make assumptions, Deborah. Anything you need to know, I'll tell you.' He rang off.

Liar. There was something he wasn't telling me. And whatever it was, I wasn't going to like it.

CHAPTER SIX

If Gerry was holding something back, it must be scary, really scary. I stood on the quayside of Bowmore's little harbour, staring down at the little white boats and the raindrops pitting the surface of water as grey as my mood. A dark shape wavered under the surface, hard to identify – you could say the same about what was going on at *Allt an Damh*.

The white wall of Bowmore distillery fronted the shore to the left of the harbour. Islay, island of distilleries, Ardbeg, Lagavulin, Laphroaig, Bunnahabhain, Caol Ila, Bowmore, Kilchoman, Bruichladdich . . . I rolled the names off my tongue. Could it be that Sir Thomas's distillery, Sròn Dubh, was included in Moran's plans? He would make an appearance soon and I'd better have my escape plan in place. I'd make a start as soon as I got back.

At *Allt an Damh*, the rain had stopped and a watery sun was struggling through the clouds. There was no sign of Gorgonzola, but I had no doubt she was watching and would join me if it suited her. I sat in the car and studied the Ordnance Survey map. A track led through the wood almost as far as the shore. That might be worth investigating. They wouldn't expect me to go to ground so close at hand.

Ten minutes later I was scuffing my way through pockets of brittle leaves in the small beech wood, enjoying the rustle underfoot. At the far side of the wood I emerged onto a small hill covered with straggly bushes, bracken and clumps of heather. The swell of the hill blocked my view of the sea, but I could hear the faint grumble of waves on the shore. The track petered out here. I'd started across the shoulder of the hill when a shout came from behind me.

'Hello-o . . .' and again, 'Hello-o. . . .'

I swung round to see Waddington waving to me from the edge of the trees. I waved back and waited till he caught up.

'Lucky . . . I . . . saw you . . . Dor . . . ward.' He was out of breath, as if he had been hurrying.

'Out for a stroll, too, Waddington?' I waited while he regained his breath and then asked, 'Is this the easiest way to get down to the sea?'

He ignored my question. 'I saw you going this way and had to warn you about Sir Thomas's project. In co-operation with Scottish Natural Heritage he's made that area' – he waved his hand in the direction of the sea – 'a wildlife sanctuary for the Anglo-Nubian feral goats. They mustn't be disturbed because the study in progress is to see the effect on them if they have no contact whatsoever with humans for a year. It's got a couple of months to run.'

I didn't believe a word of it. I smiled, 'Glad you told me. I wouldn't want to mess up an experiment. Now that the sun's come out, I'll just sit here for a bit till it's time to go back. See you at dinner.'

That put him in a bit of a quandary. I'd made it clear I assumed he was going back to the house. I knew he wanted to keep an eye on me to make sure I didn't go down to the sea, but he had no excuse to stay with me.

'Er-yes.' He turned and strode off into the trees.

I sat on one of the many small grey stone outcrops, making sure I was facing the wood. He would be watching from cover. After a few moments I narrowed my eyes as if against the glare, and under lowered lids studied the edge of the wood. Yes, I could just detect the faint outline of a figure standing well back amidst the trunks. Face turned up to the sun, I thought about how to investigate that piece of shoreline.

'Loada bunkum that,' said a nearby stone outcrop topped by a fringe of coppery bracken.

I stared at the stone, patched with palest yellow, fried egg-shaped splodges of lichen.

'He's watching you from the trees,' said the stone.

'Yes, I know.' I got up and sat on its flat top. All I could see of the man crouched behind it was an old-fashioned trilby hat. The crown was flattened as if battered by some giant fist.

'There's nothing down there but otters and seals,' the hat volunteered.

I took a chance. 'I think there's something down there he doesn't want me to see.'

'That'll be the new shed in one of the little bays on the headland. For the past week a boat's been coming after dark to bring stuff to it. I've been down there making a film for the Tourist Board – I'm calling it *Creatures of the Night*. Otters, swans, ducks, they don't spend the night sleeping like we do, you know.'

I gazed dreamily at the trees. 'You seem remarkably well-informed for a stone. Do you come here often?'

The hat tilted to reveal alert blue eyes set in a weather-beaten face fringed by a wiry grey beard streaked with brown and ginger. 'This is one of the best places on this side of the island to view wildlife, but for the past couple of weeks I've been warned off by the staff of the big house. I don't pay any attention, of course, just take cover – thought you were one of them. I go down to the bay any time I want to watch the otters, fascinating creatures. About a week ago, early morning, I was crouched behind a boulder watching them, when I heard voices and hammering from further along the shore.' His voice rose. 'Ignorant buggers! A racket like that must have scared away any otter for miles around. Even the slightest noise or careless movement and they're gone.'

'Sound carries,' I warned. 'He's still there.'

'Guilty as charged.' His voice dropped to a murmur once again. 'I like to keep tabs on anything that affects wildlife, you know, so I thought I'd go and have a shufti.'

'Shufti?' I said.

'A look-see, a dekko, the once-over. Army slang. Before your time, lass.' The eyes twinkled. 'They were putting up a shed. But here's the interesting thing. They covered it with a camouflage net – but that shed wasn't a bird or otter hide.' He tapped a finger on the side of his nose and winked.

'It wasn't? How do you know?'

He chuckled. 'No windows!'

After a moment I said, 'You'll have an infrared camera to film wildlife in the dark?' The hat nodded. 'And a boat comes during the hours of darkness?' The hat nodded again. 'You wouldn't happen to have seen what the boat's delivering, I suppose?'

My casual tone didn't deceive him. 'You're asking a lot of questions, lass. Now let me ask you one.' The blue eyes bored into mine. 'That fellow who's watching you, why don't you want him to know that we're having this little talk?'

I gazed steadily back. If he was the enemy, he wouldn't be hiding from Waddington and wouldn't be telling me all this. What I said next could lead to a breakthrough. 'Possibly for the same reason that you don't want him to know you're lying behind that rock.'

The sharp *chuck chuck chuck* alarm call of a blackbird broke into the silence that followed.

'Big stakes, eh? You're wondering if I can be trusted.' His gaze didn't waver. 'Let me tell you this. In the war I was in Intelligence, working behind enemy lines. Takes one to know one, lass. Now just what kind of Intelligence are you in?'

'*Them that ask no questions*. . . .' I quoted, smiling.

'*Isn't told a lie*.' He nodded approvingly. 'Shouldn't have asked. Sandy Duncan, at your service.

'Elizabeth Dorward.'

'Aye.' The eyes twinkled again. 'We always had a *nom de guerre*. Safer that way. But you'll find *me* in the telephone book.'

I walked slowly back to the gardener's cottage, having arranged to meet Sandy Duncan at midnight to investigate the shed in the bay. In this kind of work, it is madness to trust someone who has not been vetted. It was something I'd never done before, something I'd never thought I'd do. I believed Sandy when he said he'd been in Intelligence – it did indeed 'take one to know one'. But whose side was he on? Had Waddington seen me setting off on the path leading to the shore, and contacted Sandy by mobile so that he could lie in wait behind a rock to feed me info about the shed and the boat, an elaborate trap to test me out? Unlikely, and yet. . . . Instinct and training told me that tonight's rendezvous with S. Duncan, Esquire, would be most unwise.

At the final turn of the path I caught a flicker of movement through the trees. Someone was walking round the side of the cottage. I quickened my step. It was Waddington and he was trying the door. I'd locked it, but even if he'd got in, there'd have been nothing for him to find. I'd made sure of that: Gorgonzola was safely outside.

He swung round as he heard me approach. 'Ah, Dorward. I was wondering if you were back.' A clever attempt to pretend that he'd gone back to the house, thereby covering up the fact that he'd lingered among the trees watching me. 'I've just heard from Ramsay.'

'Ramsay?' I said, frowning as if I couldn't recall the name.

'The gamekeeper on the neighbouring estate.' An impatient wave of his hand. 'I told you about him yesterday.'

'Oh, yes.' I bent down to brush some bits of bracken from my trouser leg, as if the news was of little consequence.

'He's going to lay traps in the wood tomorrow. So my advice is to keep clear.'

Behind him in the shrubbery, the lower leaves of a rhododendron bush twitched. A gingery face peered inquisitively out.

He looked at his watch. 'I'm off to collect Sir Thomas's guest at the airport. We'll be back here in about two hours, so you'd better come over to the house in good time.' He turned to go. In another second he'd see Gorgonzola.

I put a hand on his arm. 'Just a minute, Waddington. You haven't given me any instructions about the visitor—' I broke off to flick my hand twice at knee level. 'Damn it! That's one of these awful horseflies.'

G is trained to respond to certain signals. She melted back into the shrubbery. The glossy rhododendron leaves came together, quivered and were still.

'Hate the things. Where's it gone?' I flapped my hands about.

He swung away impatiently. 'Bloody fuss about nothing. What instructions do you need? Just do the same as for Sir Thomas and Ms Robillard.'

'I need to know whether the guest is male or female. A lady will expect me to unpack her case and—'

'Just come across a quarter of an hour before your usual time so that you'll be there to greet us.' He turned away without answering my question. 'Oh, and be sure to wear gloves. Good impression, that's what Sir Thomas wants.'

The entrance hall door's stained-glass prevented me from seeing the car's arrival, but the crunch of tyres on gravel was signal enough for me to open the door and stand at the top of the steps to greet the guest.

I'd hoped that Sir Thomas's guest would be male, possibly Louis Moran, though he'd not bear much resemblance to the photo on our files. But out of the car stepped a slim Oriental woman whose expensively tailored black tunic suit would not have been out of place on the catwalk of a London fashion show.

Waddington took a small suitcase and a computer bag from the boot and followed her up the steps, depositing the luggage at the foot of the hall staircase.

'The butler will see to your cases, Ms Chang. I'll inform Sir Thomas of your arrival.' With a nod in my direction, he ran lightly up the stairs.

'Welcome to *Allt an Damh*, madam.' I gave a little bow. 'Let me show you to your room.'

She studied me for a moment, gaze lingering on my face as if storing the image in a memory database, then with a peremptory gesture indicated that I should go ahead. I picked up the suitcase and reached for the computer bag.

She snatched it away. '*I* take this.'

In silence we ascended the staircase. Silently from on high the stags' heads stared down at us. The room allotted to her was at the far end of the upper corridor, and though the same size as Gabrielle's and comfortably furnished, was noticeably less luxurious – lacking the four-poster and canopy, the overstuffed pillows, the fatly upholstered armchair and mirrored wardrobe. In their place Ms Chang had been allotted a bed with plain padded headboard, a duvet with red and green tartan rug throw, and a wooden chair with a padded seat. Whereas Gabrielle had the pleasure of a vase of expensive orchids, here a simple bowl of purple heather adorned the top of the chest of drawers. The difference in quality of the rooms might be of no significance at all, but I found it strange that Gabrielle, a mere acquaintance of Sir Thomas, should take precedence in room allocation over Ms Chang, a high-powered business associate.

I put the suitcase on the luggage stand. 'Shall I unpack for you, madam?'

'You put clothes in chest.' Again the imperious gesture. 'I not have many. Not stay here long.'

I was aware of her watching me as I took each item out of the case and placed it in the drawer.

I held up the toilet bag. 'The guest bathroom is on the other side of the corridor, madam. Shall I put the toilet bag—?'

'No. You leave bag here.' Her tone was sharp and impatient.

'If that's all, then, madam?'

The only reply was a dismissive wave of her hand.

I sighed to myself and turned to go. It was bad enough putting up with Gabrielle's temperamental moods, but it seemed I now had not just her, but her clone on my hands.

I met Waddington as I made my way back along the corridor and as I started down the stairs, heard him tap at her door and call, 'Sir Thomas is waiting for you in his study, Ms Chang.'

Ms Chang would be one to watch. Gerry would be very interested in Sir Thomas's business dealings.

Thunk thunk thunk. Something had obviously upset Chef. The ringing slam of metal on wood was penetrating as far as the hall. I eased open the kitchen door. *THUNK THUNK THUNK.*

I shouted above the din, 'All right to come in, Chef?'

He looked up, heavy knife poised over a cucumber, then chopped viciously down. 'Not if you have come with yet another last minute change to tonight's menu.' The knife crashed down again, sending the end of the cucumber flying off onto the floor. 'Does that bastard Sir Thomas care that I'd spent *hours* on tonight's bloody meal? He bloody well does *not.*'

THUNK THUNK THUNK. Pieces of cucumber shot into the air and landed back on the board. 'The venison stew was ready to go in the oven and he phones down to say that Her Majesty Ms Chang is demanding a Chinese meal.' Knife poised, he glared at me as if I was the offending lady.

'Oh dear,' I said, somewhat inadequately, searching for words that wouldn't add fuel to the flames.

'I'm bloody well not spending any more time on dinner. It's going to be a stir fry – they can take it or leave it.' He seized a jar and emptied out a handful of red chillies onto the chopping board. 'And this'll hot things up a bit, give a nice little zing to the dish.'

Seeing my look, he said, 'I'm not worried about getting the sack. He knows he won't get another chef in a hurry, so what will those guests of his do, eh?' *Chop chop chop.* He swept the fragments of chilli into a bowl. 'And when we have our supper, it's us'll be having the venison stew.'

I had half an hour before I needed to be back at the house to prepare the table. I hurried over to the cottage, anxious to feed Gorgonzola in case she was tempted again by the lure of the kitchen. A full belly would not, of course, take away entirely the risk of her making another raid on the kitchen. G, like all cats, got a kick out of going where she knew she was not wanted. It was a challenge, a game that kept the mind alert, boredom at bay. An exciting game, but at *Allt an Damh* likely to be a fatal one.

I threw my white gloves onto the table. To safeguard my uniform from spots and splashes, I unhooked my apron from the back of the door and set to work opening a tin of salmon. Gorgonzola leapt onto the table to supervise the operation, an anticipatory droplet of saliva already forming at the corner of her mouth.

'Cats are not allowed on the table, G,' I said, focused on the task of tugging at the ring pull and folding back the top. There was no soft thump of furry feet landing on floor. 'Cats are *not* allowed—' I said, looking up.

Gorgonzola's attention was no longer on the tin of salmon. Head down, she was sniffing delicately at one of the gloves I'd cast aside.

'Hungry enough to eat gloves, eh, G?'

Salmon tin forgotten, I stared at her, for from her throat was coming the distinctive crooning purr that indicated a drug find. There was no doubt about it. Something I'd handled with these gloves had been in contact with drugs: Chang's suitcase.

'Clever girl, G.'

I opened a second tin of salmon and added it to her bowl.

CHAPTER SEVEN

Somewhat to my disappointment at the time, I didn't find out how Sir Thomas and his two guests reacted to Chef's red-hot chilli rice. After I'd removed the soup plates, I stood unobtrusively against the wall listening intently to the conversation without appearing to, observing the interplay between Robillard and Chang, resplendent in a stylish black silk cheongsam. The relationship between them seemed somewhat cool. Ms Chang was occupying Waddington's chair. Had he been told that he wasn't wanted?

Ann-Marie brought in two trays of a Chinese banquet and scuttled out again. I arranged the dishes of food on the table, placed the bowl of lethal rice centrally and was about to step back, ready to become part of the furniture again when Gabrielle frowned and picked up a fork.

'What *are* you thinking of, Dorward? Where are Madame Chang's chopsticks? She will not know 'ow to eat with a knife and fork like we do.'

'I stay at best hotels in Hong Kong, New York, London. Always I am eating with knife and fork. Not difficult.' Chang's tone made it clear that she did not suffer fools gladly and that Gabrielle fell all too clearly into that category.

'I do apologize, madam,' I said smoothly, 'but there are no chopsticks at *Allt an Damh*.'

Sir Thomas waved a dismissive hand. 'You may go now, Dorward. We won't be needing you again tonight. Just arrange for filter coffee and liqueurs to be in the drawing room.'

As I closed the door, I heard, 'Now we can get down to business, Chang.'

It was a stroke of luck to be dismissed early. Too bad I'd miss the venison stew, I'd make my excuses and get in a couple of hours' sleep before I met Sandy Duncan at our rendezvous point where the path through the wood emerged from the trees.

I stood in the shadow of the beech and sycamore trees, looking out over the straggly bushes, bracken and heather of the moonlit hillside. In the bluish light of a full moon, the pale lichen splodges on the stone outcrops seemed to glow with an eerie luminescence. The *swish* . . . *swish* of the waves on the shore carried clearly in the still air.

The eerie call of a night bird startled me. Furry ears swivelled in the rucksack. It heaved as Gorgonzola tried unsuccessfully to force her shoulders past the zip. I reached a hand over my shoulder and stroked her head.

'Think our friend will turn up, G?' I murmured.

'Just what I was wondering about you.' A figure detached itself from the trees off to my left. The silhouette of the hat was unmistakable. Then, 'You're not alone.' Sharp and suspicious. 'Who are you talking to?'

'Only to the cat in my rucksack.' Aware of how this sounded, I moved forward into the moonlight.

Again the alarm call of the night bird, loud in the silence. He remained in the shadows.

If he thought I was some kind of oddball, he'd break off contact, steer clear of me. He held vital information about the little boat and the activity at the shed, and to discover what it was meant I'd have to take the considerable risk of blowing my cover – and G's. But then, I'm a pretty good judge of knowing when to trust somebody. My life depends on it.

'The cat's trained to sniff out substances,' I said quietly.

A few seconds of suspense, then, 'Very useful.' He moved out to join me. No probing questions, after all those years he was still the professional. 'Now, if we cut across the hillside down towards the beach, we'll come out above the shed I was telling you about. . . .

'. . . Shed's down there, behind that outcrop,' Sandy whispered. 'You can just see its roof. Fishermen come into the bay now and then to check their crab and lobster pots, but it's in a hollow and screened by bushes.'

Suspended above the horizon, the huge moon rolled out a silver carpet across the dark waters of the bay. Spent waves lapped lethargically against a stretch of ashen sand, stirring into motion a ragged line of seaweed washed up by the tide. We picked our way along the beach, jumping across a small stream that twisted and turned in a deep channel across the sand.

I pointed to the trail of footprints behind us. 'A bit of a giveaway, aren't they?'

'Tide's coming in. They'll be washed away before the boat comes, and now that we're over the stream we can keep to the soft stuff where the red deer come down for the seaweed.'

We were halfway towards the shed when G decided she'd been confined too long. Thump. The rucksack heaved and twisted against my back in a way that could not be ignored. I swung it off my shoulders, pausing with my hand on the zip as a thought occurred to me.

'What if the boat comes in tonight?'

He nodded slowly. 'More than likely it will, because it's a bombers' moon. You won't know that term, lass, you're too young. We used it during the war to describe the full moon the bomber pilots needed to see their target. Yes, that lot'll probably come in tonight. They don't want to prang that boat of theirs on the reefs in the dark, do they?' A throaty chuckle. 'They'd lose their precious cargo.' He gestured at the rucksack. 'Aye, let the beast out. Let's see what it can do. We've a couple of hours yet. They never come before 0300 hours so we've plenty of time.'

G didn't wait for the zip to be fully opened. She forced her way out and bounded across the sand towards the tufty grass edging the beach.

'She's detected *something*, all right. It'll be a fat and juicy field mouse.' I could hear the smile in his voice.

He was probably right. And that might very well be all she'd detect tonight, for what the boat was bringing to the shed wouldn't be drugs. Sir Thomas would be smuggling whisky.

Sandy grabbed my arm. 'Keep still!'

'Seen something?' I whispered.

'*Ssht*! Otters!' He pointed to a trail of bubbles curving through the water close to the shore.

The smooth surface of the water rippled and a dark head broke through. An otter reared up holding a writhing fish between its paws, tearing at its head, then it swam to the shallows and dragged the carcass across the sand.

Mia-a-ow. Gorgonzola rushed past us, intent on theft by snatch and grab. The otter turned to fight, its razor-sharp teeth white in the moonlight.

Sandy's reactions were faster than mine. '*Hishht.*' He raised his arm and brought it chopping sharply down.

The sound and movement were enough. Abandoning its meal, the otter turned and splashed into the sea, launching its body along the surface like a skater sliding across ice. Head . . . shoulders . . . back . . . submerged, rump and tail the last to disappear.

A grunt from Sandy. 'That was a close one. It would have cut your cat to ribbons.'

Unaware of her narrow escape, G pounced on the fish and carried it in triumph up the beach.

I tried to make a joke out of it, but I heard the tremor in my voice. 'You've saved the taxpayer a lot of money. Thanks.'

He smiled his understanding as we walked on.

As Sandy had said, the grey prefabricated shed was well camouflaged by a thick clump of juniper bushes. There were no windows and the door was on the side facing away from the sea. The strong padlock would have been easy work for my picklocks, if I'd been allowed to bring them with me to Islay.

The soft earth of the low bank on the landward side of the hollow was rutted and torn up by the wheels of the motor vehicle necessary to transport heavy cartons of whisky bottles.

'Looks like there's been a motor bike or a quad bike down here.'

Sandy came over to inspect. 'Aye, it's a quad bike and trailer. Can't film the otters when the noisy bugger comes during the day with his roaring engine. Had to give up a couple of times recently.'

I was convinced I was right that Sir Thomas was engaged in whisky smuggling. He'd make a tidy sum by avoiding excise duty. And with the rocketing demand worldwide for premium whiskies. . . . It all fitted: the white van I wasn't supposed to see on the day I arrived would have been bringing a consignment of whisky to be taken down to the shed.

We walked round the hut and stood looking out at the moonlit waters of the bay.

'The boat that slips in at night. . . .' I said. 'The question is – are they also bringing stuff in as well as taking it away?'

'Can't help you there, lass.'

Something brushed against my leg. I looked down. A mangled fish head had been deposited at my feet and G was sitting, head on one side, contemplating the shed.

'That's very generous of you, G,' I said, leaning down and tickling her behind an ear.

Sandy turned from scanning the bay with his night binoculars. 'Are we going to see her in action?'

'Might as well, but I really just brought her along to keep her from wandering in the woods. Waddington, the man you saw yesterday, got the gamekeeper to lay out traps.' I fastened G's working collar round her neck. 'I don't expect her to find anything, though. I think the shed is used to store whisky and that's not what she's trained to sniff out.'

She looked up at me. I pointed. 'OK, G, search.'

Tail erect, she walked daintily round the shed, circling it once, then sat down and wiped her face with her foreleg.

'She's nothing to report, then?' He sounded disappointed.

'Seems not. Whatever's in there, or has been stored there, it's not drugs.'

In a leisurely fashion Gorgonzola finished her ablutions and circled the shed again. She sat down in front of the door and crooned the purr that indicated a find. There might or might not be whisky in that shed, but there definitely was drugs. Because her nose had been desensitised by eating the stolen fish, she hadn't picked up on it the first time.

'Something wrong with the cat?'

I smiled. 'No. What you're hearing is Gorgonzola in action.'

With Gorgonzola safely zipped into the rucksack, sleeping off her stolen meal, we took up position on the hillside behind the earthwork of an ancient hill fort from where we had a clear view of the beach.

We'd been holed up for an hour, when I heard it – the faint *rrrr* of an auxiliary engine out at sea, the boat itself undetectable in the shimmering wavelets of moonlit water.

'To the left of that islet.' Sandy passed his night glasses to me. 'Take a look, but be careful that the moonlight doesn't catch the lenses. The crew will be scanning the dark landmass.'

I focused on the area he'd indicated. Even with the aid of night glasses the boat was a mere speck amid the flickering waves. As it came closer, I made out the low white hull of a small yacht and a thin black line of mast swaying against the quicksilver water. With engine throttled back to a murmur, it slipped into the sheltering arms of the bay and nosed into the shallows in line with the shed.

'Seabed shelves steeply there,' Sandy whispered, his head so close that his beard tickled my ear. 'This class of yacht needs less draught.'

A dark figure leapt over the gunwale, splashed ashore and guided the bow to ground lightly on the sand. He held it there while another crewman jumped into the water and carried a mooring line across to make it fast among the straggle of bushes.

Another shadowy figure emerged from the cabin with the first of twenty small packages. One by one they were piled on the beach. I took the opportunity to study the hull through the binoculars, searching for something that would identify the yacht and could be passed on to Gerry. It was frustrating not to make out the name, partially obscured as it was by a net draped over the bows. All I could decipher were the first letters, *Ir* – and the last – *es*. But the guardrail on the bow, on the portside, was bent out of alignment. That might be enough.

Sandy murmured, 'They've opened up the shed.'

I lowered the binoculars. So far there had been no attempt to move the packages, which were still piled in a heap on the beach. There was movement in the dark rectangle of the open door of the shed. Two men emerged, each carrying a cardboard box, heavy by the look of it, to contain whisky bottles. They trudged down to the water's edge and dumped their load beside the pile of packages. Whisky made sense. There'd be a payload both ways – drugs in, whisky out.

I tried to work it out. 'Ten boxes with twelve bottles to a box . . . that's one hundred and twenty bottles. Coming from Islay, you'll be a whisky man. Any idea how much that lot could be worth?'

He thought for a moment. 'A bottle of good quality whisky can fetch anything from forty to sixty pounds, sometimes more. So that little lot could bring in about seven thousand pounds – at a very conservative estimate.'

'Hmm,' I said. 'That's not much at all. Chickenfeed. Drugs organizations are only interested in deals worth hundreds of thousands.'

Sandy chuckled. 'But these bottles could be worth a lot more than seven thousand. When you think that it's six thousand pounds a bottle from something as rare as a final cask of 50 Year Old Balvenie . . . if these bottles are from one of the last few casks of a distillery that's closed down, what we could be looking at here is a total of more than half a million.'

And that certainly *would* interest Louis Moran.

Now they'd started carrying the packages into the shed. The man on the boat disappeared into the cabin and emerged with metal poles and a net.

'Thought they'd have difficulty hoisting the boxes on board,' Sandy whispered. 'That'll be a pulley.'

The small packages were stored, the shed padlocked, then one by one the heavy cardboard boxes were carried out to the yacht, lifted into the waiting net and loaded on board, two at a time – a slick operation tonight, but not so easy if a high sea was running. Even in this calm sea the weight of the boxes dangling from the net caused the yacht to list.

A mere half an hour after it had nosed into the bay, the yacht slipped out again. When the murmur of its engine had died away, we turned to go. The incoming tide was sliding smoothly over the sand where the boxes had lain, washing away all trace that anything or anyone had ever been there.

CHAPTER EIGHT

That left me with only a couple of hours' sleep before beginning my morning duties. Thirty minutes before the alarm was set to wake me, G's paw patted me softly but insistently on the cheek.

'Gerroff,' I growled, pushing her off the bed and pulling the duvet up over my head.

I knew that she wouldn't give up, that she'd try again. I lay there tensely waiting . . . I'd been wrong. I relaxed and was drifting off again when *thump*, she leapt onto the bed. Heavy paws plodded down towards my feet. A hard bullet-head pile-drove its way under the edge of the duvet cover and a furry body burrowed its way in, to settle itself snugly against my back. As rhythmic snores rumbled from under the cover, I attempted in vain to snatch the precious minutes of sleep left.

Needless to say, it was in somewhat ruffled mood that I made my way over to the big house for breakfast. Would there be any breakfast? Was Chef still here, or had Sir Thomas sacked him after last night's fiery repast? As I crossed the gravel I had my answer – someone was whistling *Flower of Scotland*. Somehow Chef had got away with it.

I pushed open the door with a cheerful, 'Still here, Chef? OK to come in?'

He looked up from stirring the pot of porridge. 'Aye, still here, and it's almost ready.' The whistling resumed.

As I sat down, Ann-Marie breezed in from the hall, slamming the door behind her. 'See the good mood he's in this morning after what happened last night with the dinner.' She sat down, leant over the table and mouthed, 'Makes a change.'

I looked from one to the other. 'What did happen? I thought Sir Thomas would be sure to blow his top.'

She giggled. 'He did, Liz. Or the chillies did. Pity you missed it. You'd just gone and we were sitting here about to tuck into the venison stew, when the intercom buzzed. "Get ready for blast off, Roddy", I said. Well, it wasn't Sir Thomas on the other end, it was the Chinese woman. At first I couldn't make out what she was saying, but it was, "You bring big jug milk *quick*".

'Roddy took his time getting the milk, didn't you, Roddy? Then I raced up the stairs. Couldn't wait to see. . . .' She dissolved in another fit of giggles. 'And there was Sir T gasping like a landed salmon, all red in the face, and eyes streaming. Stuck-up Gabrielle looked a real sight with mascara smudged all over her cheeks. Oh dear, oh dear.' Her own eyes streaming with laughter, she spluttered to a halt.

I looked over at Chef who was ladling the porridge into bowls. 'Well, don't keep me in suspense. How come you're not walking down the drive with your suitcase right now?'

He grinned. 'Because I'm a clever bastard. Western Chinese cuisine is very spicy and I thought, didn't I, that if Ms Chang was from that area, she'd appreciate some home cooking?' One eyelid closed in an exaggerated wink. 'And I'm a lucky bastard too, because Ann-Marie heard Chang tell Sir Thomas that she was indeed Western Chinese. The joke is that she assumed Sir High-and-Mighty had ordered the blow-your-head-off Szechuan cuisine especially for her. Absolutely delighted, she was.' He slid the porridge bowls across the table and pulled a chair out for himself.

Ann-Maire smiled at Chef and mimicked Ms Chang's high-pitched staccato tone. 'West China people like hot, hot food. Cook he very, *very* good.'

He grinned. 'Sir Thomas had to go along with that. Couldn't lose face, could he? Don't know what he was complaining about. If I'd thrown in a handful of Szechuan peppercorns, now. . . .'

'Hotter than chillies, are they?' I passed him the jug of milk.

'I'd say so. And there's a delay, you see, before the fire kicks in, so he'd have taken more—' He broke off at the sound of footsteps on the flagstones of the corridor.

The door handle turned and Waddington stood in the doorway. Unsure of his reception, he cleared his throat. 'Er . . . Sir Thomas is a little out of sorts this morning, Chef Burns, and er . . . will not be requiring his usual breakfast.' His hands twisted nervously, presumably anticipating that offence might be taken.

Chef scowled.

Waddington added hastily, 'Sir Thomas will have toast and tea. That will save you some trouble, won't it? And er. . . .' Chef's ominous silence produced more hand twisting, 'as it's going to be a fine day, I'm going to be driving Sir Thomas and the ladies around the island. Would you kindly make up picnic lunches for four?' A nervous swallow. 'If that's all right? We'll be leaving at ten-thirty.'

Hwhaat. Chef's hand slapped down on the table. He rose slowly to his feet.

'Well, er . . . right.' Waddington backed hastily through the doorway. We heard rapid footsteps retreating along the flagstoned corridor.

Chef grinned. 'Works every time with that one.'

At 10.25 I stowed the picnic hamper, the cool box of champagne bottles and several plastic-backed travelling rugs in the boot and stood, hand on the open car door, awaiting with some impatience the departure of Sir Thomas's party. This was the opportunity I'd been hoping for. While they were out of the house, Gorgonzola and I would have the chance to do a little snooping in the bedrooms.

I planned to smuggle G into the house hidden in the wicker basket I'd brought with me to *Allt an Damh*. Chef would be in staff quarters taking his break, so there'd be no awkward questions from him. Ann-Marie presented more of a problem: she'd be upstairs making the beds and tidying the rooms. I knew she had a set routine, starting with Sir Thomas's room and working her way along the corridor. By the time I came over from the cottage after collecting G, Ann-Marie would have moved on from there. It shouldn't be too difficult to avoid her.

I stood at the top of the stairs listening to the *hummm* of the vacuum cleaner from Gabrielle's room. Then, confident that Ann-Marie would be occupied for some time, I nipped into Sir Thomas's bathroom and let G loose. I'd had plenty of opportunity to go through his bathroom cabinet when I was running the bath and checking that the towels were warm, but drugs hidden in a bathroom are difficult to find without doing obvious damage to the fitments. If I'd missed anything here, G would find it. She nosed round the bath panel, then leapt up on the cistern. Nothing. I held her up to sniff at the cabinet. Nothing.

I eased open the bathroom door. *Hmmm* told me that Ann-Marie was still busy with the vacuum cleaner. Carrying G in the basket, I walked quietly along the corridor to Sir Thomas's bedroom, turned the handle and slipped inside.

This room was as luxuriously furnished as Gabrielle's, but in much more masculine style: same type of four-poster bed, but cover and canopy in black and gold with heavy cord tassels; black-shaded lights on the bedside tables; overstuffed black leather armchair with high back and headrests; and heavy oak chest of drawers with oval swing mirror on top.

I put the wicker basket on the floor and let Gorgonzola out. She jumped onto the bed, stretched out a tentative paw and patted playfully at a canopy tassel.

'You're on duty, G.' I fingered her working collar as a reminder.

She gave a final pat at the tassel, then jumped off the bed and strolled towards the wardrobe. 'Search!' I opened the wardrobe door for her and while she was investigating it, pulled open the bedside table drawer.

It contained only a packet of condoms and a few boxes of daily-use contact lenses – small vacuum-sealed sachets each containing a tiny jellyfish of a contact lens floating in a blue-tinged sterile liquid. I always take note of everything, no matter how unimportant it seems. The box was almost full. I dropped two of the sachets into my pocket, sure that they wouldn't be missed.

I turned my attention to the other bedside cabinet. It contained a couple of packets of prescription pills. I picked one up and studied the label. *Atenolol 50mg tablets. One to be taken twice daily*. It had been issued by an Edinburgh pharmacist to Sir Thomas Cameron-Blaik in August this year. The packet had already been opened. I extracted the information leaflet and skimmed through it . . . *treats high blood pressure, angina, irregular heart beat, protects the heart after a heart attack*. The other packet, *Ikorel*, also treated angina and high blood pressure. Outwardly Sir Thomas looked healthy enough, but of course, you never can tell. One thing for sure, those bursts of temper wouldn't be doing his health any good at all.

Gorgonzola had emerged from the wardrobe and was prowling round the room while I snooped in the chest of drawers. There was no need to watch her – if she found anything, I'd hear that crooning purr. We both drew a blank. Whatever Sir Thomas's connection with the drug smuggling ring, he didn't appear to be a drug user himself.

G wasn't too keen to return to the wicker basket, but when she knows she's on duty, she makes only a token fuss, knowing that her reward will come later. I opened the bedroom door a crack. The vacuuming had stopped but the sound of running water from Gabrielle's bathroom pinpointed Ann-Marie's position. From there, she'd move on to Ms Chang's room. The coast was clear to give Gabrielle's room the once-over.

I sifted through Gabrielle's bedside cabinets while G was nosing around. Nothing but an uninteresting clutter of beauty paraphernalia – manicure set, nail varnish, hairdryer, etc etc. In the top drawer of the dresser were three books – a copy of the *Whisky Bible* giving the quality ratings for different whiskies in the current year, the Scotch Malt Whisky Society's *Short Guide* and the current bottling list, *Outturn*, available only to members of Edinburgh's The Vaults. Like millions the world over, she must have developed a taste for Scotch whisky and Sir Thomas, as a member of The Vaults, had given her the tasting notes.

There was nothing here of interest. Gorgonzola thought so too. She was sitting on the comfortable armchair looking bored.

'More fun in the next room, G,' I said. The traces on my gloves after I'd handled the clothes in Chang's suitcase guaranteed that.

I opened the door a crack and put my ear to it. The sound of furniture being moved indicated that Ann-Marie had progressed from Gabrielle's bathroom to Chang's room. I wasn't too comfortable about having to wait here till she was cleaning Chang's bathroom, but there was nothing else for it. I might as well examine those booklets from The Vaults again to see what I could learn about the price of whisky. I flicked through the tasting notes of the bottling list – Lowland . . . Highland . . . Speyside.

'Wow, listen to this, G! A bottle from cask number 7.48, *Cold Nights and Warm Fires*, is priced at – wait for it – a hundred and eighty pounds!'

The tongue industriously licking her foreleg paused, then resumed.

'That's eleven pounds for a *dram*, a tiny little glass.'

I was treated to a slow, I'm-not-impressed ya-a-wn, displaying ridged palate and glistening fangs.

The hum of the vacuum drifted through the closed door almost drowning out the faint sound of Ann-Marie singing. When the vacuum stopped, I held the basket lid invitingly open. 'OK, fun time, G.'

In Chang's room I placed the basket on the floor near one of the bedside tables, and opened the lid. This time, there was no point in me searching the room myself: a professional, as I suspected Chang was, wouldn't have left anything incriminating for the maid to find. What she might very well have left were hard-to-spot indicators that would show someone had been snooping. Chang had definitely been in contact with something illegal and if it was here, G would find it before I did.

'Search, G!' I indicated the room with a sweep of my hand.

She leapt lightly onto the bed, sniffed at the tartan throw and the padded headboard, then jumped down to burrow under the valance. I waited.

A few moments later, I heard the hoped for *mwerwrrraouw*, muffled a little by the thick coverings.

'Attagirl, G.' I knelt down, lifted up the valance and peered in the direction of the purr.

She was crouched near the head of the bed looking up at a small package attached to one of the wooden struts acting as mattress supports. I stretched out flat on the floor and was on the point of wriggling under the bed for a closer look when I realized that the noise of the vacuum had stopped.

The words of Ann-Marie's song were now distinct, no longer a murmur. '*O my dear, my native isle, Nought from thee my heart can wile. . . .*'

The singing was louder . . . she was coming along the corridor.

'*O my dear, my native isle. . . .*'

I grabbed the wicker basket and rolled under the valance. Even though the door was at the other side of the bed, if she came in and walked towards the window, the movement of the valance would betray me.

The door handle rattled.

'*. . . My heart beats true to Islay.*'

She was in the room. I lay on my back. Had her singing drowned Gorgonzola's astonished squeak when I bumped against her? If Ann-Marie thought there was a mouse under the bed. . . .

I heard the scrape of the bowl being moved on the chest of drawers, the rustle of dried heather husks, and a muttered curse. A pause, then the vacuum's loud *hmmm* sent its vibration through the carpeted floor-boards.

The valance at the foot of the bed shook as the front of the vacuum thrust its way beneath the fabric almost touching my shoe. An involuntary snatch away of my leg brought my knee in sharp and painful contact with one of the bed struts.

A final thrust of the vacuum, then the motor was switched off. I lay there listening to the squeak of the machine being rolled away and the click of the latch as the door closed.

'O *my dear, my native isle. . . .*' receded along the corridor and down the stairs.

I pushed the basket out from under the valance and wriggled after it, holding up the fabric for G to follow.

'That was close, G.' I tickled the top of her head and behind her ears, her favourite spots. 'You stayed still when I rolled against you. You're a very good girl.'

I tried not to think what would have happened if a startled G had shot out from under the bed. The reappearance of another 'feral' cat in a guest's bedroom would have caused a hell of an uproar – though not nearly as much as the discovery of the butler under the bed!

I left the package in position without disturbing it. Chang would be sure to check to see if it was still there, and G's nose had told me that it contained illegal drugs – all I needed to know.

With Gorgonzola tucked safely away in the basket, I made my way downstairs and returned to the cottage without encountering Ann-Marie. Things had gone well. Discoveries had been made and, best of all, nobody knew I had been in the house.

CHAPTER NINE

My intention had been to make a further reconnaissance of the grounds in preparation for the quick departure that would be necessary once I had identified Moran, but heavy rain started just before I got back to the cottage. Warning drops spattered on the leathery rhododendron leaves, leaving clear circles on the dusty surface. As I closed the door behind me, the heavens opened. Rain draped a grey curtain over the chimneys of the big house, ricocheting off the brick path like tiny silver bullets, drumming on the roof of the bathroom extension and drowning out the muted rumble of the kettle as it came to the boil. Gorgonzola hated getting wet. She'd be safe for another day from the lurking danger of gin traps and snares.

One of the things in the cottage that hadn't been modernized was the fireplace. It still had the black Victorian cast-iron fire grate and basket piled with small logs and kindling. A couple of matches soon set a good fire going. I closed the curtains to shut out the depressing weather and any prying eyes, made myself a cup of tea and with G curled up on my lap, settled down to read the magazine I'd bought on the ferry. Fashion . . . cooking . . . gardening . . . the fun quiz *How human is your pet?*

'Let's see, G, how you rate on this.' I read the first question to her.

'*If your pet misbehaves, and you tell it off, does it:*

a) Look ashamed?

b) Pretend nothing has happened?

c) Fail to understand what you're getting uptight about?

d) Give an unmistakable "Up Yours" sign?'

Her ears rotated 180°, an eye slowly opened and half-closed again. As far as G was concerned, the answer was *d)*.

I scanned the next question. It was a good one.

You put a plate of its favourite food on a high table and leave the room.

'*If* I was foolish enough, G, to leave a piece of salmon on the table, would you *a)* eat it as soon as I've gone out?'

The half-open eye closed.

'That's a no, then. How about *b)*? Would you eat it even before I've left the room?'

No response. Her sides rose and fell in slow rhythm. 'Or would you, *c)* Leave it untouched?'

A gentle snore. That meant no, again.

'Well, that leaves *d)*. You'd eat it and shift the blame by placing a piece in another pet's bed. Well, would you, G? Is that right?'

Unsheathed claws stabbed gently into my thigh.

Shifting the blame, that's exactly what G had done. It was not long after I'd taken her on as a trainee sniffer with the dogs. A fish had disappeared from the kitchen worktop and I'd later found the head wedged through the mesh around the dogs' kennels.

Again the sharp claws dug gently into my thigh. Was she remembering, too?

A flurry of rain battered at the window. If Sir Thomas and his party had been caught in this, it wouldn't do his temper any good at all. The flames flickered up the chimney as a log collapsed in on itself. I leant back in the chair and closed my eyes. Drained by last night's lack of sleep, I dozed off. . . .

Brrr Brrr Brrr Brrr. The fire had died to a smouldering heap of charred wood and ash. *Brrr Brrr Brrr Brrr*. It would be Waddington, or, worse still, Sir Thomas, ringing through on the intercom to find out why I had neglected to prepare the table for dinner.

I leapt up, avalanching Gorgonzola in a furry heap onto the floor. With a reproachful *hwaaar* she wasted no time in reclaiming the warmed seat of the armchair.

I snatched up the receiver. 'Dorward here.'

It took a second or two for me to realize that it was not Waddington at the other end of the line, but Gabrielle, shrill and petulant.

'*Mon dieu*, 'ere I am shivering, *shivering*. I am wet through to the skin. I want the hot bath and the warm towels, and I want them *tout de suite*. Now, you understand? Why 'ave they not been made ready? What were you thinking, Dorward?' Her voice rose to a strident shriek.

I held the receiver away from my ear, letting her rant on with a long catalogue of what she expected of a butler and detailing how very far short I had fallen from her expectations.

'You 'ave not even switched on the towel rail. *Imbecile*! Did you not see the rain? We 'ad to return early. Even a *fool* would know we are wet.'

She paused for breath, enabling me to insert a polite, 'I'm so sorry, madam. I'll be right over.' I put down the receiver before she could resume the tirade.

Silly woman. Her bath would have been ready and the towels warming up by now if she'd run the bath herself and switched on the towel rail instead of wasting time haranguing me on the phone.

I was just coming down the stairs with an armful of Gabrielle's wet clothes, when I heard the entrance gate intercom buzz and saw the CCTV screen light up. I hurried down the last few steps to see who the visitor was before Waddington answered from his office and the screen went blank.

Buzz. The screen was still live. The overweight man on camera was obviously very angry. His face was flushed, his mouth compressed into a tight line.

Buzz. Buzzz. Waddington didn't answer. He must be changing out of his wet clothes, perhaps still relaxing in his bath.

Buzz. Buzzz. Buzzz. The visitor's rage was increasing by the second. He appeared to be shouting. Suddenly the face filling the screen disappeared as he turned on his heel. He strode to his car and reached in through the open window to press hard on the horn. Before I could answer the intercom, he abandoned that tactic, rushed at the gates, grabbed the bars and shook them violently.

Whoever the man was, he was not Louis Moran. Ample girth could be faked with padding, but even a master of disguise couldn't cut a foot off his height and shorten his arms and legs. No, not Louis Moran, but somebody who had pressing business with Sir Thomas. Should I play safe and continue on my way to the utility room with Gabrielle's clothes, or should I answer the intercom? Would that arouse suspicion, jeopardizing HMRC's operation? I decided that it would be the natural thing for a butler to do: somebody with obviously important business with Sir Thomas couldn't be turned away.

I picked up the receiver. '*Allt an Damh*. May I enquire your name and your business with Sir Thomas?'

The face appeared once again on the screen. 'The name's Winstanley. I demand to see Cameron-Blaik and don't damn well tell me I can't.' The angry words tumbled over each other. 'I've been down at the distillery. He'll know what it's about.' His face thrust closer to the camera. 'And if I don't get a bloody good answer, tell him the next stop's the police.'

This was better than I'd hoped for. Much better. Sir Thomas's reaction when I announced the imminent arrival of the enraged Mr Winstanley would tell me a lot.

I pressed the button to open the gates. 'Please drive in, Mr Winstanley. I'll inform Sir Thomas that you are here.'

I took my time taking Gabrielle's wet clothes to the utility room. Sir Thomas and Waddington were unaware of the storm that was about to break. If I could delay informing them till I'd let the enraged visitor into the house, they would be caught off guard, have no time to fabricate a convincing defence to a matter serious enough, in Winstanley's opinion, for the police to be called in.

Slowly I ascended the stairs. At a leisurely pace I walked along the corridor under the impassive gaze of the stags to Sir Thomas's study. There was no reply to my light knock. No reply either from the bedroom.

I tapped on the bathroom door. 'Sir Thomas, I'm sorry to disturb you, but' – I chose my words carefully – 'a Mr Winstanley has just called from the gates on very urgent business. I've just opened them to let him drive up.'

The roar of 'Opened the gates!' was followed by a loud surge and splashing of water, and a string of curses. A few moments later, Sir Thomas wrapped in a Cameron tartan robe, face red as the tartan with anger and the heat of the bath, flung open the door.

'Winstanley? Never heard of him. What the bloody hell do you mean by opening the gates?' His eyes blazed. 'By God, you'll pay for this, Dorward.' He raised his voice. 'Waddington! Waddington, where the hell are you, man?'

I adopted an expression of surprise mingled with consternation. 'I'm sorry, Sir Thomas,' I stammered, 'but he said he would call the police if you didn't see him.' Not *quite* Winstanley's words, but the very mention of 'police' should exonerate me, and with luck, precipitate hasty and perhaps rash action.

Without a word, he pushed past me and at the same moment

Waddington appeared at the top of the stairs, out of breath, his hair plastered to his scalp by shower or rain.

With a barked, 'In here, Waddington,' Sir Thomas flung open his bedroom door. As the door closed behind them, I heard, rapped out, urgent, 'The name Winstanley mean anything?'

Buzz. The intercom announced the arrival of the unwelcome visitor at the front door.

I tapped on the bedroom door. 'That's Mr Winstanley now, Sir Thomas. What do you wish me to do?'

A pause, then a flustered Waddington poked his head out. 'Take the gentleman into the billiard room. Sir Thomas will be down shortly.'

I walked away, but when the door clicked closed, darted back and put my ear to the panel. I was in time to hear Waddington bleat, '. . . here in the diary. His name's down to visit the distillery. I didn't think it mattered if—'

Bzzzzzzzz. I didn't hear the rest. I hurried down to open the door before the delay aroused Sir Thomas's suspicions.

Before I had the door even half-open, Winstanley hurled himself through it. 'The bugger's bloody well not going to get away with stealing my casks. I'm going straight from here to the police.' Nostrils flaring, he looked wildly round. 'Where is he? Take me to—'

'Follow me, sir,' I interrupted soothingly. I opened the door to the billiard room.

He brushed me aside and strode in, fists clenched. 'Where the hell are my casks, you bast—?' Realizing he was addressing an empty room, he swung round belligerently.

'Sir Thomas will be with you very shortly, Mr Winstanley.' I gestured towards the bar with its row of bottles. 'While you're waiting, can I offer you a whisky?'

The violence of his reaction took me by surprise. 'Whisky!' He swept his arm across the billiard table, scattering the triangle of balls across the baize. 'What's happened to *my* whisky? That's what *I* want to know.'

'Whisky?' I frowned, hoping to get more out of him before Sir Thomas appeared.

'The ten casks my father laid down fifty years ago. They'll be worth six figures now. When I called at the distillery today to inspect them, not one cask had my number on it. I walked up and down the rows but—'

'Ah, Mr Winstanley.' Sir Thomas's voice, smoothly urbane, came from behind me. 'So sorry to keep you waiting.' He advanced, hand outstretched. 'I'm just back. I was caught on the hills when the heavens opened and soaked to the skin. Had to change.' He turned to me. 'That will be all, Dorward.'

Winstanley pointedly ignored the offered hand. As I made my way slowly out of the room, I heard him snarl, 'Where the hell are my casks? And don't think you can fob me off with something else. First thing I'll do is send a sample off to Tatlock & Thomson for analysis.'

I closed the door very, very slowly so as to see and hear as much as I could.

'Your casks?' Sir Thomas's hand stroked his chin.

'Yes, my casks, ten casks, ten bloody casks with my number on them missing from the bloody warehouse. Explain *that* away.' Through the closing gap I could see the veins standing out on Winstanley's temples like ropes. His face had turned an alarming shade of puce.

I closed the door loudly against the jamb, but held the handle so that the latch didn't engage, then pushed the door open a crack and pressed my ear to it, conscious that Waddington would be back at any moment.

'Ah, your number,' Sir Thomas was saying. 'Now, there's an explanation for that. Since your last visit, due to the rapid upturn in business, we've had to build an additional warehouse. We've moved the older casks there, more stable maturation conditions, of course. So important for the quality of the whisky. If you give me your cask number, I'll phone my secretary to bring down the warehouse list from my office.'

I left the door a fraction ajar and moved rapidly away. When Waddington came hurrying down the stairs, file folder in hand, it was to see me emerge from the corridor leading to the kitchen.

'Ms Gabrielle wishes me to attend her,' I called out. 'Will Sir Thomas be needing me any more?'

He didn't seem to hear me. Sweat beaded his hairline. The fingers clutching the file were white with pressure.

'Will Sir Thomas be needing me any more?' I repeated.

As if his mind was on something else, something much more weighty, he said abstractedly, 'Sir Thomas will see the visitor out, Dorward.'

Out of sight of the entrance hall I waited at the top of the stairs, listening for the billiard room door to open again.

'Dorward!' Sir Thomas's shout came floating up from the entrance hall. 'Dorward!'

I waited a moment or two to give the impression I had been busy in one of the rooms, then hurried down the stairs. Sir Thomas and Winstanley were standing in the doorway of the billiard room. Waddington was nowhere to be seen.

'See Mr Winstanley out, Dorward.' Sir Thomas turned to him and shook his hand. A jovial, hearty, 'Well that's settled, then. I'll call for you at The Harbour Inn tomorrow at eight o'clock, take you to the new warehouse to inspect your casks, and have you back at Port Ellen in time for the morning ferry.'

'And the car hire to come all the way out here? I wasn't expecting that expense when—' Winstanley's voice still held a trace of its former belligerence.

'Waddington will reimburse you and see to the return of the car. Just give him the receipt tomorrow. No need to worry, George.' Another firm handshake. 'Everything's going to be taken care of.' He went back into the billiard room. The door closed quietly.

I held the front door open. 'I trust everything has been settled to your satisfaction, sir.'

Winstanley grunted. 'We'll see.'

I watched as he wedged himself behind the wheel. Without a backward glance he sped off down the drive, gravel spurting from under the wheels.

I made my way upstairs to see what mess Gabrielle had left for me. Along the corridor, her bathroom door stood open, wafting out clouds of scented steam. I entered to find, as usual, wet towels lying on the floor where they'd been carelessly dropped and the bath full of water – it being beyond milady Gabrielle's strength to pull out the bath plug.

'Think we handled that pretty well, eh?' Sir Thomas's voice came from the top of the stairs.

A murmur from Waddington.

I turned the bath taps fully on. The sound of rushing water would signal that Elizabeth Dorward, butler, was fully engaged in her official duties. Far from her mind the visit of Mr George Winstanley.

At dinner that evening conversation was desultory. Sir Thomas for once had little to say; Ms Chang, dark eyes inscrutable, spoke only when spoken to; Waddington, present this time, said nothing at all; Gabrielle, normally so quick to criticize my failings real or imagined, made no comment on the drop of wine that fell on the tablecloth. They all seemed preoccupied, merely picking at Chef's *tour de force*, a whole salmon ornately decorated with an elaborate design in crème fraiche and dill.

Whatever was on their minds, I was not to be party to it. I'd crunched the serving spoon through the crust of a magnificent Baked Alaska when Sir Thomas said irritably, 'Leave it, Dorward. We'll help ourselves.' As I turned to go he added, 'Oh, and tell Chef, I want breakfast at six-fifteen tomorrow.'

That meant a rise at dawn for chef and myself. I wasn't looking forward to telling him the bad news.

Bad news too for Gabrielle. '*Mon Dieu*, Thomas! Six-fifteen? That eez the middle of the night!'

He reached over and patted her hand. 'That's just for Waddington and me, my dear. We've to allow time to get to Bowmore and take Mr Winstanley to the new warehouse to show him his casks. After that we'll drive him to Port Ellen to catch the ferry. No, no, I wouldn't expect you and Ms Chang, here, to breakfast so early.'

Since my presence was no longer required, I made my way downstairs to the kitchen. I, too, had plenty to think about: Winstanley's 'missing' whisky casks, to be exact. Sir Thomas's explanation had been very convincing – on the surface, that is. But I couldn't forget his alarmed, almost panicky reaction when I'd first informed him of the visitor's imminent arrival. Such a strong reaction suggested that he might indeed have something to hide: Winstanley's conviction that his casks had been stolen could well prove correct.

As soon as I pushed open the kitchen door, I could see something was wrong. Chef sat, silent and brooding, at the head of the long wooden table. His Medusa curls writhed, angry black vipers, above drawn brows and narrowed eyes. The dark shadow of stubble added to the air of menace. The target of his glowering gaze was the four plates of barely touched salmon lined up in front of him, silent testimony of the diners' verdict on his cooking. He clearly felt that the hours spent creating the dish had been a complete waste of his valuable time.

'Don't take it to heart, Roddy,' Ann-Marie was saying soothingly. 'They weren't hungry, that's all.' She sat down beside him and patted his arm.

'Yes,' I said, adding my bit of consolation, 'it's because you were too generous with their picnic hamper.'

Chef growled something rude regarding the picnic hamper and where Sir Thomas could put it.

'It wasn't the *picnic hamper* that put them off their food,' Ann-Marie cried. 'That's not it at all!'

His eyelids slowly raised, the glower transferred itself to her. 'Ar-r-re you meaning—?' The rolling 'r' a danger sign of explosion pending.

She didn't let him finish. 'It's because of what happened this afternoon.' She turned to me. 'That's right, isn't it? Tell him, Liz.'

'Sir Thomas had an unexpected visitor,' I said cautiously. 'And . . . er . . . it seems to have upset them all.'

Chef's expression lightened infinitesimally.

'The man said he was going to the police,' Ann-Marie breathed, her eyes round with excitement. 'He was ranting on about Sir Thomas stealing his casks of whisky.'

Damn. She must have been lighting the fire in the drawing room when she'd heard the commotion in the entrance hall. I'd been going to keep quiet about Winstanley and his threat to call the police over his missing casks.

'There's no smoke without fire. Sir T's as guilty as hell.' A solemn nod. 'I always felt there was something *fishy*—' She nudged Chef, pointed at the offending plates and gurgled with laughter.

He almost smiled. The prospect of Sir Thomas being dragged off in handcuffs was obviously pleasing.

Though I joined in Ann-Marie's laughter, I was worried. Sir Thomas was playing for high stakes. With my own eyes I'd seen the evidence: those boxes of whisky in the shed on the beach, whisky that was being traded for drugs. He'd not hesitate to take action against anyone who posed a threat to him. Ann-Marie was treading on dangerous ground. If she gossiped about the missing casks, her sudden and untimely death was a real possibility.

I tried to defuse the situation. 'I'm sure everything's above board. After all, Sir Thomas is a respected distillery owner. There's bound to be a simple explanation.'

'Like what?' Ann-Marie snorted, patently unwilling to be cheated out of a juicy piece of scandal.

Now was my chance to test Sir Thomas's story on someone with local knowledge. 'Like . . . like . . . Mr Winstanley was looking in the wrong warehouse for his casks.'

'Wrong warehouse?' She looked at me as if I had taken leave of my senses.

85

'Well,' I said, 'perhaps Sir Thomas has two warehouses. Maybe he's built a new one since Mr Winstanley was last here.'

'Good try, Liz, but there's only one warehouse, and it's half empty. Why on earth would he build another warehouse? They say that the Sròn Dubh distillery's been losing money for years.'

'Well, you could be right then, that something's going on. But we'd better keep quiet about it for the moment till we see what happens,' I said slowly. 'You know Sir Thomas's temper – if he finds out we've spread rumours, he'll sue us for all we've got.'

'I don't think so!' Chef rose from the table and fetched a sharpening stone from a drawer. *Sschwee sschwee sschwee sschwee.* He honed the cleaver razor sharp till its cutting edge glinted in a thin silver line.

'Sue *me* for all I've got? That'll be right. I haven't got anything!' Ann-Marie raised two rude fingers in the direction of the dining room and its occupants.

Chef cheered up after that. The three of us tucked into the salmon along with a bottle of Sir Thomas's best wine which I liberated from the cellar.

Later, I took the little that remained of the salmon back with me to the gardener's cottage, ostensibly as a picnic snack for tomorrow.

'With the compliments of the chef, G.'

She delicately selected each morsel from the plate, her rolling *purr* a token of appreciation. Unlike Sir Thomas and his guests, Gorgonzola had an appetite for best Scottish salmon when it came her way.

Now that I knew from Ann-Marie that there *was* no new warehouse in which the missing casks would be found, the reason for the lack of appetite at dinner was clear: Sir Thomas, Waddington, and Gabrielle, Moran's partner-in-crime, were preoccupied with the threat posed by Winstanley to their very profitable scheme.

A thought occurred to me, and it concerned Chang. Why had *she* been off her food? I was as sure as I could be that she knew nothing about the whisky scam, or George Winstanley. So what was on *her* mind?

I didn't get much sleep that night between thinking about Chang and worrying about Chef and Ann-Marie. Would they take my advice and keep quiet?

CHAPTER TEN

At a quarter to eight next morning, an hour after Sir Thomas and Waddington had driven off in Sir Thomas's 4x4, I found out what had been on Chang's mind. The intercom buzzed when I was in the kitchen giving Chef a hand with the washing up after our own early breakfast, and Ann-Marie had bustled off to change the sheets and clean Sir Thomas's room.

'If that's madam demanding her breakfast half an hour early, she'll be getting a one-minute boiled egg and non-boiling water for the tea.' Chef didn't seem to be joking. 'And,' he added, 'no toast, only bread.'

I laughed. 'How would I explain that? Sudden electrical failure in the kitchen, perhaps?'

'It could be arranged.' Chef's eyes strayed to the main fuse box.

But Chef didn't get the chance to flick the switches on the fuse box: it wasn't Gabrielle on the intercom.

'It is Ms Chang. Please to order taxi for ferry. I go now.' The words staccato, sharp with tension. 'Taxi come soon?'

I managed to conceal my surprise. 'We are a considerable distance from Port Ellen, madam. I'd think it would take the taxi' – I did a rapid calculation of the time it had taken me – 'forty-five to fifty minutes to get here, and the same to get back to Port Ellen. I'll order the taxi straight away. You should be in there in plenty of time to catch the ferry.'

I carried Chang's bag out to the taxi and watched it drive off. First chance I got, I'd take a look under her bed and see if the package had gone with her.

I was in the kitchen preparing Gabrielle's breakfast tray when Ann-Marie came through the door with an armful of sheets and dumped them in a heap in front of the washing machine.

'Well, that's the lord and master's room done. When Robillard and Chang deign to get up, I'll get their sheets too.'

'You can get Ms Chang's right now.' I placed a single-stemmed rose artistically across the corner of the breakfast tray. 'She's just left to catch the ferry.'

'Lucky for her she's not gone to catch the plane.' Ann-Marie stuffed the sheets into the washing machine and pushed the start button. 'While I was making the bed, I heard on Sir T's radio that this morning's flight's been cancelled.' She glanced out of the window. 'Probably because of the low cloud. Planes don't land when it's like that.'

I stared thoughtfully out at the heavy sky. What Ann-Marie had just said could affect me too. It confirmed my doubts about the wisdom of making the plane my first choice when the time came to escape from *Allt an Damh*. Not only would Moran find it easy to track my car – and intercept it – on that long straight road to the airport, there was now the possibility of bad weather to consider. My escape from Islay might very well have to be by ferry.

That was not what Gerry had planned. At the briefing, his pen had doodled a circle. 'You are to leave by ferry *only* if for some reason you can't get on a plane.' A horizontal bar completed the doodle. A no-entry sign in any language.

'What's happened to the sacred expense account?' I'd joked.

He hadn't smiled, only sighed in exasperation.

'Really, Deborah, can't you work it out? It's simple. Moran will stop at nothing if he thinks you are a threat. I'll spell it out so you realize fully the danger you'll be in when you identify him. The best I can do to protect you, if you travel by the ferry, is to have a man detailed to act as bodyguard, but neither he nor you will know who among the crowd of passengers might be Moran's men – or women. There are too many opportunities for ambush on that two-hour crossing. Think about it. Am I right?'

I'd nodded. Gerry was always right. HMRC undercover agents under his control had good reason to be grateful for his meticulous attention to detail and his forward planning for even the most unlikely eventualities. His nickname of Belt-and-Braces Burnside was well-earned.

'You are to leave by *plane* because it offers the best security. Your safety is my priority, so to make sure your departure goes smoothly. . . .' He'd ticked off the points on his fingers as he made them. 'One: from the day after your arrival, on every flight from Islay a seat will be booked under the inconspicuous name of Smith. Two: on the flight that you actually take, all passengers will have had to have pre-booked their seats and any stand-by seats will be cancelled. Three: all you will have to do at the airport is supply a codeword to gain high security clearance – you won't need a passport in the name of Smith. Four: you will be kept out of sight of waiting passengers and public and be boarded first.'

Gerry had had it all cut and dried on how I was to leave the island, but up to now I hadn't done anything about his warning that I might first have to go into hiding. Finding a place to lie low was something that couldn't be postponed any longer. I'd do something about it as soon as I was free today.

Before I delivered the tray to Gabrielle and while Ann-Marie was busy dusting downstairs, I took the opportunity to slip into Chang's room. I didn't bother to lie on the floor and squirm under the bed, but flicked up the valance and cast a cursory glance along the bed struts, sure that Chang would have taken that valuable package of drugs with her.

She hadn't. It was still there, and much as I thought about it, I couldn't fathom out why.

My discovery of Sir Thomas's trade in whisky-for-drugs had not been enough to warrant the risk of an urgent phone call to Gerry, but Winstanley's accusations against Sir Thomas and this morning's sudden departure of drug dealer Chang had changed all that.

I planned the phone call carefully: I'd inform Gabrielle that her bath was ready, then take off in the car to the phone box in Bowmore, a safe distance from *Allt an Damh*.

It didn't work out that way. Before I even got as far as running the bath, things went wrong. When I laid the tray on Gabrielle's bed, she grumbled as usual about the weather, the breakfast and the layout of the tray. I let it all wash over me and prepared to leave.

My hand was on the door handle when she called out, '*Un moment*, Dorward. That *imbecile*, Winstanley, 'as *ruined* my day, ruined it!' She smacked her teaspoon hard on the boiled egg smashing the shell. The yolk trickled down the side and formed a sticky pool on the tray cloth. She scowled. 'Because Thomas and Waddington are taking 'im to the distillery, they will 'ave the car till lunchtime, eet now seems. Sir Thomas 'as been *most* inconsiderate. 'Ow am I to visit the famous reserve for nature at Gruinart? Last night eet was all decided that 'e takes me there this morning. And now my day eez ruined! Unless. . . .' She studied me, calculation in her dark eyes. 'Yes, that eez it. After my bath I 'ave a job for you. Why do I not think of this before?' She broke off a piece of toast and dipped it in the boiled egg. 'You will be my *chauffeur*, Dorward. Yes . . . you will bring your car to the front door at ten thirty. And 'ave Chef make up a picnic as we will not return till after four.'

'Certainly, madam.' I bowed and closed the door quietly behind me.

Gabrielle had just made it impossible for me to phone Gerry today. Unless . . . I made some rapid calculations. I *could* just make it to the nearest phone box, the one outside the Ardbeg distillery, if I ran the bath now with the hottest water, no cold added. In twenty minutes it would be just the right temperature.

I set the control box for the gates to manual operation and by half past nine I was speeding away from *Allt an Damh* towards Port Ellen.

The needle-points of Ardbeg's chimneys were lost in sea mist. In the gap between the distillery buildings an angry sea dashed against the reef, sending spray fountaining up from the rocks. Heavy grey clouds threatened rain – not at all the weather for even the keenest of bird-watchers to visit the Gruinart Nature Reserve. Why was Gabrielle so determined to go bird-watching on a day like this? Up till now, the only interest she had shown in feathers was as a hat decoration. I pushed the matter to the back of my mind. There'd be time to think about that after I'd made the phone call.

I parked the car in the distillery car-park and hurried back up the hundred yards to the phone box. If timing hadn't been so critical, I wouldn't have used it, but it should be safe enough: Sir Thomas and Waddington wouldn't be coming this way for another couple of hours. It would take them that time to go to the distillery and then see Winstanley off on the ferry.

While I waited to be passed through to Gerry, the seconds ticked by, emphasizing what little time I had to get back to *Allt an Damh* before I was missed. As soon as he came on the line, I launched into my report.

'. . . but,' I finished, 'I can't work out why Chang didn't take the packet of drugs with her on the ferry. Strange, isn't it?'

There was a moment's silence. 'She wouldn't, if she was planning to go by air.'

I should have thought of that. She'd not take the risk of being caught with drugs at airport security.

'So,' Gerry said, 'she's trying to cover her tracks. And that means—?'

Time was too short for brain exercises. 'It means,' I snapped, 'that she's done a runner from Cameron-Blaik. She waited till he'd gone off to his distillery. Therefore he doesn't know yet that she's gone.'

The 'Well done, Deborah,' sounded abstracted, preoccupied.

I knew him only too well. 'OK, Gerry. You're now going to tell me something I won't want to hear, aren't you?'

For a moment he didn't reply. Then, 'The police have identified the woman buried on Portobello beach.'

Why did he hesitate before telling me that? Why did he think it would upset me? 'And so?' I said, glancing at my watch.

'Forensics found a laundry mark on her dress and from there it was just a matter of confirming identification by dental records.'

He was leading up to something, definitely preparing me for a shock.

'Out with it, Gerry,' I hissed, 'I've got to get back.'

He sighed. After a long pause he dropped his bombshell. 'Dental records prove her to be Lady Amelia Cameron-Blaik.'

To say I was stunned may be a bit of a cliché, but I can't think of a better description. Before this revelation my mission had simply been to wait for Moran to appear and then get out fast. Sir Thomas's illegal activities had been of lesser importance than the capture of Moran. But the murder of Lady Cameron-Blaik had now changed everything.

Gerry was saying, '. . . so I persuaded the police to delay informing Cameron-Blaik for a week. Now that we're so close to getting our hands on Moran, what we don't want is a police investigation and newspaper headlines. I've a feeling Lady Amelia's death may be linked to whatever's going on at *Allt an Damh*. I don't have to tell you to be very careful indeed, Deborah.' The gravity in his voice said it all.

I'd just pushed open the door of the phone box and was about to step out, when a black 4x4 roared past and before I could read its number plate, disappeared round a bend. I stared after it.

There's no need to worry, I told myself. Sir Thomas won't be coming this way for another couple of hours. It's your imagination running riot.

Nevertheless, that 4x4 was on my mind all the way back to *Allt an Damh*, increasingly so as I neared the gates. If it had been Sir Thomas in the car, the gates would now be controlled from the house and I wouldn't be able to get through. But when I pushed at them they swung silently back. All was well. I put my foot on the accelerator, and palms moist with sweat, pulled up at the front door with a minute to spare.

The bird-watching at Gruinart had been underway for half an hour without any noticeable enthusiasm on Gabrielle's part. She stared moodily through the windscreen at the geese floating on the grey waters of the loch.

'This eez so so boring. Nothing to see but water and grass and seabirds – or perhaps they are ducks?' She lowered the binoculars and tossed them onto the back seat. 'I 'ave seen enough birds, Dorward!'

Since it had been clear from the moment we'd arrived that she had not the slightest interest in birds, except those served up on a plate, why were we here? Was there an ulterior motive to keep me away from *Allt an Damh*? I'd test her out.

'Perhaps you would prefer to go back to *Allt an Damh* now, madam?'

'*Non*, Dorward. Thomas was most clear. We must not return till four. Drive me to some other place.'

To hide my elation I turned away, pretending to adjust the wing mirror. She had inadvertently revealed that the trip to Gruinart was no spur-of-the-moment idea, but in fact a prearranged plan. While we were away from *Allt an Damh*, something was going on, something that Sir Thomas wanted kept secret. Could it be that they were moving the consignment of drugs delivered to the shed by boat? So would that van be making another visit?

She pulled the guidebook from the glove compartment and thrust it at me. 'Find a more interesting place, Dorward.'

I flipped through the pages. 'Finlaggan's not too far from here. It says that from medieval times this place was the seat of power of the Lords of the Isles who—'

'*Merde* to all that boring history!' She snatched the book from me. 'Just *drive* there, Dorward. What are you waiting for?'

It wasn't the best of days to visit Finlaggan either. A cold, blustery wind was whipping the long grasses and ruffling the grey water into angry peaks. Dark clouds in a leaden sky pressed on the surrounding hills and threatened rain. A large black bird wheeled slowly overhead, its harsh *kaar kaar* scratching at the brooding silence. We sat gazing through the windscreen, this time at the locked and bolted visitor centre. The only other sign of man's intervention was a narrow muddy path curving its way over a low rise and disappearing in the direction of the loch.

Gabrielle made it clear she had no intention of leaving the comfort of the car and making the short walk to view the island and the ruined chapel.

'Ugh! 'Ow could anyone choose to live in this place?' She shivered despite the warmth of the car. 'What Thomas wants eez not possible. Drive me back *now*, Dorward.'

It was two o'clock when we returned to *Allt an Damh* only to find the gates standing wide open. When we'd set off for Gruinart, they had been on manual and I'd carefully closed them behind me. Who had left them open? It certainly wouldn't have been the security-conscious Sir Thomas.

Gabrielle had come to the same conclusion. She glared at me. 'Dorward, you did not close the gates correctly. It eez simple for *anyone* to drive in. Thomas will be *furieux* when I tell 'im.'

She droned on about the dire consequences of carelessness. Useless for me to say that there had been no mistake – that I had definitely heard the latch click, and that the heavy gates could not have swung open of their own accord.

I let her out at the front door and was taking the uneaten packed lunch out of the boot, when she came flouncing back down the steps.

'No one eez answering the door. 'Ow am I to get in?' She flung herself into the car and sat there, arms folded. 'Do something, Dorward.'

With an effort I fought back a rude reply. I managed a civil, 'I'll go over to the staff quarters, and—'

'Action, Dorward, not words!' She slammed the car door shut. '*Vite!*'

Round the corner of the house and out of sight of the car, I slowed to a walk. Let her wait, this was supposed to be my time off. In front of the kitchen window someone had carelessly parked a quad bike with the nearside front wheel crushing a small rosemary bush. A machine like this would leave just the kind of tracks I'd seen behind the shed on the shore. I'd been right in thinking that they'd been moving the drugs while we were safely out of the way at Gruinart.

I found Ann-Marie in her room. Before I could ask her for the key to the back door, she burst out with, 'Guess what, Liz! Sir T and that creep Waddington came back about half past eleven. I was in the drawing room tidying up the mess they'd made last night, and the first I knew about it was when his lordship came barging in, shouting, 'Where's Chang?

Where the hell is she?'

'I was that surprised, I just looked at him. He went quite red in the face and bawled, 'Speak up, woman, can't you! Where's that bloody Chang gone?'

'Well, if he'd asked me nicely, I'd have told him, but he wasn't going to get away with talking to me like that. "Miss Chang?" I said. "I don't know where she is *now*".' Her eyes sparkled as she relived the scene.

' "Has she gone, you stupid woman?" he howled.

' "Oh, yes, sir", I said acting stupid, "yes, she's gone".

' "Gone *where*?" He could hardly get the words out. He grabbed me by the shoulders and shook me.

'That did it. After *that* I wasn't going to tell him she'd gone off to catch the ferry, was I? "Well, she's gone on the plane to Glasgow", I said, "but I don't know where she was going from there, sir. She didn't say".'

She giggled, but that innocent lie to mislead Sir Thomas could have very serious consequences for Chang. If she *had* gone to the airport and the flight had been delayed for some hours, she might still be there when Sir Thomas and Waddington came in search of her, as they undoubtedly would.

I managed a laugh and delivered the expected response. 'Good for you, Ann-Marie. Serves him right.'

'Got a little of my own back there. You should have seen his face. He swore something frightful, and rushed off shouting, "Waddington! Waddington!" loud enough to waken the dead.'

I frowned. 'I wonder why he was so upset?' The cause was clear to me, but this way I might get something more out of her.

'*I* think' – she lowered her voice to a whisper – 'Chang's gone off with something that belonged to Sir T.'

There's nothing like injecting a little doubt to make someone give more information. 'Oh, surely not!' I said encouragingly.

'Well, listen to this. I heard him say, "Go and check, man. Go and check!" Then I went off to the kitchen, had to tell Roddy, didn't I? And through the window what did we see?'

I shook my head to indicate that I hadn't a clue.

'Waddington roaring off on his quad bike.'

'Quad bike – what on earth would he want with a quad bike?'

'Dunno. Handy for carrying things round the grounds, I suppose.

Anyway' – Ann-Marie was not to be diverted from a juicy story – 'off he goes. And about half an hour later just as I was finishing in the billiard room, the bike roared back.

'He comes rushing into the hall and up the stairs shouting, "It's empty! Not one left". Then I heard them both running down the stairs, the front door slammed and they were gone. Wasting their time. They're not going to catch her at the airport, are they?'

I shook my head and pretended to be amused.

I collected the key and went back to the car to be greeted with Gabrielle's petulant, 'Why do you take so long? I am dead with hunger. Bring the picnic and I will 'ave it in the *salon*.'

I didn't get permission to escape back to the cottage till the grandfather clock in the hall was striking three. But at least she had told me I could have the whole of Saturday off. She had other plans that didn't involve me, it seemed.

Ms Chang listened carefully to the announcement on the airport public address system. The English words did not sound quite the same as when she had learned them in Hong Kong, but she recognized 'flight' and 'depart' and 'three o'clock'. One more hour and she'd make her escape from this island and the dangerous man who would kill her because she had robbed him of his very valuable consignment of drugs.

This morning she had panicked when she'd arrived at the airport to find the flight had been cancelled: she didn't understand the reason at first, though the girl behind the desk had tried to explain. It was only when the girl had made a drawing of hills with a layer of cloud over them and a plane flying above, that she understood.

She'd been very frightened then. 'Ferry? Ferry?' she'd asked frantically. But by then it had been too late to catch the ferry. She had burst into tears and the girl behind the desk had looked sorry for her and said she thought the plane would go later perhaps at two o'clock.

She'd tried to calm herself. After all, the man Blaik would not come back to the house for some hours and then, because she had been clever and told the servant woman that she was going to the ferry, he would think that is what she had done and that she was now many miles away, somewhere on the mainland. No, he would not look for her here at the airport. There was nothing to worry about. And in less than an hour she would be gone.

She walked over to the little café, sat down at a table and studied the menu.

'Come with me, Chang,' the voice said quietly from behind her. 'If you don't make trouble, you just *might* stay alive.' Something sharp pressed painfully into her back below the ribs.

CHAPTER ELEVEN

Waddington phoned across to the cottage at half past four. He sounded flustered. 'Sir Thomas and Ms Robillard have . . . er . . . received an invitation to dine out this evening, Dorward, so . . . er . . . your services at dinner will not be required. I myself will be driving them. And . . . er . . . in view of your extra hours on duty today, Ms Robillard is kindly giving you the rest of the evening off.'

This unexpected phone call was very welcome. When Gabrielle had commandeered my services as chauffeur, I'd resigned myself to having to postpone for another day the search for an emergency place to lie low. Now my plans to scout around could go ahead. I must be quite open about my intention to leave the estate, but of course, I'd lie about where I was going.

'Well, I'd quite like to take a drive to Port Ellen and have dinner at a hotel or visit a pub, if that's all right with you.'

His reaction took me by surprse. 'Er . . . er . . . I hadn't thought. . . . Er . . . well, I suppose . . . Yes, yes. I'm sure Sir Thomas won't object.'

'*Object*? But why would—' I laced astonishment with a hint of outrage.

'No, no, of course . . . I mean of course *not*,' Waddington floundered. 'Er . . . just a turn of phrase.' He put the phone down.

I didn't set off immediately. A Persian cat needs to be groomed every day, otherwise the coat becomes painfully tangled, and my trip to Gruinart and Finlaggan with Gabrielle had prevented this morning's brushing session. When she saw me pick up the brush, Gorgonzola leapt onto my lap and stretched out, ready to be pampered.

I was still brushing her when the phone rang. When I answered, it was Waddington again, this time his usual smooth self.

'I think it may have slipped your mind about the gates, Dorward. I will leave them at manual for the next hour, but please remember that Chef Burns will have to stay on duty to let you in, so it is only courtesy to return within his normal duty hours, that is by ten o'clock at the latest. Er . . . have a good time.'

I put down the receiver and resumed the brushing of G's coat. 'Waddington seems a bit worked up, don't you think, G? Something odd's going on.' I made half-a-dozen vigorous passes with the brush. 'And how very thoughtful of Gabrielle to think of me and give me the rest of the evening off. It's *so* out of character, eh?' I turned her over and brushed her other side with long slow strokes. 'She hasn't a thought in her head for anyone but herself. If I had a nasty suspicious mind, I'd say that they didn't want me over at the house tonight. Do you think I'm right?' I interpreted the loud *prrr* as complete agreement.

I laid aside the brush and reached for the map. There were five hours or so of daylight left. In the long drive to and from Gruinart I'd had plenty of time to decide whether I should look for a hideout close to *Allt an Damh*, somewhere so close that they wouldn't think to search there. In the end, I'd decided that wouldn't be a good idea. It would mean leaving the car parked in its usual place, thereby indicating that I was somewhere within walking distance. And if I left the car here, how was I going to get to airport or ferry?

So I'd decided that the best plan would be to conceal the car somewhere between here and Port Ellen and get Sandy to pick me up. In the few hours I had at my disposal this evening, I'd see if there was any suitable spot between here and Port Ellen.

I used Gorgonzola's back as a book-rest to study the map. . . . Between *Allt an Damh* and Port Ellen there was only one side road off the main road. I traced with my finger the short stretch, almost a track, leading to an ancient monument site at Kildalton and then petering out near enough to the sea for Sandy to spirit me away by boat.

'Fancy a little stroll, G?'

Her limp, relaxed body tensed, sprang off my knees and was at the door before I'd had time to fold the map.

'Oh, no, you don't.' I scooped her into the rucksack. 'It's carrying time for you till we're well away from the danger of those snares and gin traps.' I grabbed the rucksack with its restive occupant and headed for the car.

*

The signpost read *Kildalton Cross*. As the map had indicated, the turn off was a very minor road, a narrow tarmac strip barely the width of the car. Some distance ahead beside a shelterbelt of trees, a tiny roofless church came into view. Both church and the surrounding shoulder-high wall were built of large grey stones, coated with pale lichen, a spectral white in the early evening light.

'OK, G, it's safe for you to have a stroll here.' I let her out of the rucksack and with an 'about time' twitch of her tail, she squeezed though the bars of the gate in the wall and disappeared among the headstones of the small graveyard around the church. I made a more conventional entry through the gate and stood for a moment taking in the scene. It was disappointingly obvious that this place would be useless as a hideaway. The church was just a shell and the roadside verges were bare of bushes or anything else that might provide concealment for the car. I was wasting my time here. A really isolated spot like the Oa peninsula on the other side of Port Ellen was where I should be looking. But that would have to wait till tomorrow. It would take too long to get there tonight.

Dark rain clouds were building over the sea. 'OK, G, time to go,' I called.

She was sniffing at the scallop shell someone had placed among the scattering of coins on the plinth of a tall, ornately carved Celtic cross. I went over, holding open the rucksack. But Gorgonzola had other ideas. She took off through the gravestones, gathered herself at the foot of the wall and with one bound was on top. She lingered there just long enough to cast me a glance that said quite clearly, 'Catch me if you can', leapt down the other side and legged it towards the road.

The wall blocked my view of her as I ran in pursuit across the graveyard and through the gate. Shit, shit *shit*. She might allow me to catch her or might disappear into the bracken and be on the hunt all night. But there she was . . . on the road that continued past the church and over a slight rise in the direction of the sea. She was running past a load of scallop shells piled high beside the road. As she drew level with the heap, I saw her come to a sudden halt, legs braced, fur bristling, and crouch down on the road facing the pile of shells. This was my chance. I put on a spurt, holding the rucksack open and ready to receive.

'In you get, G, and then it's home and your favourite dinner, *fish*.'

The word 'fish' normally got her full attention. This time, though her head turned in my direction, she didn't move. Outweighing the bribe of a fishy meal, a creature must be lurking among the shells, something alluring like a field mouse – or more alarming, something dangerous like a stoat or a snake.

'Gotcha!' I made a grab for her.

That was a little premature. She evaded my clutching hands and scampered lightly to the top of the mini-mountain of shells, from where she peered down at me with round, frightened eyes. Something had definitely spooked her and no amount of wheedling and cajoling had any effect. The top of the pile was well above my head. I reached up and dug both hands into the shells, scrabbled for a foothold and attempted to heave myself up. Shells slid from under my foot, my hands lost their grip and I slithered back down to the road caught up in a mini-avalanche. A second attempt fared no better. I tried to excavate a couple of steps in the pile. Once more the shells cascaded down.

A landside would deliver her into my waiting hands either before she realized what was happening or when she sensed the shells moving and jumped down. Then I'd have her.

I couldn't dig without a spade. I looked back towards the church. Perhaps in the graveyard. . . . But the graves were old, some of them centuries old, there'd be no recent burials there. There might be something in the car.

I came back with a hub cap. Using it as a giant scoop, I dug into the scallop shells. Irritation with G combined with frustration at my failed attempts to scale the heap erupted into what I can only describe as 'shell rage'. Like one possessed, I hurled the shells aside. The scallops beneath Gorgonzola began to shift. I redoubled my efforts. One more scoop and. . . .

I saw something that made me catch my breath. At the back of the hole I'd excavated was a black leather shoe, a man's shoe. Nothing too sinister about that – discarded shoes are regularly found on city streets, under hedges and on waste ground. But inside the shoe was a dark red sock, a sock with a distinctive design of blue interlocking circles. I'd seen such a sock only this morning: it had been worn by George Winstanley.

Scruusssh, the shells avalanched down. G stirred and made a flying leap to the ground. Drymouthed, I dug once more into the heap of scallops. When the shoe reappeared, I rammed the hub cap into the shells to form a protective ledge above it. Tentatively I put forward a finger and touched the sock. Beneath the cotton fabric was flesh and bone.

Winstanley and his accusations against Sir Thomas had been overshadowed by Chang's sudden departure and the consequent uproar at *Allt an Damh*. He had posed a threat to a very profitable scheme. And now he was dead.

I tugged the hub cap out of the shells and watched them slide down to fill the hole. Once more the sock and the shoe were hidden from view and the heap of shells were as they had been.

A harsh metallic *cheeoouugh* from the trees behind the churchyard startled me. I whirled round to see a large black bird fly down into the field near the wall. In the failing light the ancient lichened stones of the church glimmered, more ghostly than ever. The bank of rain clouds had advanced and were now filling the sky to the north and east, and a gust of wind heralded the approaching rain. It ruffled Gorgonzola's fur as she crouched beside the abandoned rucksack, eyes round and staring.

Uneasily, I looked up and down the road before turning back to the heap of shells. Did the killers plan to leave the body here till it was discovered weeks, perhaps months later, or were they intending to move it to a place where it might never come to light? Could *this* be the 'engagement' Sir Thomas and Waddington had for tonight?

It was time to get out of here. I scooped G up and stuffed her into the rucksack. She didn't resist. It was as if she, too, wanted to get away from this place of death as quickly as possible. Using the hub cap as a shovel, I carefully scraped any stray shells back into the heap, leaving no evidence of disturbance, and drove back to *Allt an Damh* pondering my next move. I came to a decision. Early tomorrow I'd enlist the help of Sandy Duncan.

It was almost dark by the time I reached there, but well before ten o'clock. I pressed the intercom button. 'It's Liz Dorward, Chef. That's me back.'

There was no acknowledgement but the gates swung silently open. He couldn't have been too pleased at having to be on duty waiting for my return. I could only hope he'd be over it by breakfast time.

*

Next morning as a fiery dawn streaked the sky with red, I headed for the bay where Sandy Duncan came to watch the otters. There was no certainty that he would be there, I could only hope. As I rounded the shoulder of the hill I could see below me the water of the bay, a smooth metallic grey pierced by snags of dark rock. Keeping a dry-stone wall on my left, I picked my way down the tussocky slope made slippery by overnight rain and a scattering of wet leaves. I was moving quietly, but a long-legged oystercatcher flew up from the shoreline, sending a strident *kleep kleep* alarm call ringing out over the water, and with a *flapflapflap* of wings, a large multi-coloured duck took off in fright to the other side of the bay. I stood on the narrow strip of sand and scanned the shoreline. The water lapping lazily at the rocks stirred the fringed clumps of olive-brown seaweed and blurred a webbed otter track in the sand. Of the otters themselves or of the otter watcher there was no sign.

Disappointed, I made my way back along the shore towards the dry-stone wall, noticing for the first time its strange construction. Bright spots of light shone through large gaps between the stones, giving the effect of a chenille scarf knitted on giant pins by a careless knitter and full of holes from dropped stitches.

A dark shape blocked one of the gaps. I had the uneasy feeling that I was being watched. Could Waddington have followed me here from the cottage and be lurking behind the wall? He'd warned me away from this area giving as a reason the Anglo-Nubian goat study, but if challenged, I would point out that there were no goats, Anglo-Nubian or other, anywhere in sight, and say I'd made quite sure of this before coming down to the shore. I stared at the wall again. I mustn't allow last night's discovery of Winstanley's body to conjure a bogeyman out of a sheep or a goat.

The shape moved and light shone through the gap. Then slowly above the top of the wall rose a battered trilby hat. Sandy Duncan did not appear at all pleased to see me.

The blue eyes were frosty. 'Fools rush in where angels fear to tread.'

'Er. . . ?' I said, somewhat taken aback.

'You've buggered up the video shot I've been trying to get for weeks.'

Oh dear. Guiltily I recalled that fresh otter track on the sand. 'Sorry, I didn't think.'

'That's the trouble with young folks nowadays, they don't *think*.' He levered himself stiffly to his feet. 'Well, I suppose you've come to tell me something, but it had better be good.'

'Murder,' I said. 'Someone's been murdered. Is that good enough?'

He stood for a moment, head on one side, considering, then gave a grudging, 'Yes, I suppose that's good enough. Who did you kill?'

'It may be a big disappointment, but you're not face to face with a murderer, Sandy. Someone has met an untimely end, but not at *my* hands.' I told him where I'd found the body, just the barest of details. 'The man, George Winstanley, arrived at *Allt an Damh* and made the mistake of creating a fuss with Sir Thomas about missing whisky casks.'

'Made what you might call a fatal error, eh? Don't need Sherlock Holmes to work out whodunit.' He leaned on the wall and stroked his beard thoughtfully. 'Beside Kildalton Church, you say ... that's old McIntyre's land. He'll be using the scallop shells as infill for land drains, helps the crops to grow.'

'And that's not all I've got to tell you. Something else happened yesterday.'

'Let me guess. . . .' He frowned as if deep in thought. 'If I'm right, does that get me a bottle of 10-Year-Old Ardbeg?'

'Done,' I said. HMRC's money was safe.

He took off his hat, studied it closely and said slowly, as if reading out the answer from the sweatband, 'What you're going to tell me is to do with the drugs in the shed. Or rather, the drugs that were in the shed. Am I right?' I nodded and, bottle secured, with a gleeful smile he gave up all pretence of it being a matter of guesswork. 'Two nights ago there was a lot of activity.' He jerked his head in the direction of the next inlet. 'There was quite a torchlight procession. They were carrying stuff out of the shed and loading it on a boat. I thought it was the *Allt an Damh* gang, but yesterday morning the shed door was hanging off its hinges. It was my duty as an upright citizen to investigate, wasn't it? I looked inside and the whole lot had been cleared out. Now isn't that info worth a bottle of Ardbeg?'

'OK,' I said, resigned to having been outwitted, 'a good *guess*.'

His eyes gleamed, and I should have been warned. 'But if I can tell you something you *don't* know about last night's activity, you'll stump up two bottles?' As I hesitated, he added, 'Double or quits.'

Eyes narrowed, I contemplated the impossibility of getting the cost of even one, let alone two, bottles of ten-year-old Ardbeg past the penny-pinching eyes of HMRC's expense account department. It was worth the gamble, though. What could he tell me that I didn't know already?

'It's a deal,' I said, confident that I was on safe ground. Assumptions again, as Gerry Burnside would have said.

'Well. . . .' He paused, savouring the moment. 'The boat that sneaked off with the drugs—'

'Was crewed by Chinese,' I broke in. Game, set, and match to DJ Smith.

'Nope.' His smile was the smile of one who has set a trap and watched his prey walk headlong into it. 'That boat was the very same one that landed the drugs here in the first place.'

'The *same* boat? You're absolutely sure?'

He tapped the night binoculars hanging round his neck. 'Affirmative. I knew that would surprise you.'

Bested. Wily old codger. I gave in gracefully. 'Can't argue with that, Sandy. The bottles are yours.'

So, Chang had been more devious than I'd thought. But had she got away with it? I needed his help to find out.

'I suspect it might all have been organized by Chang, a Chinese woman who arrived at *Allt an Damh* a couple of days ago. She sneaked off suddenly yesterday morning without telling Cameron-Blaik.'

He looked thoughtful. 'So the lady's done a runner. . . .'

'The thing is, this morning Cameron-Blaik and his henchman Waddington discovered the shed had been emptied and went haring off to the airport after her.'

In mellow mood after the success of his Ardbeg gambit, Sandy came straight to the point. 'You'll want me to go to the airport and see if she was among the passengers who took off for Glasgow on yesterday's delayed flight?'

'I'd certainly like to know if there's the possibility of another body turning up,' I said.

'While we're on the subject of bodies, what do you propose to do about that little problem with the . . . um . . . scallop shells?'

'I'm thinking about it,' I said. Screaming newspaper headlines and the accompanying police enquiries would put paid to any chance of Louis Moran turning up at *Allt an Damh*. 'A strategic delay in reporting it might be on the cards.'

'Roger, and out. Rendezvous for debriefing. Edge of the wood at thirteen hundred hours.' He bent down and picked up his camcorder. 'Ardbeg 10-year-old, mind. Don't try to fob me off with something else.'

He started off up the hill and a few minutes later disappeared among the trees.

CHAPTER TWELVE

I watched Chef as I ate, trying to gauge the state of his temper. There'd been no slamming down of implements, no drawn brows. I was somewhat surprised. He didn't seem to bear me a grudge for having to stay on duty to open the gates last night. Nor did he seem to be at all upset that, after all the effort he had spent preparing it, the evening meal had been cancelled at short notice. The thought occurred to me that perhaps he'd been given a lot more warning than I had.

My dawn stroll by the shore had given me an appetite. I scraped my bowl clean and held it out for more.

Ann-Marie looked at me sideways. 'All right for *some* to be given the evening off last night, wasn't it?'

'You mean *you* weren't?' I said, avoiding looking at Chef.

He ladled a dollop of porridge into my bowl. 'We were and we weren't,' he said cryptically.

'But if they were going to dine out, surely. . . ?'

Chef smiled grimly. 'When the little creep stammered that Sir Thomas had given me the evening off, he seemed to think I'd be *pleased*.'

Ann-Marie giggled. 'Roddy threw one of his wobblies when Waddington told him that the food he'd been slaving over wouldn't be needed. "Four o'clock!" he roared, so loud that Waddy jumped a foot in the air. "Four o'clock! What time is this to tell me? I've been slaving for hours preparing this meal, and *now* you tell me I've been wasting my time and needn't have bothered".

'It was like commissioning a painting from an artist, and then when it's half-finished telling him not to bother. He's wasted his time, and all the materials too,' she said earnestly. 'Roddy's an artist with food, aren't you, Roddy? So you can understand why he would throw a strop, can't you?

He picked up his meat mallet and smashed it down on' – her eyes grew round in excited recollection – 'on one of those big tomatoes. And it spurted *all over* Waddy's white shirt. So that got rid of him. He couldn't get out of the kitchen fast enough.

'And *then*,' her voice rose to a squeak, 'if that wasn't enough, half an hour later the intercom buzzes and Waddington says in that stuck-up voice of his, "Sir Thomas has changed his mind. He's going to stay at home. Tell Chef that dinner's on again". And before I could say, "Tell him yourself", he puts down the phone.

'I don't mind telling you that I was scared to tell Roddy, but when I did, he just laughed and said, "They'll be having a one course meal, omelette, tonight, then. You can tell them I got the message too late, and I'd thrown away all the food".'

'But you hadn't?' I said.

'Of course not. Put it in the fridge. That way, I'd be able to put my feet up today.' He winked. 'And, of course, that gave me my night off too.'

So it had been Waddington who had operated the gates to let me in. Why, then, had I been led to assume that it had been Chef?

'They did go out later,' Ann-Marie said, 'just after ten o'clock. Maybe they wanted a fish supper. The mobile Nippy Chippy's in Port Ellen on Fridays. I knew they'd gone out because the headlights lit up the room while Roddy and me were watching *Casualty*. Last night was the first time since we came here that we've been able to see it.' She launched into an interminable account of disasters suffered by characters I'd never heard of.

Busy with my own thoughts, I soon tuned out. Could Sir Thomas's sudden change of dinner plans have had anything to do with me telling Waddington that I was intending to go off to Port Ellen? I had been pressured into coming back before ten o'clock . . . was it significant that someone had left *Allt an Damh* only *after* I had returned?

'What do you think of that, then?' Ann-Marie was looking at me expectantly.

I sought for words that would adequately cover the over-wrought situations of a TV soap. 'How *awful*!' I cried.

The *click click click* of Chef's whisk stopped.

'What's so awful about Roddy baking me a birthday cake, then?' She jumped to her feet and stood hands on hips.

'No, no, no,' I said hastily. 'You've got me wrong. I only meant that I had no idea that it was your birthday; I haven't got you a birthday present.'

The *click click click* of the whisk resumed.

'Oh.' She sat down again. 'Well, it's not till next week, so you've still got time to do some shopping.'

I opened the rucksack. Like a champagne cork out of its bottle, Gorgonzola popped out and shot into the long grass for a gin-trap-free forage. She would come back when I whistled. I'd plenty to think about as I sat on a fallen tree trunk waiting for Sandy. Why had a car driven away from *Allt an Damh* so late last night? Had the driver waited till I had returned so that our cars wouldn't meet on the road? Could he – or they – have been *en route* to Kildalton to move the body? Or had it something to do with the sudden departure of Chang?

With a sharp *crack* a twig snapped behind me. I jumped to my feet and whirled round.

'That was careless of me.' Sandy was standing only a few feet away, his dark clothing a perfect camouflage in the shadows. 'Never leave your back unprotected. One of the first rules of combat training.'

'I knew you were there all along,' I lied.

This was met with a sceptical, 'Uh-huh?' and raised eyebrows.

I sat down again on the log. 'What did you find out at the airport?'

He sat down beside me. 'Your Ms Chang was on the passenger list, all right.'

'So she left by plane and they didn't catch up with her. I must say I'm glad about that. I wouldn't like to think there'd been another murder.'

'I wouldn't assume that,' he said, in an unwitting echo of Gerry Burnside. 'I said her *name* was on the list, but there was no Ms Chang on the delayed flight that left for Glasgow at fourteen hundred hours.'

So much for the Burnside theory that she'd left the drugs under the bed because she intended to travel by air. Gerry had got it wrong for once. Chang had indeed taken the ferry.

'Having her name on the list,' I said confidently, 'will have been a ruse to mislead enquirers like Cameron-Blaik, have him rushing off to the airport, as he did, while she actually went off by ferry.'

He shook his head. 'Got to shoot you down in flames on that. She did arrive at the airport. The staff remember her because she was so upset at the flight being delayed for some hours.'

I stared at him. 'At the airport, but didn't get on the flight?'

'Just disappeared,' he said. 'When the flight was called she didn't turn up. They had to unload her bag.'

Though the sun was warm, I felt cold. Chang had disappeared, and without a body there'd be no evidence that murder had been committed, no evidence at all.

Except for Winstanley's body, hastily hidden under the heap of shells – if it hadn't been moved.

Sandy's car, and even more importantly his camera, was half an hour's walk away, and Kildalton a further forty-five minutes. If I was to take a photograph of the body and be back at *Allt an Damh* in time to go on duty by five o'clock, there was no time to lose. I whistled for Gorgonzola, but I'd underestimated the temptations of the undergrowth. After waiting a minute for her to appear, I whistled again. Again there was no response.

'She hears, but does not obey. Court-martial offence, I'd say.' Sandy rested chin on hand as if prepared for a long wait.

'She's wary of men.' I said defensively. 'She's probably frightened of you.'

'No sign of that last time we met at the shed.'

'It was dark,' I said. 'She didn't notice.'

A snort of derision. *Tchk Tchk Tchk.* He clicked his tongue against his teeth and called softly, 'Come to Daddy, Gorgonzola.'

Almost immediately, the grasses swayed, parted. Ignoring me, she danced over and with a loud *purr* rubbed lovingly against his leg.

'Who's afraid of big, bad men then?' he said, bending over to tickle her between the ears.

I scooped her up and bundled her unceremoniously into the rucksack. 'I don't know what's got into you, G,' I hissed in her ear. But, of course, I did. Tired of being restricted to the confines of the cottage, she was asserting her independence. Every so often, when one of us feels miffed by the other's behaviour, we play the one-upmanship card.

'The shells are on the side of the road just past the church,' I'd said. But they weren't. When the lichen-white stones of Kildalton Church came into view, the grass verge stretched ahead, empty of anything higher than a stunted bush. Only a thin layer of scattered and crushed shells marked the spot where the heap had once been. I was too late.

We got out of the car. 'So much for the photographic evidence,' I said.

'If only we had got here earlier. . . .'

Sandy stirred the fragments with his foot. 'If McIntyre had found a body when he moved the shells, the place would have been buzzing with police by now.'

Cameron-Blaik and Waddington had gone out to shift the body last night. I'd been right. 'It could be anywhere now,' I said, gloom descending. 'Miles away. . . .'

'Possibly only yards.' He was looking towards the roofless church. 'It was dark, they didn't have much time . . . and they'd need more than a spade to dig a hole in this rocky ground.' He marched off down the road, the words drifting back, 'Why wouldn't they take the easy way out? If there's a graveyard on your doorstep, use it.'

I grabbed the rucksack and hurried after him. G had found Winstanley's body yesterday, perhaps she could do so again.

The rusty hinges squealed loudly as he pushed open the gate. Otherwise there was no sound at all, not even the chirp of a bird. The leaves on the trees behind the church hung dusty and motionless. It was as if the sleepers in the churchyard were holding their breath. . . .

Sandy stood looking around. 'If I'm right, and the body's here, they've chosen a good place. Any traces they might leave would be put down to all those visitors poking around. Can't let things be, some of them.'

I let him lead the way. 'Visitors?' I said. 'Are there many here?'

'Oh, yes.' He ran a finger over the weather-worn carvings on the imposing Celtic cross. 'Twelve hundred years old, these carvings, they say. This one shows a murder, Cain killing Abel, and here's an attempted murder, Abraham about to sacrifice Isaac. Nothing changes, eh?'

I set down the rucksack and lifted Gorgonzola out.

He looked down at her. 'Trained to sniff out bodies as well as drugs, is she?'

'No, but. . . .' I told him how she had reacted to the body hidden in the shells.

'Might as well give it a try.' He didn't sound too convinced.

We watched as she picked her way towards three flat slabs lying half-hidden in the grass.

Sandy shook his head. 'I don't think the body's underneath one of these. There'd be pretty obvious signs of disturbance. They couldn't crowbar up a slab that's been there for hundreds of years without tearing up the grass that's bonded itself to the stone.'

110

Gorgonzola had no idea she was supposed to be searching for a body. She was enjoying herself – pouncing on an invisible prey, playfully snapping at an insect or trying to catch it with a paw, crouching to stare intently at a gap between the stones in the wall. The minutes passed. I looked at my watch. How much longer could I give her?

Sandy had been leaning against the dry-stone wall watching these antics. 'Aye,' he said 'it's time we did a bit of looking ourselves. The creature's mind's not on it.'

I sprang to her defence. 'She's not trained to search for dead bodies. If it was drugs, now, I'd put her special collar on, tell her to search and she'd quarter the ground methodically. When she knows she's on duty she's not distracted by *anything*.' This was not *quite* true. On rare occasions she had indeed succumbed to temptation.

I rummaged in the rucksack for G's collar. 'That's what I'll do. I'll tell her she's looking for drugs, then if she tries to avoid a grave, we can take a look.'

'Try over there, then.' He pointed to an overgrown burial plot surrounded by rusty railings, the entrance gate long gone.

I fitted the collar, walked across with G and put her down. The fluffy-headed grass that had taken over the railed area stood tall and untrampled. It was obvious that there'd been no digging at this grave.

'No one's been here.' I bent down to scoop her up.

But G had other ideas. Collar signified Duty and Search and, more importantly, Reward afterwards. And 'Search' was what she was determined to do. She wriggled out of my outstretched hands and began sniffing the ground near three sunken slabs depicting two soldiers wearing pointed helmets and a sort of kilt.

'Come and look at this, Sandy. They're straight out of the Bayeux Tapestry.'

'Mmm. . . .' He didn't look up. He was poking about round three table-type gravestones raised above ground level by a foot high wall of upright slabs placed on edge. 'There are bigger and better carvings like these inside the church itself. But I'm afraid you won't have time to look at them today. Bring the cat over here. This is exactly the kind of grave our body-snatchers would make use of.'

I clicked my tongue to attract Gorgonzola's attention. 'Over there, G.' I pointed to the three table-gravestones. 'Search.'

She looked over at Sandy, then up at me, but made no move.

'Really, G,' I said crossly. 'Now's not the time for temperament.'

I grabbed her, stomped across and dumped her down on top of one of the lichen-blotched table-stones.

'The vertical slab at this end's missing. Gap's been filled with large stones, probably taken from the wall.' He knelt down. 'Take a look at this. There seems to be a cavity behind them.'

But I was looking at Gorgonzola. She had leapt off the table-stone and was crouched on the ground a short distance away, coat bristling, eyes round and frightened.

'G's telling us that we've found the body,' I said.

I picked her up and held her close. She was shivering, her heart thumping. 'There, there,' I whispered, rocking her gently and feeling guilty. I should have remembered how much distress she'd been in when she'd detected Winstanley's body in the scallop shells. 'Yes, Sandy, this is definitely the place.'

I carried her over to the rucksack. She cowered down into its depths. 'There you are, G. Nice, dark, snug.' I zipped it up and left it in the shade against the wall of the church.

When I got back to the table-stones, Sandy had heaved aside three or four of the boulders and was peering into the void.

'There's quite a bit of space under here. Pity we've not got a torch.' He took off his hat and placed it carefully on the table-stone, then lay down and reached into the gap. 'There's something. . . . If I can just. . . .' He grunted with the effort. 'Almost got it . . . almost. . . . Nope, just out of reach.'

He wriggled back and leant on the table-stone to heave himself to his feet. 'I'll poke the camera in and we'll be able to see if it's worth investigating further. Might just be a bag of rubbish somebody's shoved in.'

We studied the pictures on the digital screen. The flash had reflected off not one, but two large black plastic bin bags.

'Two bags. Probably *is* just rubbish.' Sandy sounded disappointed.

I shook my head. I knew by Gorgonzola's reaction that the bags contained something other than rubbish. What she had smelt was death. 'No, if there are two bags, there are two bodies. One of them must be Chang.'

I'd expected Sandy to be shocked and even, perhaps, feel it was too dangerous to help me any further, but his only reaction was to pick up his hat and study it thoughtfully. 'Battle plans get nowhere without accurate reconnaissance.' He placed the hat back on his head. 'If we want to see who's in those bags, we're going to have to crawl in there and pull them out.'

It transpired that when he said 'we', he meant me, DJ Smith.

When I didn't immediately step forward to volunteer, he said apologetically, 'It's a matter of logistics, Ms X. My physique prevents me from squeezing far enough into the space to get a sufficiently firm grip of the bags to haul them out. Therefore, regrettable as it is. . . .'

'It will have to be me who crawls in,' I finished.

'Got it in one. Now what I suggest is this. . . .'

I'm all for equality of opportunity between the sexes, but I would have put aside my principles and allowed him to do the grisly deed if there had been any other way.

'It will only take thirty seconds,' I told myself firmly as I lay flat and prepared to squirm in under the heavy slabs, 'probably less. As soon as I get a good grip on a bag, he will pull me out.'

Digging my elbows into the ground for leverage, I inched my way forward, head scraping against the rough stone above, chin just clear of the damp earth, shoulders blocking out most of the light. I don't suffer from claustrophobia, but the irrational sensation of being entombed brought out a film of sweat on my forehead and set my heart racing.

It'll only take thirty seconds, I'd told myself, but it felt like thirty minutes before my fingers at last touched plastic. I steeled myself to stretch out my hand and run it over the surface, feeling for a body part that would give me a firm grip when Sandy pulled me out. My fingers touched something hard, definitely a shoe, a man's shoe by the size. I tried not to think about the foot inside it.

I felt for the ankles and took hold with both hands.

'OK, Sandy. Ready.' It came out as a hoarse gasp. Fortunately the underlying tremor in my voice would be muffled by the thick walls of my stone sarcophagus.

He gripped my legs and pulled. Just in time I half-turned on my side to prevent my face ploughing a furrow in the earth. My body straightened and slowly . . . slowly . . . I and the plastic bag with its grim contents were dragged towards the daylight.

At last the backward movement stopped. I'd closed my eyes and now I opened them. My hands and part of the bag were clear of the slabs.

Sandy helped me to my feet and together we pulled the bag out onto the grass.

'You'll want a picture of the face.' He took a knife from his jacket pocket and slit the plastic.

Winstanley stared blankly up at us, like the blood from his face, all anger drained away. I've seen quite a few dead bodies, but I was surprisingly upset. A couple of days ago Winstanley had been alive, radiating rage, a whirlwind of fury; the most important thing in the world for him had been to find his missing whisky casks. And now . . . the vanity of human wishes. . . . Would he have valued those casks more than his life?

Sandy raised his camera. 'This your man?'

I nodded. After the pictures had been taken, I gently replaced the flap of plastic and returned Winstanley once more to the anonymous world of the body-bag dead.

To retrieve the second bag necessitated even more of a nightmare struggle in the depths of that narrow space. This bag was full of gases and it was difficult to grasp the shoe. Again, a man-sized shoe. Whoever it was, it was not Chang.

I took a grip of the ankles and called a warning to Sandy. 'This one's been dead for some considerable time. The bag's full of gases. Gently does it. We don't want the bag to tear.'

As Sandy dragged me out, the gas-filled bag rubbed against the rough stone. Each moment was an eternity of anxiety in case it split and released the foul air inside. Immediately my hands were clear of the table-stone, I released my grip and scrambled to my feet. Together we eased the body out into the open.

'I'd stand over there, if I were you. This is not going to be pleasant.' Taking position upwind, Sandy took his knife, hesitated, then slit the plastic over the face.

I was six feet away, but that was not far enough.

He seemed to be immune. 'Had to get used to this sort of thing in the war. You don't need to look.'

He flipped back the plastic. 'Aye, he'll be difficult to identify. Been dead for some weeks. No harm in taking a photo, though. At least there'll be evidence if they move the body again.'

I'd recovered a little. 'They'll have removed any identification in the pockets, but take a photo of the clothes—'

I was seized with a fit of retching as he lengthened the slit and pulled the plastic aside to reveal a dark-green Barbour jacket and a maroon silk cravat knotted at the neck.

'One of the hunting, shooting, fishing fraternity. I haven't heard of anyone missing on the island, though. Must be a visitor. Hello, what's this?' He bent over to examine the arm folded across the chest. 'If I take a close-up and zoom in on the screen, I might just be able. . . .'

Together we looked at the picture. It showed a broad gold ring sunk deeply into the swollen flesh. A ring with some sort of design.

'Zoom in more,' I said.

The image now filled the entire screen. It was of five arrows tied together into a bundle rather like a sheaf of corn, the whole surrounded by a broad buckled belt. And below, a three word Gaelic motto.

He frowned. 'I've seen a ring like that somewhere before. . . .' After gazing thoughtfully into the distance for a moment, he shook his head. 'Nope. Can't place it, but it'll come to me.'

He put the camera in his pocket and pulled the plastic bag together as best he could. 'Right. If you want to delay informing the police, we'd better get them stowed away again before anyone chances along.'

Gallantly he took hold of the shoulders of the mystery victim, leaving me to deal with the legs. We heaved the body-bag into position and shoved it headfirst into the void under the table-stone. We did the same with Winstanley and had almost finished rolling the large stones into position, when we heard the hum of an approaching car.

'Our luck's run out. That'll be tourists coming to see the cross and the carved warriors.' He whipped out the camera. 'Time to play the visitors ourselves.'

I grabbed the rucksack, and we made our way over to the roofless church. When a man and a woman wandered through the doorway to join us, it was the cue for Sandy to take a photo of the large warrior carving wedged into a recess in the wall.

I said loudly, 'Did William the Conqueror and his soldiers get as far north as Islay?'

Sandy shook his head. 'Some say so, but I don't agree. They're not Norman. I think they're linked to the Viking raids on Islay.' He looked at his watch. 'Come on, we're running late. I want to take another picture of the cross.'

'Slickly done,' I muttered as we made our escape.

It was as he was driving me back that Sandy had his eureka moment. He'd been silent for some time and I too had been lost in thought, pondering the identity of the other murder victim. Suddenly he let go of the wheel with one hand and slapped his knee, sending the car veering dangerously close to a shallow ditch.

'Got it! Knew I'd seen something like that ring design before.' Just in time he grabbed the wheel again. 'That's the Cameron badge. It's likely that Sir Thomas is wearing one himself.'

Was he? I thought about it. There was a ring on his finger, but I hadn't paid it any attention. Tonight when I got back, I'd make it my business to take a closer look.

'Are you *listening*?' Sandy showed his irritation. Justified, I must admit, when you're enthusing over a pet theory and the listener isn't paying rapt attention to every word. 'As I was saying, all we have to do is find out who in the Cameron clan has gone missing. If Cameron-Blaik has bumped off that whisky guy and the Chang woman because they got in his way. . . .' He turned towards me, in his excitement oblivious of the approaching bend in the road. 'It'll be one of his relatives returned to Islay from the back of beyond, say Australia or South America, to claim his rightful inheritance. That should narrow the search—'

'If we don't take the bend, neither of us will be doing any searching because we'll hit that tree.' I pressed my feet hard against the floor mat in an automatic stamp on the brakes.

He pulled the wheel round, and not thinking our near brush with death worthy of mention, let his imagination run riot, conjuring up a life history of Cameron-Blaik's Cousin X: a scenario involving misspent youth, family shame, exile, sudden unwelcome reappearance and blackmail – entertaining, but decidedly in the over-the-top B movie, Victorian melodrama category.

But the Cameron ring was a different matter. Sandy *had* hit the mark there. Only a Cameron would wear such a ring, and Sir Thomas was, at the very least, accessory to the murder of the owner of that ring. Here was a man, on the surface a pillar of society, an upright citizen, who had been revealed in his true colours as a whisky smuggler, drug runner and cold-blooded killer of Winstanley, and Chang, for I was sure that she too was dead. It was a catalogue of crime worthy of Louis Moran himself.

Though Moran had not yet arrived at *Allt an Damh*, Cameron-Blaik was definitely in constant communication with him and following his instructions. I'd have to—

The car lurched violently to the right. I flung up my arms in the approved airline brace position and closed my eyes.

Instead of the expected crash of splintering glass and torn and twisted metal, I heard a chuckle, loud and prolonged.

'That's got your attention, eh?'

I lowered my arms and opened my eyes. We were driving along an absolutely straight stretch of road and a glance in the wing mirror showed not a bend or obstacle of any kind.

'Gotcha! Gets your attention every time.' More chuckles as he adroitly passed off as intentional the previous close encounters with the ditch and the tree. 'I was saying that I know the very place for you to lie low when things get too hot and the powder keg goes off.' He certainly had my full attention now. 'It's within walking distance of the ferry – just the other side of Port Ellen, near the beach they call the Singing Sands. Looks like the balloon's going to go up soon, so when do you want to give the place the once-over?'

'Make it tomorrow. The earliest I can meet you is eleven.'

I'd a feeling I was going to need that place very, very soon.

CHAPTER THIRTEEN

In spite of Gabrielle's attempts to introduce various topics of conversation, the atmosphere at dinner that night could only be described as tense. I myself had a lot on my mind. As Sir Thomas took his soup, I positioned myself where I could study his hands. He wore a wedding band on his left hand, and on his right, a ring with some kind of clan badge. It was going to be difficult to get a surreptitious closer look. When I placed the fish course before him, I did get an opportunity, but his hands were in his lap, hidden by the tablecloth.

My next chance came with the meat course. I waited till I'd served the venison steak, then picked up the pepper grinder and offered it first to Gabrielle.

'And you, Sir Thomas?' I poised the grinder over his plate.

As he watched the pepper drift down, the position of his hands shifted, giving me a good view of the ring on his finger. The design was a sheaf of arrows encircled by a broad buckled belt. At a cursory glance it could have been mistaken for the Cameron badge as it was indeed a sheaf of arrows, but the arrows on this ring were horizontal, not vertical, and held in a fist rather than tied together with a ribbon.

'That's *enough*, damn you, Dorward! Do you want to make the food inedible?' He pushed the grinder away impatiently.

It fell from my hand onto the table knocking over his glass of wine. I dabbed vigorously at the tablecloth, hastening to take the blame.

'I'm so sorry, Sir Thomas. That was very clumsy of me.'

He held his napkin clear of the table and I got another look at his ring. As I'd thought, it was not the Cameron badge although very similar. Underneath the horizontal arrows, the motto was only one word instead of three. I could think of no reason why he would be wearing the ring of another clan, so probably this was just another version of the Cameron coat of arms. First chance I had, I'd see if there was something on the Camerons and their history in the billiard room library. I always check up on anything that doesn't seem to fit.

I retired back to my position against the wall, giving the impression that I was gazing into space, my mind a blank, but in reality studying the diners. Waddington seemed to have lost his appetite, merely toying with the food on his plate. He wasn't, however, showing the same lack of interest in the consumption of wine. Twice he'd motioned for me to fill up his glass. Was Winstanley's death weighing on his mind?

A large quantity of wine on an empty stomach might very well precipitate a useful indiscretion. Every time the level in his glass dropped below halfway, I sprang forward to top it up.

It was during the dessert course that my plan bore fruit. Gabrielle was expounding at tedious length on the shopping expedition she'd made in Edinburgh before she came to Islay. Neither of the men seemed to be listening. I moved forward to refill Waddington's glass.

'I *do* think that 'arvey Nichols eez the only place to shop. Where else would—?'

'No more for you, Waddington! You've had enough.' Sir Thomas's brusque interruption provoked the outburst I'd been waiting for.

'Enough? Yes, I bloody well have!' Waddington, face flushed, violently pushed away his dessert untouched. The stemmed glass dish toppled over, spilling fruit salad onto the tablecloth. 'I should never have agreed to work for you, Blaik! Yesterday when—'

The flat of Sir Thomas's hand slapped down hard on the table. '*Enough!* You're drunk.'

A shiver ran up my spine. He hadn't raised his voice, but the unnatural quietness of the delivery gave his words an air of menace.

Despite his drunken state, Waddington felt it too. The colour drained from his face. Mouth open, Gabrielle looked from one to the other. Face expressionless, I stepped forward to pick up the toppled dessert dish.

Sir Thomas waved a dismissive hand. 'We'll attend to that, Dorward. You can go now. That will be all for tonight.'

'Very good, Sir Thomas.'

No one spoke as I made my way to the door and closed it quietly behind me. The thick wood cut out all sound from within.

I stood there for a few moments thinking about what I'd just witnessed. Cameron-Blaik was a rich man motivated by greed or financial straits to barter whisky for drugs, and capable of a whisky futures fraud. He had let his mask slip, revealing a side of himself I'd suspected but not personally experienced. When threatened with exposure he might very well have resorted to murder. It was clear he was a very dangerous man indeed.

I pushed open the billiard room door. This was my chance. Before they left the dining room, there'd be time to see if there was a book on the shelves showing variations of the Cameron clan badge. The difference in the ring design was bothering me.

Before dinner I'd closed the curtains and switched on a table lamp near the fire in readiness for the after dinner coffee. The room was in darkness, illumined only by the warm glow from the table lamp and the flames of the log fire leaping up the chimney. I switched on the light and was on the point of closing the door when I thought better of it. Though I hoped to be gone before I was discovered, I took the precaution of leaving the door ajar so I would hear a warning burst of conversation if the dining room door opened. That would give me time to shove the book back onto the shelf and excuse my presence by saying that I'd assumed Sir Thomas's 'That will be all for tonight' applied only to the dining-room duty, so I was waiting to serve the usual coffee and drinks.

I crossed over to the bookshelves. Philosophy . . . literature . . . botany . . . geography. . . . As I'd thought, the books were mainly old tomes, some with Latin titles, chosen for the ornamental effect of their tooled leather spines. I scanned the titles in the history section. *Flodden and its Aftermath*, *History of the 'Forty-Five Rebellion*, *The Clearances*, *Kings and Queens of Scotland*, *The Scottish Clans*. Time was running out. I pulled that last volume off the shelf.

Resting the heavy book on the edge of the billiard table, I ran my finger down the contents page to *Clan Insignia*. On each page of that chapter was a paragraph of clan history beneath a representation of the clan badge. Clan Cameron's badge was indeed, as Sandy had recognized, the vertical sheaf of five arrows and the three-word Gaelic motto meaning 'Unite'.

So that ring of Sir Thomas's wasn't Clan Cameron. But arrows in a fist must be the badge of another clan. I flipped back to the beginning of the chapter and leafed quickly through the clans. *Anderson . . . Armstrong . . .*

Buchanan ... Buchan ... Bruce ... Brodie ... I stared down at the Brodie page. There it was. The three horizontal arrows grasped in a fist with motto 'Unite', a single word in English. What reason could there be for a Cameron to wear a ring with the insignia of a different clan? None that I could think of, unless the man calling himself Sir Thomas Cameron-Blaik wasn't Cameron-Blaik at all. Which meant that the body in Kildalton churchyard, the wearer of the authentic Cameron ring, could very well be Sir Thomas Cameron-Blaik.

So who was the man who had taken his identity?

'I didn't expect to find you here, Dorward.' It was said quietly, with that same tone of underlying menace I'd heard him use to Waddington.

I whirled round. Cameron-Blaik was behind me. His shoes had made no sound on the thick carpet.

His eyes travelled from the open book to my face. 'I told you to finish off for the night.' It was a statement, not a question, the words spoken slowly and with an edge.

'I assumed you were referring to my duties in the dining room, Sir Thomas, and that you would want coffee and drinks served here as usual.' My mouth was dry, my heart beating fast.

Again his gaze travelled from the book to my face, from face back to book open at the Clan Brodie page, telltale evidence that I'd noticed his ring and was curious about it.

For a long, long moment he said nothing. .... The clock above the bar *tick tocked* the seconds away. A burning log exploded with a sharp *skrak*.

He turned away. 'As you're here, you might as well stay. Coffee and a Bruichladdich 15 Year Old for both of us.'

I found it distinctly unnerving that he had said nothing about either the book or the page it was turned to.

Gabrielle was hovering in the doorway. Now she advanced into the room and flung herself down on one of the sofas.

'Make eet a very large Bruichladdich, Dorward.'

No reference was made to the scene that had occurred in the dining room, but there was tension in the air. I stood behind the bar, straining to hear their murmured conversation, but could catch only a few words.

'... and he's a liability ... have to. ...'

'But, Thomas, that would. ...'

Something Gabrielle said next seemed to anger him.

She put a calming hand on his arm. 'You must play the snooker,

Thomas. Eet eez always good for you when you are cross.'

He rose abruptly from his chair, seized one of the cues from the wall-rack and shrugged off his jacket. 'Put on the table lights, Dorward.'

He moved to one end of the table and stood there, impatiently chalking the cue while I walked over to the switch on the wall.

Gabrielle swung her legs up onto the sofa. 'And put out the main light. We'll 'ave only the table lamps, then you are like the actor on the stage, Thomas.'

The powerful lights shone down on the smooth green baize, throwing the rest of the room into shadow. He leant over the table, spread his fingers wide and sighted along the cue. A second later the cue ball smashed into the triangle of red balls, sending one rocketing into a pocket. 'Going for the blue,' he grunted. *Click.* Effortlessly he sank the targeted ball.

Gaze concentrated on the table, he rapped out, 'Put up the balls for me, Dorward.'

I took a pair of white gloves from the cupboard, pulled them on and replaced the blue ball on its spot. One after the other he fired the balls into the pockets with the ferocity of a gunman eliminating his chosen victim; Gabrielle greeted each successful pot with a clap of her hands and a 'Bravo, *chéri*.'

Only the black was left. He walked round the table studying the angle of the cue ball on the black. Taking aim, he stretched over the table, then stepped back. 'Hand me the spider, Dorward.'

He positioned it on the baize and rested the cue on it, lining up for the final shot. Caught up in the drama of the moment, I paused at the other end of the snooker table. He was stretched out across the baize, sliding the tip of the cue back and forth two or three times, concentrating on the exact spot to make contact with the cue ball.

Glass in hand, Gabrielle uncurled herself from the sofa and came over to stand beside me. As his gaze concentrated on the two balls, his eyes appeared to bore straight through us. Under the strong overhead lights the blue seemed shadowed – and a thin brown circle of iris was now showing round the contracted pupils.

I should have been able to maintain an expressionless butler's face, but I'd never seen anything like these eyes. Taken off guard, I stared, completely failing to hide my astonishment.

He registered this at the very moment that he made his stroke. Instead of striking the ball cleanly, he miscued. Instead of the black arrowing straight into the pocket, it cannoned off the side cushion and rolled slowly to a halt halfway down the table. What frightened me was his reaction: he didn't swear or display any sign of annoyance, just stood there looking at me.

Gabrielle's cry of disappointment, '*Quel dommage*! Do not take eet so much to 'eart, Thomas,' hung heavily in the air.

She chattered on, but I don't think he was listening. I certainly wasn't.

For at last I was face to face with Louis Moran.

The last piece of the puzzle had clicked into place. It all fitted – the drug running, the ruthless elimination of anyone who posed a threat to business or self, the masterly disguise. I had totally failed to make the connection between Cameron-Blaik and Moran. And it was due to one of those false assumptions Gerry was always warning me against. Moran was a master of disguise, I'd been prepared for that. But I'd assumed, taken for granted, that whatever his appearance, his eyes would be brown. The blue eyes of the man facing me had done what he'd intended – thrown the forces of law and order off the scent. With a sinking feeling I remembered that I'd found the contact lenses in his bedside drawer. The blue of the contact lenses had been masked by the blue-tinged solution in the capsule. I'd slipped the lens sachets into my pocket and forgotten about them.

Gabrielle was saying sharply, 'Dorward! Why are you dreaming? I told you to bring Sir Thomas another Bruichladdich.'

My hand was shaking, an admission, a fatal admission, that I'd recognized him. As I poured the whisky some of the liquid dribbled down the outside of the glass.

I fought to bring my nerves under control. He must be used to a surprised reaction. It couldn't have been the first time that someone had stared at the effect of strong light on his contact lenses, so perhaps he wouldn't realize that I'd seen through his disguise and recognized him as being Louis Moran.

What *would* betray me was any trace of fear. I turned to put the bottle back on the shelf and took several deep breaths. By the time I carried the tray over to the sofa, I was again Elizabeth Dorward, impassive, unruffled butler.

'Your Bruichladdich, Sir Thomas, just as you like it. Will there be anything else?'

For a moment he didn't reply, seeming to be lost in thought. I put the tray down on the side table and for an instant our eyes met. In the subdued light of the table lamp and the leaping flames, his pupils had once more dilated and the irises had returned to their usual blue.

With a dismissive wave of his hand and a brusque, 'Switch off the table lights as you go,' he turned away as if he'd lost interest in me. But I knew he hadn't.

CHAPTER FOURTEEN

That short walk to the door was one of the longest in my life. I could feel his eyes on me. Each moment I expected a hand to grip my shoulder, spinning me round.

Once outside in the hall my immediate reaction was relief. I'd got away with it, but for how long? My life would depend on making the right decision. Since Gabrielle had given me Saturday off, the alarm would be raised only when I didn't turn up to carry out my morning duties on Sunday morning. So should I grab Gorgonzola and make a bolt for it tonight?

I'd already realized how difficult it would be to conceal any car, especially one as conspicuous as mine. If I abandoned it here at *Allt an Damh* and met up with Sandy tomorrow, that would mislead Moran and buy me more time. They'd find the car on Sunday, think I must be close by, and make an extensive search of the surrounding area with dogs. By then, with a day's start, I'd be off the island and safe.

There was only one snag. Sandy wouldn't be at the rendezvous till eleven tomorrow, so there was no point in blundering through the woods in the dark. I might as well stay in the cottage till morning. I'd have plenty of time to work out with him how to get to the airport unobserved, or to one of the ports to catch the ferry. And if things didn't go according to plan, I could hole up in that cottage he was going to show me.

There was another argument in favour of delaying my departure. Gerry had stressed time and time again that one must consider *all* possibilities. Moran might send Waddington on some pretext or other to visit the kitchen. If he did, he'd find me talking and laughing as if I had nothing important on my mind. The decision was made. I'd leave tomorrow and keep to my usual routine of supper in the kitchen with Chef and Ann-Marie.

We were finishing chef's venison pie. Ann-Marie had just launched into her favourite pastime, Gabrielle Robillard.

'That woman's mouth never stops, does it? When I brought in the venison course, she was droning on about shopping at Harvey Nichols and she was still going on about it when I brought in the fruit salad. If she goes shopping in Port Ellen, she'll find that a bit of a comedown.' She adopted an exaggerated French accent. ' "Tonight no veneeson for me, I go to get zee takeaway from zee Neepy Cheepy. I weel only 'ave zee 'aggis zat was shot ziz morneeng. A beeg fat 'aggis 'Arvey Nichols qualeety. I weel 'ave 'aggis and zee French fries, and Toe-mas weel—" '

Without warning the kitchen door opened. Gabrielle Robillard stood framed in the doorway, a bright red spot of anger flamed on each cheek.

She glared at Ann-Marie who smiled back, not at all embarrassed at being caught out. Loftily ignoring this show of defiance, Gabrielle addressed me.

'Oh, there you are, Dorward. Since I 'ave given you Saturday 'oliday because of our visits to see the so boring birds and that awful lake, please to remember to tell the maid that *she* must perform your duties.' With another glare at Ann-Marie she swept out.

What was it about Gabrielle's visit to the kitchen that made me so uneasy? On the face of it, she had come to make sure I hadn't forgotten to tell Ann-Marie to deliver her breakfast tray, but I was sure it was merely an excuse. Behind that visit was Moran. As I'd thought he might, he had wanted to know if my routine had altered after seeing the ring on his irises. If I hadn't been taking a meal with the others as usual, that would have been enough for him to act. Well, his suspicions should have been allayed. Gabrielle had found me in the kitchen, seemingly relaxed. My decision to wait till the morning had been the right one.

It was after ten o'clock when I closed the kitchen door behind me and made my way back to the cottage. A gale had blown up. I felt it even in the shelter of the shrubbery. Branches of trees creaked; leaves whispered in heated argument; clouds scudded across the sky, fitfully revealing and obscuring the moon. High winds always make me feel on edge, perhaps that accounted for the sudden unease I couldn't shake off.

I locked the cottage door behind me, switched on the table lamp and pulled the curtains tightly shut. And didn't feel any safer. Gorgozola seemed to tune in to my mood, for she twined herself round my legs and remained pressed to me without any welcoming *purr*.

I turned on the TV and sat back with G curled up on my lap, stroking the top of her head gently with my finger. *Had* my decision to remain here tonight really been the right one? I stared unseeingly at the changing images on the screen. . . . Something about Gabrielle's visit to the kitchen was still bothering me. What was it?

It was the very fact that there'd *been* a visit. That meant Moran did indeed suspect that he'd been recognized. I knew from the briefing file that Moran lived by the gangster's rule of thumb – if in doubt, rub 'em out. Though my decision to wait till morning had bought me a little time, I knew now it had been the wrong one.

I switched off the TV, gathered up Gorgonzola and leapt to my feet, cursing myself for my stupidity. 'Time to go, G.'

I grabbed the rucksack and stuffed her into it, snatched my waterproof fleece from the hook on the back of the door and left, flicking off the light and locking the door behind me. I didn't stop to take anything else.

If I had, they would have caught me.

A large dark cloud was covering the moon, but there was just enough light from the sky for me to pick out the more solid columns of tree trunks and the irregular shapes of bushes. The gravelled drive between stable block and cottage was a faint grey ribbon weaving through the dark mass of rhododendron shrubbery.

I was still within a few yards of the cottage when I saw the bobbing beams of two torches playing on gravel and flicking across leaves and trunks. I had barely thirty seconds. I dropped to my knees and wriggled into the heart of the nearest rhododendron bush. The thin whippy branches closed behind me and I lay there in close conversation with Mother Earth, the side of my face pressed into the damp mat of leaf mould. The rucksack on my back heaved and twitched as Gorgonzola adjusted herself to her suddenly horizontal position. At my whispered, 'Quiet, G', it too was still.

I heard the *scrunch scrunch scrunch* of gravel under running feet, the *thud thud* as shoes met the harder surface of the brick path and slowed. Lying on my side, I could see torch beams playing on the cottage door, could not quite make out the whispered words.

The darkness behind the closed curtains gave the impression that I was still at home, had gone to bed. If they thought I was asleep, perhaps they'd think that they could safely wait till morning to deal with me. It would be only a temporary reprieve, for when they came for me in the morning and found the cottage empty, they'd bring in the dogs.

I'd make a break for it into the wood as soon as they'd gone. I knew exactly how I could cover my tracks and fool the dogs. *Allt an Damh* got its name from the stream that ran through the trees down to the bay. I'd seen a stag walking in the stream, and I could too. Once at the bay, I'd keep to the shallow waters till near the rendezvous point on the track that led up from the shore.

The whispered consultation ended. One of the figures stepped forward and knocked loudly, the other flattened himself against the wall to the right of the door.

'It's only me. Waddington. The intercom's developed a fault, so I've come over to tell you that. . . .' He dropped his voice to a level that would have been indistinct to me inside.

They waited. Then *Bang Bang Bang*. He hammered on the door again. 'Wake up, Dorward.' *Bang Bang Bang*. 'It's Waddington. Open the door.'

After a moment I heard Moran say quietly, 'She's not going to come out.'

He fished in his pocket. I heard the *click* of the lock turning. Light flooded out onto the path as the door crashed back on its hinges. He rushed in. Waddington hung back a moment, then followed him inside.

I pressed myself deeper into the leaf mould and turned my face away from the cottage. If I could see them, the pale blob of my face might be visible enough to attract their attention. In the beam of their torches, I'd be like a rabbit caught in the glare of approaching headlights – and as doomed.

The crash of splintered furniture and smashed crockery spilled from the open doorway as Moran vented his rage on the contents of the cottage. Suddenly they were outside. Very close. Too close.

'She's gone.' Moran spat out the words.

I heard the sharp *sthaat* of fist against flesh and a gasp, then Waddington whined, 'It's nothing to do with me. It's not *my* fault that she's done a runner.'

Another *sthaat*. 'You bloody fool, Waddington. It has everything to do with you. I caught her in the billiard room looking up the ring in a book. My explicit instructions to you were to buy a *Cameron* ring, arrows tied together and the motto Unite. You bought a Brodie ring, you bloody fool.'

'I'm not taking this, Blaik.' Waddington was showing more defiance than was wise in the circumstances. 'A badge with arrows and the motto *Unite*, that's what you said, and that's what I got you. What was wrong with tha—?' By the sound of the choking gasp, Moran had gripped him by the throat.

'The Cameron motto is in *Gaelic*, imbecile. I don't tolerate mistakes. If she's not caught, *you're* next in the firing line. Do – I – make – myself – clear?' The effect was of a terrier shaking a rat.

'She won't get far tonight in the dark.' The tremor in Waddington's voice undermined the confidence of the words.

'I hope for your sake she doesn't. Get the gamekeeper to send over a dog at first light tomorrow. That'll flush her out.'

Waddington gave a shaky laugh. 'Dog and gin traps, she doesn't stand a chance, does she?'

Even though they appeared to have gone, I waited another half-hour before easing myself out the far side of the rhododendron bush. I brushed off the leaf mould and shivered, for the first time aware that the damp leaves had seeped through my thin butler's trousers. Dare I take a couple of minutes to dash into the cottage and pull on thick trousers and boots?

Just a few yards away light was still streaming from the open doorway, offering easy access to that clothing. Oh so tempting – and possibly a trap. Waddington could be somewhere out there in the darkness waiting . . . waiting for the fleeting silhouette of a figure against that yellow rectangle of light. I thought about it. If I had to hide out in the woods, these thin shoes and clothes were totally unsuitable. I'd minimize the risk by entering through the bathroom window at the rear.

But my first priority was to reassure Gorgonzola. I felt my way deeper into the surrounding shrubbery, shrugged the rucksack off my back and zipped it open. She didn't try to struggle out of the narrow gap, just sat there. I cupped her head gently in my hands.

'Good, good girl,' I whispered into her ear. 'Don't move, I'll be back.'

She seemed to understand and settled into the depths with the faintest *miaow*. I closed the zip and left the rucksack under the largest bush where I'd find it again.

Keeping to the edge of the shrubbery, I moved slowly and cautiously round to the back of the cottage till I stood looking up at the square of glass faintly illuminated by the light from the main room. I was about to turn burglar. The bathroom window was positioned quite high off the ground, but I could just reach to push up the lower sash to its full extent. The aperture was small, very small, and reminiscent of a giant cat flap. I retreated a few paces. A run, a leap, an undignified scramble, and my head and shoulders were through – followed by a painful headlong tumble onto the bathroom floor. I was in.

Trusting to the overturned table and chairs to screen me from the open doorway, I crawled along to the chest of drawers and extracted warm trousers, thick shirt and woollen jersey. By stretching out a hand I managed to retrieve my boots neatly lined up beside the bed. I changed in the bathroom and exited by the window as awkwardly as I had entered.

The electric light had ruined my night vision and now the bushes merged into one black mass. I found my way back to G by sheer luck. With whispered words of comfort, I swung the rucksack onto my back, and eyes straining to penetrate the darkness, groped my way towards the woods.

The moon had set. Though my night vision had returned, my progress through the wood was painfully slow, keeping to the path to avoid the gin traps much more difficult than I'd expected. Bushes and trees were merely denser black on black, the ground underfoot a pool of darkness. Again and again I stumbled over uneven ground, spreading tree roots, or tussocks of grass bordering the path.

When I calculated that I was far enough into the woods to use the emergency torch kept in the outer pocket of the rucksack, I switched it on. The bulb glimmered faintly, flickered and died. *Shit.* I'd last used the torch on the visit to the shed with Sandy, and hadn't checked that the sliding switch was fully off. Without light I was condemned to this snail's pace.

There was no doubt about it, I was tiring: at times tripping over a half-buried stone or fallen branch, lurching off the path and finding it again after several heart-stopping minutes, the rucksack a constant weight pulling at my shoulders.

At last, off to my right I heard the rippling burble of the stream. From previous reconnaissance I knew it was a mere hundred yards away across the bracken-covered hillside, but even in daylight the intervening ground was a minefield of concealed boulders and ankle-turning holes. It was just the place a gamekeeper would choose to set his murderous gin traps. Even if I reached the stream safely, to attempt to walk down its bed slipping and sliding over unseen rocks in the dark would be courting a broken leg, or concussion, and face-down, risk drowning in the water.

With dawn would come the dog. I closed my eyes, took a deep breath and slowly let it out again. Paralysing panic subsided to a mere cold sweat. I sat down with my back against a tree, clasping the rucksack to me. As soon as it was light enough to make out the ground ahead, I'd find a thick stick and stab it down at the ground before each step: the gin trap's cruel teeth would bite into wood rather than bone. . . .

In the grey pre-dawn light, the bracken-covered hillside and the trees lining the stream were a flat monochrome. It was Gorgonzola heaving about in the rucksack that had woken me. I opened my eyes, for a moment my mind a blank with no recollection of last night's events. Then it all came rushing back. I leapt to my feet, horrified that I'd allowed myself to fall asleep. I should have been away from here an hour ago.

The rucksack almost twisted out of my restraining arms as with a loud demanding yowl G forced the zip apart with her shoulders. A large furry paw hooked itself into the fabric preparatory to leaping out.

'Sorry, G, but I'll have to put you on the short lead.' That would restrict her to the edges of the path. I fumbled at the rucksack pocket with stiff, cold fingers. 'Can't risk you wandering off among the gin traps.'

She submitted to the collar and lead with ill-grace and retired to excavate a hole in the leaf mould under the trees. Next on her agenda would be a good scratch at the bark of a tree before she went on the hunt for breakfast, but there wasn't time for that. As soon as she'd covered her traces, I tugged on the lead and reeled her back, ignoring her indignant protests and dragging feet. Expecting squirming resistance I reached out to scoop her up.

She was standing very still, ears swivelled back the way we'd come. Then I heard it too. The distant barking of a dog. A branch snapped further back along the path. A deer making its way down to the bay? Or a man hunting DJ Smith?

I didn't wait to find out. I grabbed Gorgonzola by the scruff of the neck, dumped her in the rucksack and zipped it closed. The nearest cover was the torn up root-plate of a fallen tree, a circle of grassy tussocks, moss, earth and dried out roots. I crouched down behind it and waited, ears straining to catch the slightest sound.

Thud thud thud. Running feet. Close and coming closer. I gripped the rucksack, hands sweating. Judging by the laboured breathing, the runner was only yards away. The running feet slowed, faltered, stopped. At first, all I could see through a tiny gap in the wall of earth and tangled roots was an empty stretch of path, then a man moved into view, face flushed, air rasping in his lungs, chest heaving with the unaccustomed exertion. Waddington. He pulled out a mobile phone and turned away to look out across the bracken towards the stream. Praying that he would move on along the path, I laid the rucksack flat on the ground and curled up on my side to offer the lowest profile.

After a few moments, when his breathing had steadied I heard, 'I'm where the path goes close to the river. No sign of her yet. What do you want me to do?' A pause. 'Right.' The *thud thud thud* of his running footsteps resumed and died away.

When he'd decided he'd missed me, he'd come back – in five minutes, thirty minutes – there was no way of telling, but he'd come back. The barking was louder now, much louder. I had no choice. I'd have to risk the no-man's-land between here and the stream. There was no time to look for that stick to detect gin traps. No time for anything but to run across the rough grass into the bracken. My only chance was to get to the stream. Once there, screened by the bushes and trees along its edge, I'd be able to make my way down to the bay.

I shrugged on the rucksack, and after a quick glance each way along the path, set off like an athlete exploding from the starting block, eyes fixed firmly on the winning tape. I shut my mind to the thought of gin traps concealed in the bracken, iron teeth biting through flesh into bone, and concentrated on racing to the stream only two hundred yards away. One hundred and fifty yards . . . one hundred. . . . Almost there. Twenty yards from the stream, my luck ran out.

The shout came from behind. I didn't stop. I heard the sharp crack of a shot and a white star spurted on the trunk of the tree ahead. I threw myself down in the bracken and crawled forward on hands and knees, pushing aside the stems, sweating at the thought of thrusting my hand into the steel teeth of a gin trap.

Another gunshot followed by Waddington's triumphant shout, 'I can see you, Dorward. Stand up and put your hands on your head.'

He was bluffing. If he could see me, that last bullet would have found its target. I crawled on, all too aware of the snap and rustle of crushed bracken fronds as he crashed his way towards me. The sounds stopped.

'Can you hear me, Blaik? I've got her cornered.' He was very close.

I flattened myself to the ground. Futile. In a few seconds he would be looming over me, gun aimed at my head.

The rustle of bracken resumed. 'She's beside the str— *Aaaa. . . .*' An awful scream sent a flock of birds fluttering skywards. 'Oh my God, *my leg, my leg. . . .*' The screams went on and on.

I rose to my knees, an instinctive reaction to rush to the aid of a suffering human being. Then I shut my ears to the terrible cries and crawled quickly on, heedless of the stems scratching at my face. I had to get to the stream before Moran – and the dog – made an appearance.

I pushed my way through the wall of bracken, and was staring at rough grass, half-buried tree roots and a line of trees. Beyond the lacy curtain of thin branches overhanging the stream, amber water bubbled and gurgled on its way down to the sea. My intention had been to go downstream, circle round the shoreline in the shallows of the bay and make my way to the road to meet up with Sandy at eleven. But that plan would be a death trap now. All Moran had to do was stand with a rifle on the hillside above the bay and take aim: I'd make an easy target.

I'd go upstream, back towards *Allt an Damh*, he wouldn't think of that. I scrambled down the bank, and slipping and sliding on the smooth boulders, splashed along, crouched low taking advantage of the screening bushes and trees. As I stumbled between the steep sides of a narrow ravine, I began to hope that escape was possible.

To my relief, Waddington's cries were fainter now, deadened by the walls of the ravine. But I wasn't safe yet. The rush and tumble of that small waterfall ahead would drown out any sound of pursuit. At any minute could come a shout of discovery, a bullet in the back, killing me – and Gorgonzola. I swung the rucksack off and unzipped it enough to enable her to force her way out – if I was hit, she'd have a chance. Hugging it to me in an awkward embrace, I picked my way over the rocks at the foot of the waterfall.

Psshchh . . . sshch . . . sshch. A shot echoed and re-echoed, bouncing back and forth against the vertical sides of the ravine. Moran had crept into the ravine and was stalking me, rifle at the ready. I ducked under an overhang carved and hollowed smooth by millennia of winter torrents. Trapped.

I closed my eyes the better to focus on sounds, straining to hear. Was that the rattle of a dislodged stone? The click of a safety catch?

At last those terrible screams had stopped. Moran had been able to lever apart the jaws of the gin trap. I wouldn't have wished that suffering on Waddington even though he had been intent on killing me. He hadn't had any choice. I couldn't forget Moran's threat, 'I don't tolerate mistakes. If she's not caught, you're next in the firing line.'

I realized suddenly that that was exactly what had happened: the shot had been fired not to kill me, but to kill Waddington. And it hadn't been to put a stop to the suffering, but to rid himself of a liability. One mistake too many, that was John Waddington's epitaph. I needed no further proof that Moran would stop at nothing.

There were no other shots. Waddington was dead and Moran wasn't tracking me up the ravine. He had assumed I had taken the obvious way and gone downstream. That gave me more time, but I knew I needed every minute. I left the shelter of the hollowed-out overhang and began to climb over the tumble of boulders at the side of the waterfall.

After emerging from the ravine I left the stream and made my way over hilly country towards the rendezvous with Sandy, keeping well clear of *Allt an Damh*. Tempting though it was to take the quickest route through the woods and down the drive, I'd be caught on the CCTV camera trained on the gates. It was now 11.30, half an hour after the time I'd arranged to meet him. Had he waited?

I topped the last rise. Below me I could see the rutted track that ran down to the shore and beside it, our rendezvous point, a tree splintered by lightning.

But of Sandy's car there was no sign. No sign at all.

CHAPTER FIFTEEN

My heart sank. Suddenly I felt very tired. The thought of meeting up with Sandy and being whisked away to the bolt-hole of the cottage had kept me going, but now . . . I trailed on downhill, trying to convince myself that we hadn't set an *exact* time to meet, that he could have been delayed by a puncture, that he'd overslept, that he'd. . . . To be honest, I was trying not to accept the awful truth that he'd come, grown tired of waiting and gone.

I stood at the side of the track, for the first time aware of just how exhausted I was. A tear trickled down my cheek. Angry with myself, I brushed it away. 'Don't be such a wimp, DJ,' I sniffled.

From somewhere low down near the splintered tree came a chuckle. 'Aha, so that's your real name, is it!'

I tried to identify the exact spot from which the voice had come, but a master of camouflage isn't easily spotted. And then I saw the sign he'd left for me. Hooked on a snag of branch was a battered trilby hat.

'You're looking more than a little the worse for wear, lass.'

He rose to his feet from behind a screen of moss, leaves and broken-off branches. Perched on his head in place of the hat was a small clump of bracken rooted in a chunk of turf torn from the banking.

'Didn't see me, did you? Works every time. Brings back memories of the war – some good, some bad.' He restored the turf to the banking with all the care of a golfer replacing a divot on the green.

'I thought you'd gone.' The tears were running freely now. And I didn't care.

He pulled a large khaki handkerchief from his pocket and offered it to me. I took it, blew my nose and said with an attempt at a smile, 'Let's get out of here. I'm leaving Islay.'

'That shot early this morning, was it anything to do with you?' When I made no reply, he looked at me thoughtfully and nodded. 'Mission complete, eh? Say no more.'

'I didn't see your car and—' I swallowed hard, not trusting my voice to continue.

'That's why I left my hat hanging up. You see, the track's good enough for a quad bike and trailer, but no use for a car if you value your suspension.' He unhooked his hat from the tree. 'Let's go. I've a flask in the car. You look as if you could do with a good strong cup of army tea.'

We walked up the track in silence. I was debating how much I should tell him, and he, I suppose, was being discreet, leaving me time to come to a decision. I was aware of covert sidelong glances, but it was only when we reached the car that he voiced what was on his mind.

'You've been swivelling that head of yours like a meerkat on watch. You're on the lookout. Is it for that fellow Waddington?'

'Waddington's dead.' I'd intended it to come out flat and unemotional. If he heard the wobble in my voice, he gave no sign, only nodded as if that was something to be expected – and not at all regretted.

Avoiding his gaze, I busied myself unzipping the rucksack. 'Gorgonzola's been shut in here far too long.'

G's cross face peered up at me. I sat in the car and lifted her onto my knee. 'There, there, G.' I ran my hand down her back in long smooth strokes. 'You've been a good girl, a very good girl.'

I turned to Sandy. 'I think we'd better—'

A wriggle, a squirm. Seconds too late I made a grab. G had leapt out, disappeared into the long grass and was gone. I fumbled in the outer pocket of the rucksack for the ultrasound whistle in the hope that training would be stronger than temptation. It wasn't. To a hungry cat the wooded hillside and its wildlife was a feline supermarket. By the strident alarm calls of frightened birds I could track her progress as she moved deeper and deeper into the woodland.

'Looks like she's gone AWOL and won't be back for a while.' He saw the tears in my eyes and his smile faded. 'Don't take on, lass. She'll come back, even if it takes an hour or two. We'll just sit here and have a cup of tea.'

'But we *can't*. He could be here at any moment. He killed Waddington and now he's hunting for me.' The words tumbled over each other in my anxiety to convince. 'Any moment now he could come along the track from the bay and—'

'Whoa, lass.' He gripped me by the shoulders and shook me gently. 'Let's get this straight. This killer, who the hell is he? Can't take evasive action if—'

'Cameron-Blaik, it's Cameron-Blaik. Don't you understand? If he sees me with you, he'll shoot *both* of us. We've got to go *now*.'

'Cameron-Blaik, eh?' I could see his interest, but all he said was, 'You're suffering from shell shock, not thinking straight. Combat neurosis, I believe they call it nowadays. You'll never forgive yourself if you don't look for the cat. Think about it – a soldier doesn't abandon his weapon when he retreats. And to you, the cat's more than a weapon. Give it five minutes and then we'll get out of here at the double.'

He was right. The momentary panic had come from exhaustion. 'OK. Five minutes.' I snatched up the rucksack and clambered up the banking. The bushy undergrowth at the edge of the trees could provide cover for an army of cats. If G was on the prowl here, I'd have little chance of spotting her. Further in, bushes gave way to stinging nettles, finely cut ferns, and ambushing thorny bramble shoots arching downward to root in the leaf mould. I paused beside a heap of moss-covered stones tumbled from an old drystone wall, a promising hunting ground for a cat on the lookout for small rodents. Gorgonzola might not be far away, might even be watching from behind one of the smooth grey trunks that stretched into the distance. But if I didn't find her very soon. . . .

It was now six minutes since I'd entered the wood, and I'd already overstayed the agreed time. I took out the whistle and blew hard and long. I waited, eyes searching desperately for the slightest movement or glimpse of scruffy red fur. Cats are independent creatures and G was more independent than most. That's what I loved about her. But this time, that independent streak could mean that I'd lose her for ever. Despondently I turned to go back.

And there she was. A short distance away, peering guiltily from behind a fallen trunk.

'Here, G,' I called. And over she came.

Contrite, she offered no resistance to being gathered up and stowed in the rucksack. Nevertheless, I didn't give temptation a second chance and zipped her securely in. I hurried back to the edge of the wood and was on the point of pushing through the bushes when I heard Sandy's raised voice.

'I'm a bit deaf. Didn't quite catch that. Could you speak up?'

I dropped to my knees and peered through the screen of leaves. Moran. Moran with a rifle slung on his shoulder. He was standing beside the car, back half-turned to me, stooping to speak to Sandy through the open window.

'I *said*, Has my friend come along the track?' He pointed towards the bay.

Sandy had been peering at Moran as if trying to read his lips. 'The track? You want to know where it goes? Down to the shore.'

Moran tried again. 'Have – you – seen – a – *woman*?'

Sandy shook his head. 'Can't make out what you're saying. Forgot to put in the hearing aids this morning. Sorry.'

'Stupid old bugger.' Moran straightened up and turned as if to look back along the track, taking the opportunity to glance into the back of the car.

'What the *hell*'s this?' He pulled open the door and hauled out a long canvas bag lying on the back seat.

'Hey!' The driver's door began to open.

With a violent thrust of his hand, Moran shoved it shut. 'Stay in the car till I tell you to get out.'

Some choice army language drifted my way as Sandy made another attempt to open the door. Moran dropped the canvas bag and slung the rifle off his shoulder.

'Poachers meet with accidents on my estate. Especially deaf ones who don't hear any warning shouts.' I heard the *snick* of the bolt.

Mouth dry, I watched from the cover of the bushes. How was Sandy going to play it?

He leaned out the window. 'Can't make out what you're muttering on about, but a gun speaks loud enough. You trying to rob me? Well, my life's worth more than a camera tripod. Take it and bugger off.'

Moran leaned the rifle against the car, ripped open the zip of the bag and tipped out a telescopic tripod onto the hard-baked earth. He prodded it with his foot then without warning, strode to the back of the car and flung open the boot. 'Let's see what you've got in here.'

His camera and other photographic equipment. Beads of sweat formed at my hairline. If Moran thought there was the slightest possibility that Sandy had been spying on the yacht and the activities at the shed. . . .

'Taking pictures?' Moran came round to the front of the car. '*Photography's not allowed* on this estate. Private means *private*.'

Sandy's irate face poked out of the driver's window. 'Private, did I hear you say? Private! Haven't you heard of the Land Reform (Scotland) Act 2003? I don't need *your* permission or anybody else's to take wildlife pictures of the otters in the bay. Who the hell are you anyway, the gamekeeper? I'm going to make a complaint to the landowner. What's your name?'

Moran's response was to flip open the back of the camera and pocket the card.

Sandy flung open the car door. 'For God's sake! That's *theft*! All my otter pictures are on that.' He put a foot down on the track.

In one smooth rapid movement Moran snatched up the rifle, the *snick* of the drawn back bolt loud in the stillness. 'So what are you going to do about it? Now get the hell off my land.'

Their eyes met. Sandy swung the other foot out of the car.

'Don't do it! Don't do it!' I whispered. I had no doubt at all that Moran would kill him – and me too if I tried to intervene. I'd be playing right into his hands. Gerry would never get the all-important message that we'd found Moran.

As if he had read my thoughts, he withdrew his foot and closed the car door. The engine started, blue smoke puffed from the exhaust, and the car jolted up the track and out of sight.

Moran laughed, and picking up the tripod, hurled it into the bushes. I watched him walk on up the track, rifle swinging loosely in his hand, head turning from side to side as he searched for any sign of me.

Though he was now out of sight, I moved back deeper into the wood. He would come back in the hope that if I was hiding near the track, I'd feel safe and come out once he'd passed by.

I allowed fifteen minutes, then made my way cautiously back towards the track. I listened for the sound of boots on hard-packed earth, but there was only the distant hum of a car on the Ardbeg road, the chirp of birds and the sough of wind in the trees. The coast was clear.

The first few bars of *The March of the Cameron Men*, strident and tinny, floated up to kill the birdsong. I dropped to the ground, squirming my way forward till I was able to peer through the screen of bushes. Only ten yards away Moran was standing, mobile to ear.

'Sorry I missed you, Callum. I've been called away to Port Ellen. I'm there now. You found the dog in the garage all right, did you. . . ? No, she didn't nose out the bird I lost out on the hill, damn it. I could have done with her longer. . . . Thanks anyway.' He flipped the phone shut and walked on down the track.

Port Ellen. Clearly he was still sure he'd find me. He was setting up an alibi for when he killed me. And I'd so very nearly given him the opportunity, made it easy for him.

One narrow escape was more than enough. Better to avoid the track and keep to the woods. But first, I'd see if I could find Sandy's tripod. Moran wasn't going to get away with that bit of unprovoked bullying. I'd noted where he'd thrown it into the bushes, so it took only a few minutes of searching before I came upon it upended in a bush and carried it triumphantly off.

A glimpse of black tarmac through the trees indicated that I'd reached the single-track main road. A short distance along it, Sandy's car was parked in a passing place with its boot lid up and spare tyre propped against the rear bumper. He was sitting in the driver's seat studying the car manual. I'd kept to the edge of the trees, now I jumped down to the road.

He looked up. 'Nothing to worry about, lass. All this puncture business is a bit of disinformation in case that bastard Cameron-Blaik shows up again.'

'Sorry about the camera card, but I liberated your tripod.'

'Just what I need to mend the puncture.' Closing the manual with a snap, he got out and heaved the tyre and tripod into the boot. 'Got the cat, have you?' I nodded. 'Then we'll be on our way.'

I clambered in. 'Fast as you can to the airport, Sandy.'

He paused, hand on the ignition key. 'It's Saturday and there's only one plane – and that went hours ago, before ten o'clock. If you want to leave the island today, it'll have to be by ferry.' He looked at his watch. 'We might just make Port Askaig in time for the boat at fifteen-thirty.'

Long before we'd even reached Port Ellen I'd dozed off, so I didn't hear the radio announcement that all Caledonian MacBrayne sailings had been cancelled due to a lightning strike by crews over a management-imposed change to their working conditions.

'OK, lass, here we are.'

I opened my eyes drowsily, for a moment disorientated. Where was the ugly ferry jetty at Port Askaig, its little harbour of fishing boats, and beyond that across the narrow Sound of Islay, the two perfect cones of the Paps of Jura?

'This isn't Port Askaig.' I was staring through the windscreen at a metal gate in a drystone wall. Beyond the gate, through a tunnel of beech trees, was the gable end of a small stone cottage.

'We're at my cottage on the Oa, near the lighthouse.' He told me about the cancelled sailings. 'You were asleep and there was no point in waking you. The trouble's been brewing for some time. Just your luck that it came to a head today.' He put a hand on my arm. 'Don't worry, lass. The first plane on Sunday is in the afternoon. I'll get you to it in plenty of time. Now come in and I'll make us a good cup of tea.'

There was no point in worrying. I'd be safe enough here for tonight. I got stiffly out of the car, and with Gorgonzola as expedition leader, her tail up and tip gently twitching, we crackled towards the cottage over a carpet of last year's brittle beech leaves and empty shells.

'My burglar alarm. Not even a cat, let alone a cat burglar, can walk silently on this.' Sandy attempted a stealthy tiptoe. *Scrunch scrunch scrunch.* 'You see, it's impossible. Nobody can get close without us knowing.'

The cottage stood in a small clearing in the beech wood. From near at hand it had a somewhat tumbledown appearance: the roof ridge sagged under the weight of years; moss and ivy clung tenaciously to the slates like a second skin; and the late afternoon sunlight slanting through the trees dappled the rough stones, highlighting the crumbling mortar. It was a building sinking slowly and gracefully into the arms of Mother Earth.

'And this,' Sandy waved a hand at a green lake of nettles and wild garlic, 'this is my vegetable garden. Nettle soup, nettle quiche, nettle tea – have you tried any of these?'

'Er, no.' I shot him a glance. Was he serious?

He laughed. 'Delicious and nutritious, I can assure you. And I've even got running water.' He pointed to a small stream burbling through the trees.

In keeping with the rest of the building, years of sun and rain had distressed the paint of the door to artistically peeling patches of green or blue on bare wood, weathered to grey. He turned the handle.

'Not locked?' I said.

'What is there that anybody would want to steal in here?' He led the

141

way into a low-ceilinged room.

Through a thick haze of peat smoke I saw two wooden chairs and a table, its surface scrubbed to creamy white, and a couple of battered but comfortable-looking armchairs positioned on either side of the stone hearth. Peat embers smouldered in the fire basket, keeping warm the contents of a large black pot. A radio and an old-fashioned glass-chimney oil lamp stood on a low cupboard in one corner of the room.

'Sit yourself down. As I said, what we both need is a good cup of tea.' He moved aside the pot to make way for an equally large kettle and with brass-studded bellows wakened the sleeping embers into leaping flames.

The tea was green and very hot and, I must admit, not as bad as I'd feared. I smiled at him over the rim of the mug. 'Now, if I could borrow your mobile. I've got to make an urgent call to HQ.'

He lifted the lid of the pot and peered at the contents. Gorgonzola, sprawled inelegantly on her back in front of the fire, twisted round and sat up, a drool of saliva at the corner of her mouth. 'Cat sat on mat, sniffing out rabbit.' He gave the pot a stir. 'The good news first, or the bad?' He didn't wait for a reply. 'The good news is that I *do* have a mobile. The bad news is that there isn't a signal here at the cottage. That's true of many places in Islay.'

I slumped back in the armchair, sunk in the despair of self-recrimination. The first thing I should have done was make that phone call to Gerry, but I'd fallen asleep in the car, and because of that I'd jeopardized the success of the operation to capture Louis Moran. He knew he'd been recognized, and he wasn't going to hang around waiting for HMRC to come and arrest him. He had probably already left *Allt an Damh*.

Sandy was studying me. 'That call's pretty urgent, eh?'

I nodded. 'I could have phoned in at Ardbeg or Port Ellen and I didn't. I've probably blown the mission.'

'*That* urgent. I see. Well, *nil desperandum* as the Roman general said. There's a spot not too far from here where the mobile *can* pick up a signal. If you're worried about Cameron-Blaik disappearing, he won't be going anywhere. There's no ferry, and no plane till tomorrow. You can make the phone call after we've put a little strength in our bones.' He lifted the pot onto the table. 'Now, the cat's ready for her supper and we are too.' He turned down the wick in the glass funnel of the oil lamp to extinguish the flame. 'No need for this now.'

The fire cast a flickering warm glow over the room. We sat beside it, washing down the rabbit stew with mugs of his nettle tea. Full of rabbit, Gorgonzola was curled up on Sandy's lap purring contentedly. I'd been abandoned in favour of the Provider of Food.

Reluctantly I put down my mug. 'I'd better make that phone call. Where did you say I could get a mobile signal?'

'Not far, not more than four hundred yards. When you go out the door, turn right through the beech wood. The path leads to a grassy field that slopes down to a bay and the Singing Sands.'

'Singing Sands? How weird.'

'They're called that because you hear a high-pitched whine when you scuff your feet. Give it a try while you're there.' He slid a foot across the floorboards to demonstrate the action. The sudden manoeuvre deposited Gorgonzola off his lap onto the floor.

'Want to come for a walk, G?' I stood up and pulled her lead from my pocket.

A twitch of her tail indicated that she'd heard and was treating the suggestion with the contempt it deserved. She stood on her hind legs, rested her paws on Sandy's knee and leapt back onto his lap. She collapsed there in a heap, eyes half-closed, sides rising and falling in sleepy rhythm. Her answer was clear: to leave the comfort of a lap and a warm fire was just plain silly.

I slipped Sandy's mobile into my pocket and closed the door behind me. I stood for a moment to let my eyes grow accustomed to the dark in the shadow of the trees. Beyond the black tracery of beech branches an almost full moon shone a silver-blue searchlight on the countryside.

Moving about in the dark doesn't usually bother me. It's something I'm used to, but for no reason I could put my finger on, tonight I was on edge. The crackle of beech leaves underfoot was unnervingly loud in the stillness and small rustlings in undergrowth had me looking over my shoulder expecting to see the dark shape of an assailant sneaking up behind. Of course, there was nobody, nobody at all. Nevertheless I was glad to move out from the shadows of the little wood onto the open space of the moonlit field.

Halfway across the field I looked back. In the dew that had formed on the grass, my feet had left a trail of silvery footprints as distinct as the mark of boots in snow. A hollow cough close by made me spin round, heart pounding, mouth dry. It had come from that two foot high outcrop of rock ten yards ahead. Whoever was there was hidden from me, must be lying on the ground. I could jump down on top of him and . . . I walked on at the same steady pace, careful not to show any sign of alarm.

As I approached, a white shape rose up from behind the outcrop, eyes glinting in the moonlight. With a startled bleat a sheep trotted off. I had let nerves get the better of me. I was in the countryside, for God's sake. What else would I expect to find behind a rock but a sheep?

That was a hundred times more likely than Moran. Either he would be holed up somewhere organizing his own escape, or still be scouring the area round *Allt an Damh* for me, and have sent someone to the airport or ferry ports. He no longer had his right-hand man Waddington, but there would be others he'd call on, such as the men who had put up the shed. I decided now that the airport – and the ferry ports – wouldn't be safe. Plan B had been for me to hole-up until Moran was captured, and that was what I'd have to do. One thing for sure, he wouldn't be giving a thought to the sparsely inhabited peninsula of the Oa.

Ahead, moonlight glinted on water but though I could hear the *swassh* . . . *swasssh* of waves breaking on the shore, I didn't see the sands until I reached the far end of the field. Fifteen feet below lay the moonlit waters of a small bay, beautiful in the moonlight, breathtaking on a sunny day. On the stretch of white wind-rippled sand, small reefs of jagged black rocks bristled like the scaly backs of giant reptiles poised to return to the sea after laying their eggs.

Once I'd made that phone call, I'd wander along the beach and try to make the sands sing for me. I reached into my pocket for Sandy's mobile and punched in Gerry's number. *Network not found. Call Failed.*

Sandy had assured me I'd get a signal here, but he must have meant on the beach. I took the narrow path leading down to the sands. My feet sank into the soft crystalline grains as I walked towards the sea, experimentally scuffing a boot in an attempt to reproduce the singing sound he'd described. Without success, until I was halfway across the beach beside a line of jagged rocks. Then I heard it – a faint high-pitched *zinnng* from the sole of my boot.

I was tempted to try for that effect again but it would have to wait until after I'd made the phone call. I mustn't get distracted. I flipped open the phone *Searching for network. Network connected*. As I contemplated the wave patterns on the moon's pathway across the water, I punched in

Gerry's number. Listening to the ringing tone, I swung my foot across the sand again.

Zinnng. The sound came, not from the sand under my boot, but from the other side of the line of rocks. I had time only to snap the phone shut and thrust it into a crevice before they were on me.

CHAPTER SIXTEEN

A fist thumped into the side of my head. I was falling . . . My head made contact with hard rock. Then nothing.

It was the throb, throb, throb pounding in my head that brought me back to semi-consciousness. No sounds. The ground beneath me was hard . . . I drifted off again. . . .

The next time I was aware of anything, the pounding in my head had died to a dull ache. I felt rough wood against my cheek. I was lying on floorboards. I opened my eyes to total darkness. I moved my hand near to my face – and could still see nothing. For a terrible moment I thought the blow to the head had blinded me. Slowly and painfully I turned my head. The blackness was broken by a faint grey line at floor level. I lay there staring at it, trying to work out what it was, but it was all too much bother. My eyes slowly closed. . . .

. . . A thin strip of bright light had taken the place of the faint grey line. I realized it was daylight seeping beneath the bottom of a door. I levered myself onto an elbow and then with difficulty into a sitting position. When the worst of the sickness and dizziness had subsided, I looked about me, trying to gain a clue as to the kind of place they'd dumped me in. It was still too dark to make out anything, so I just sat there with my head on my knees, eyes closed, trying to recall what had happened.

I'd been on a beach of white sand looking at the moonlight playing on the sea . . . why was I there? That was it, the phone call to Gerry. I frowned. Had I made the call? Did he know that Louis Moran was at *Allt an Damh*, and was HMRC even now *en route* to Islay to arrest him? I'd heard the ringing tone and then . . . then I'd heard the sands sing, warning of the presence of someone.

I raised my head and stared at the line of light, now the golden brightness of sunlight. HMRC wouldn't be on their way, there'd be no cavalry to the rescue. I hadn't spoken to Gerry, given him the message. He *didn't* know about Moran.

I fought back tears, not of fear, but of rage and despair. I didn't expect to escape from here with my life. Death was ever a possibility in undercover work, I accepted that. But to lose my life to no purpose . . . and it *would* be to no purpose if Moran escaped and once again went to ground, whereabouts unknown. I'd been so close to success. So very close.

The bar of light under the door faded in intensity and slowly brightened again as clouds drifted across the sun, a reminder that there was a world out there and if I wanted to be a part of it again, I'd better do something about it. Where there was a door, there was the good chance that there would be a light switch. I crawled across the floor and using the door handle for support, hauled myself to my feet.

A light switch would be somewhere about here . . . I swept my hand up the wall. Click. Dazzled by the sudden flood of light, it was several seconds before I took in my surroundings. Familiar surroundings. I was back in the gardener's cottage. I stared across the room at Moran's handiwork: the overturned table, the couple of chairs with splintered and broken legs, the smashed plates and cups lying scattered on worktop and floor in the kitchen recess.

The door was of solid construction, the lock modern and tamperproof. I staggered over to examine the blocked-out windows. No hope here: they had been securely boarded up on the outside with plywood nailed to the frame. There was no escape route. This was my prison and they had the key.

While I worked out what to do when they came back for me, I'd resort to that traditional standby in emergencies, a cup of tea. The electric kettle looked as if it had survived Moran's onslaught. If I could find an undamaged cup . . . I hauled the table upright, and five minutes later, sipping tea and munching on a chunk of cake found in the cake tin, I sat on a surviving chair and considered my options.

They hadn't killed me at the Singing Sands. That meant only one thing: Moran wanted to know who I was and who had sent me. Then he'd kill me. Any attempt to remain silent, and he'd know for certain that

I'd guessed his identity. He'd try to torture me into revealing who had sent me, and I wasn't sure if I could withstand the pain. In fact I was damned sure I couldn't. To avoid torture I'd have to convince him I was harmless, concoct a story to hide the fact that I was an HMRC agent who had come to Islay in search of him – and had found him.

I didn't have long to wait. The rattle of a key being inserted in the lock gave me enough warning to psyche myself up for the encounter. The door began to open. . . .

'The light's on, guv.' The accent was English, the voice one I didn't recognize.

A curse, then, 'Out of my way.' The door crashed back against the wall.

Moran stood framed in the doorway, behind him two thugs of villainous appearance, black hair, black stubble, black hearts. They would enjoy inflicting pain, revel in it, prolong it.

I let out a cry of alarm, allowing my face to show a trace of the real fear that was, in the old cliché, turning bones to jelly, blood to water, for this fitted the role that I'd decided was my only chance of surviving the next hour.

Then, as if just registering who he was, I leapt up from the chair smiling a tearful welcome. 'Oh, Sir Thomas, thank God it's you!'

My reaction was not at all what he had expected. He frowned, disconcerted. Just as I'd hoped.

'L-last night somebody attacked me, I don't know why. . . .' My voice shook and it wasn't all an act. 'I was knocked out and . . . and I found myself back here. Locked in.' I looked round the room and stifled a sob. 'They . . . someone . . . seems to have wrecked the cottage. I don't know what they expected to find. I mean, there's nothing here of much value, is there?' I sank back onto the chair and burst into tears. This isn't how undercover agents are supposed to behave under pressure, but it was a safety valve for the terror I was fighting to control. I didn't feel too badly about it as tears fitted perfectly with the role of distraught and harmless female.

I'd half-expected Moran to interrupt, grab me by my jacket, smash his fist into my face. But there was only silence. Unnerving silence. The blue eyes bored into me.

After a moment he said brusquely, 'On Friday night, where were you?'

'Friday night?' My surprise was carefully judged to be just enough, not overdone. 'I went to see the otters. As you will know, Ms Robillard told me I could have the whole of Saturday off in recompense for spending most of Thursday on duty. It was an ideal opportunity to stay out all night and study the otters hunting by moonlight – they're very shy and I've never had much luck catching sight of them during the day.'

How was I doing? I could tell nothing from his expression.

'I see,' he said slowly. 'So you didn't come back to the cottage?'

I clapped a hand to my mouth and stared at him. 'You mean that if I had been here in the cottage on Friday night, or on Saturday, I would have been here when—? Oh, my God.' I paused as if contemplating the horror of it, and then continued, 'No, it was such a nice morning that I decided to hitch-hike to Ardbeg distillery's café for a late breakfast.' Though a thin story, it might buy me time.

For a long moment Moran stared at me. Then, 'You say you were attacked? Did you see who it was?'

Behind him, the two thugs glanced at each other.

I shook my head and winced at the resulting pain. 'Whoever it was came from behind.'

'So you weren't attacked here?' As if he didn't know.

I started to shake my head again before remembering that was not a good idea. 'On the way to Ardbeg I got a lift from a local man.' I'd tell him Sandy's name, if necessary, but give the impression that he was a mere chance acquaintance. Damage limitation. He was in real danger now that he was linked with me – I should have realized that Moran had been suspicious after the confrontation with Sandy on the track and had traced him, and then me, by that distinctive speckled beard of his. Anyone round about Port Ellen would have recognized his description, know where he lived. 'We had something at the café and then he offered to take me to look at the highland cattle and feral goats on the Oa.'

That didn't explain why I had still been there at Sandy's cottage at night, long after I'd have been able to see little more than the shapes of the dark-coated cattle or feral goats. My story was full of holes, thin as the thinnest layer of ice on a pond.

I saw that, so did he.

His expression hardened. 'So . . . you were studying the goats in the dark, were you?'

The refined civilized air of Sir Thomas Cameron-Blaik fell away. In its place was the cold ruthlessness of a man who gave as little thought to murder as he gave to throwing away a cigarette end.

I'd known from the beginning that my story would have to satisfy him a hundred per cent, that the slightest suspicion would be enough for him, more than enough. I'd been skating on thin ice – and fallen through. I'd tried my best and lost.

Without turning his head he said, 'Close the door, Eddie.'

One thug moved toward the door, the other looked at Moran for instructions. Mouth dry, palms sweaty, I pressed my back against the hard bars of the chair in an instinctive bid to distance myself from the violence to come.

The slightly muffled notes of *The March of the Cameron Men* took us all by surprise.

'*Shit!*' Moran pulled the mobile from his pocket, studied the display, then put the phone to his ear. 'I *told* you not to ring me . . . *What!*' His lips tightened into a thin line. 'Say that again. . . .' He cut short the agitated twittering. 'I'll be there right away.'

He thrust the phone back into his pocket and bent down to my level. 'Whatever your name is, it's not Dorward. When I come back, you'll tell me the truth – and who sent you. Eddie here will see to it.'

The tone was matter-of-fact, quietly confident. It was that, more than anything else that set my heart pounding. I didn't bother with a futile, 'I don't know what you mean,' just watched as he motioned to his men and strode out. At the door Eddie turned and smiled. A smile of anticipation.

The key turned in the lock. Voices murmured. Silence fell.

A grey predawn light was filtering through the thin curtains. For a moment Sandy stared vaguely at the brown ash in the grate. He'd fallen asleep in the chair, silly old buffer. He eased himself stiffly into a more comfortable position.

Wahhh. Miaow. Needle-sharp claws pierced his trousers and dug into his leg, jolting him fully awake. He stared down at Liz's cat. The cat stared crossly back at him. For a moment he couldn't quite recollect why it was there. Yes . . . he remembered now. Liz had gone out last night to the Singing Sands to get a signal for the mobile. She must be away making another phone call. Sandy and the cat dozed off. . . .

It was the *chook chook chook* of an alarmed blackbird that woke him again. A stray sunbeam was poking a mischievous finger through a chink in the curtains, caressing the thin layer of dust on the radio and playing on the glass chimney of the oil lamp.

He yawned and stretched. A shifting of the weight on his knees reminded him of the cat. All of a sudden the weight lifted: Gorgonzola had darted across to the door.

'Message received and understood.' He heaved himself out of the chair and let her out.

He stood in the doorway taking deep breaths of the cool clean air. It was going to be a fine day. He turned to go back inside, it was time to get the porridge ready. Liz should be back soon. He hadn't heard her going out this morning. He hadn't heard her come back from making that phone call last night either. He frowned. She had come back last night, hadn't she? Of course she had. Why wouldn't she?

Half an hour later he sat at the table spooning the porridge from the bowl. The pebble of disquiet had developed into a boulder of worry. He went to the door, looking along the path to the field beyond the trees, hoping to catch sight of an approaching figure. But there was nobody. He sat down again at the table. He'd give her a little longer – till he'd finished the bowl of porridge. No doubt there'd be some simple explanation to account for her absence – watching the antics of the otters or seals, for instance. After all, he hadn't set a time for having breakfast, so there was no necessity for her to be back at the cottage by now.

He swallowed the last spoonful of porridge. It was no use. Fear had ousted worry. He knew she'd gone to the Singing Sands – what if she'd fallen and twisted an ankle, easy enough in the dark? She could have been lying out there all night. He should have thought of that before. He'd take the cat with him. He leapt to his feet and snatched up the cat's lead hanging on the back of a chair. It wouldn't do at all if the cat went AWOL. The cat would be the first thing she'd ask about.

From the top of the track leading to the beach, he could see that the Singing Sands appeared deserted. He hadn't realized just how much he'd been counting on finding her here, paddling in the sea, or sitting on a rock or walking up and down on the beach. Could she be lying with a twisted ankle or, God forbid, a broken leg, hidden from view behind one of the outcrops of rock?

Once on the beach, he looked down at the cat. 'You'd find her if you were a dog. Well, have a bit of fun while we're here.' He unclipped the lead and watched as the cat stalked a seagull perched on one of the dark ridges of rock. 'You've no chance there, lass.'

He shook his head in amusement and turned to look along the beach. There were no fresh footprints: the wind-blown, powdery sand was already smudging the cat's tracks. Shallow hollows, ghost footprints, were the only trace of previous visitors, human or animal, with no indication of how recently they had been made. He'd have to look behind each of the saw-edged outcrops running in parallel at right angles to the sea.

It didn't take long. She was definitely not here. There was nothing else to do but go back to the cottage and wait. She must have had her own reason for going off, but she'd be back. She wouldn't have left without her cat.

Catching the cat was more difficult than he'd expected, a lot more difficult. In fact, it seemed to take a perverse delight in eluding capture, treating his efforts as a game. The dangled lead was playfully tapped, the come-to-me whistle studiously ignored, the lightning grab easily evaded, the wheedling plea treated with contempt.

'Come here, you insubordinate bugger!' He made a desperate lunge. 'Gotcha!' His hands closed round the furry body, only for the fiend of a cat to squirm out of his grasp. A leap and a scrabble, and it was looking smugly down at him from a rocky pinnacle.

He looked up at it, eyes narrowed. Perhaps a more subtle approach . . . 'You want *rabbit*, you want *fish*? Follow me, you ginger bugger.'

He turned to make his way back to the cottage. Something glinted in a crevice in the rock. He prised it out. What the hell was a mobile phone doing—? He flipped it open. That otter display: the phone was definitely his. Shaken, he stood staring down at it.

How long did I have before they came back? I'd have to act quickly. Nevertheless, for what I had in mind, I had to allow time for them to get well away. Before I got up from my chair, I made myself wait. I stared at my watch and willed the minutes to pass . . . At last. I crossed the room and listened at the door and the windows.

Moran and his gang seemed to have gone – but one of the thugs might still be on guard outside. I flicked off the light switch. In the dark the thin bar of daylight stretched the width of the door, unbroken by the shadow of feet. That didn't rule out someone standing against the cottage wall or within earshot. There was only one way to find out.

I put on the light, seized a pot from the kitchen cupboard and pushed up a front window, exposing the sheet of plywood. The squeal of the wooden sash shrieked, 'She's trying to escape!' But there was no angry shout, no key inserted in the lock.

Now to set my plan in motion. I crashed the pot against a bottom corner of the plywood. *Bang Bang Bang. Bang Bang Bang.* If I could loosen one of the nails pinning the board to the window frame, it might be possible to use one of the broken chair legs as a lever to force off the plywood sheet. *Bang Bang Bang. . . .*

. . . *Bang Bang Bang.* I stopped and wiped the back of my hand over my brow. My desperate efforts had had little effect apart from dents in the plywood and a barely visible length of nail. What was needed was something to target the force of my blows: the smaller the diameter, the greater the force applied, the stiletto heel effect. My eye fell on the broken chair leg. I seized it and, using it as a make-shift punch, pressed it to the plywood and hammered its end vigorously with the pot.

One nail loosened and fell out. Encouraged, I attacked the next one. *Bang Bang Bang.* This one was a bit easier to dislodge. Two down, but many more to go. How much time did I have before Moran returned or one of them heard the noise and came to investigate?

Not long, as it turned out. After a third nail had fallen out and then a fourth, the plywood moved outward a fraction under the pressure of my hand. It would need more than that. I shoved the table over to the window and climbed on top. I held onto the curtain rail to steady myself. *Thud.* I slammed the sole of my boot into the hardboard with all the force I could muster.

A small gap opened up along the right-hand edge of the plywood sheet. At the same time a startled, 'What the *bloody hell*?' came from outside.

Eddie had come back! I scrambled down from the table and looked round for something to defend myself. The broken chair would do. Off with the light. Faced with darkness when he flung open the door, he'd be momentarily at a disadvantage. I'd rush at him and do my best to smash the chair down on his head.

I waited for the key to be inserted in the lock. Outside, only silence. I put down the chair and crept towards the window, feeling carefully with my feet for ambushing chair legs or anything that might trip me up. Daylight shone through the narrow gap I'd forced between the plywood and the window frame. I applied my eye to it.

Staring back at me was another eye.

CHAPTER SEVENTEEN

I leapt back with a shriek. A sharp intake of breath from outside was followed by, 'Who's in there? Is that you, Liz? What the hell's happening?' It was a voice I recognized.

'Roddy!' I sagged against the wall, close to tears. This was no time for hysterics. I fought to control my breathing. 'Cameron-Blaik attacked me and shut me up in here. He's going to come back . . . and . . . and. . . .'

No questions, no laughing it off as a joke, no humouring of someone deranged.

'*Bastar-r-rd.*'

Strong fingers gripped the loose edge of plywood. Grunting with the effort, he prised the board away from the frame until, with a sharp *crack* like a rifle shot, it split in two, catapulting him backward into the shrubby embrace of an accommodating rhododendron bush. The narrow gap he'd made didn't look quite big enough, but I eased my head through, careful to avoid the splinters. Roddy grabbed me by the shoulders, pulled and I was out.

'I'm not making it up about Cameron-Blaik,' I said, trying to keep my voice steady. 'You do believe me, don't you?'

Roddy studied me. 'Yup! You've a lump on your head the size of a quail's egg, and a br-r-uise on your face the colour of raspbe-r-ry coulis.'

I started to shake, delayed shock.

He put his arm round my shoulders. 'That shit of a bastar-r-rd won't look for you in the house itself. You'll be safe there just now. I saw his car going down the drive.' He steered me towards the path through the shrubbery.

I stopped short. 'The dog! When he finds I've broken out, he'll bring in the dog. He'll soon know exactly where I've gone.'

'No pr-roblem.' Roddy swung me up into his arms. 'You can't leave a trail if your feet don't touch the ground. Anyway, Blaik won't be able to borrow the dog from the next estate. The big shoot starts today. That's why Callum collected her from the garage yesterday. And he won't be lending her out again till it's finished.'

He carried me through the shrubbery to the back of the big house. Once in the kitchen he put me down and locked the door behind us.

'We don't want surprise attacks from the rear, eh? And better check in case that bloody Waddington's back. He went off on some ploy or other yesterday.' He popped his head out into the passageway. 'OK, the coast's clear.' He took a large old-fashioned key from a hook. 'There's a room along here that used to be the housekeeper's when there was one. We can go there.'

What had once been the housekeeper's spick-and-span command post, now looked forlorn and shabby. The musty smell of long disuse hung heavy in the air. The tiled fireplace with its ornamental fire screen and set of fire irons; the patchwork cotton coverlet on the bed in the bed recess; the high-backed wing chair with its dusty needlework cushion; the faded sepia pictures hanging crookedly on the wall – all spoke of an era vanished for ever. As I sank down onto the armchair, a cloud of dust swirled up catching my throat and making me cough.

'I'll get Ann-Marie and we'll have a council of war over a good cup of tea.' He turned with his hand on the door. 'Unlikely, but the Robillard woman might just take into her head to explore the house. Lock the door behind me to make sure nobody comes in. I'll tap like this to show it's me.'

He was a man in the Gerry Burnside mould, acting on the principle that if there's a possibility something can happen, it may well do so. How much did Roddy need to know? It must already be obvious to him that Cameron-Blaik was a dangerous man. There would be nothing to be gained by telling him that Waddington was dead. Nothing.

The council of war was held at a little round table just big enough to hold the tea tray. Roddy poured the tea and handed me a mug.

'So Sir T *attacked* you?' Ann-Marie burst out. 'I just knew he'd completely lose his rag one day. What on earth *happened*? Tell me all!'

'Let her tell us in her own time.' He cut a large slice of fruitcake and passed it to me.

I sipped the tea while I thought about how to make it credible that the fake Sir Thomas had attacked me. It would have to be something that would make them think that I was the only one in danger, and that the police would soon intervene. Then they would be able to act normally when Moran returned to *Allt an Damh*.

To give myself more time to think, I asked a question that would involve a lengthy reply. 'What happened this morning when I didn't turn up for duty?'

Ann-Marie took a sip of tea, and leaned forward. 'We thought you'd overslept, alarm not gone off or something. I said I would cover up for you by taking Milady Gabrielle her breakfast tray.'

'Didn't work, though.' Roddy cut her another slice of cake. 'Ann-Marie was late taking the tray up because first she had to get the breakfast room ready for Blaik and serve him, so it was me that got the earful on the intercom from Lady Muck. Got my own back though. Let her rant on for five minutes, then when she ran out of breath, I gave out I hadn't heard a word.' He cupped a hand to his ear in re-enactment. ' "Hello? Hello? Anybody there?" Then I indulged in a fine bit of effing and blinding and shouted, "Bloody intercom's faulty again", and clicked off the switch.'

'All right for you, Roddy.' Ann-Marie tossed her head. 'It was *me* who had to take up her tray after that. A fine temper she was in, I can tell you. "Dorward, why 'ave I been waiting till I starve to— But you are not Dorward! Where eez she? Why 'as she not come with zee tray"?' Ann-Marie's smile faded and she fell silent, eyes on my bruised face. 'Something awful happened, didn't it?'

I'd had time to think up my story. 'Well, yes.' Gingerly I felt the lump on my head and winced. 'Since I was given Saturday off, I thought I'd spend the afternoon sightseeing. There's an illustrated guidebook on Islay in the billiard room library, and I was sure Sir Thomas wouldn't mind if I consulted it. While I was sitting in one of the high-backed armchairs reading about the terrible shipwrecks, he and Waddington came down the stairs and stood talking in the hall. I wasn't paying much attention till I heard them mention Winstanley and—'

'Winstanley? That's the guy who was sounding off about Sir T stealing his whisky, wasn't it?' Ann-Marie helped herself to yet another piece of cake.

My story gathered momentum. 'We could hardly forget him, could we, with all that shouting and accusations! I heard Waddington say that Winstanley had phoned to say he was about to pay another visit to the distillery to take a sample from his cask and send it away for testing. Waddington was all panicky because the whisky in the cask was only one year old, not fifty.'

Ann-Marie held out her hand, palm upwards. 'You owe me five pounds, Roddy. I was right when I said Sir T was up to something!'

He scowled. 'For God's sake, woman, stop interrupting.'

I continued hastily, 'Sir Thomas just laughed and told him there was no need to worry, it would be easy to stamp Winstanley's number on the genuine cask of fifty-year-old whisky kept for the purpose. He said, "We've done that before and we can do it again".' I thought I was pretty close to the truth there. The real Sir Thomas had probably been running that particular scam for years.

'Changed the number, I like it!' Roddy raised his mug in a toast of admiration.

'When I heard all that, I thought, My God! I hope they don't find out I'm listening.' I paused for dramatic effect.

'But they did, eh?'

'It was my own fault. The guidebook slid off my knee onto the floor, no hope of them not hearing it. Waddington hissed, "There's someone in the billiard room", and Sir Thomas came rushing in. Before I could even get up, he hauled me to my feet and threw me against the wall. I don't remember much else. . . .' I passed a weary hand over my eyes. 'I came to in the cottage and found it all boarded up.'

Well, that should do it. That would convince them that Sir Thomas had attacked me to cover up serious fraud and GBH, but it gave no hint that he was a ruthless criminal capable of murder. I sat back, congratulating myself on the way I'd handled a tricky situation.

Both of them were silent, thinking it over. Ann-Marie, hanging on every word, had obviously swallowed the story whole. I wasn't so sure about Roddy.

After a long moment he said, 'I can see why they would want to stop you informing Winstanley or the police, but why would they go to the bother of carrying you off to the cottage and boarding up the windows?'

I stared at him, my mind a blank, unable to think of anything to say. My carefully constructed story had been demolished like a soufflé hit by a draught of cold air.

It was Ann-Marie who came to my rescue. 'It's obvious, Roddy. They were going to do a runner. Couldn't let her go, could they, or she'd spill the beans? Don't you see? They left her there to *starve to death*.' I could see she was revelling in the sheer horror of it.

'Bullshit! If they were going to kill her, they'd have done it right away in the billiard room.'

'Yeah, and I'd have just dusted round her without noticing, I suppose!'

They glared at each other, forgetting me for the moment, and more importantly, taking Roddy's mind off that big flaw in my story.

'There could be *something* in Ann-Marie's theory,' I said. 'I think Sir Thomas has realized the game's up and he's going to disappear with as much money as he can take with him. He didn't kill me because fraud's one thing, but cold-blooded murder is quite another. Once he was well away, I'm sure he'd have sent a message to someone about where I was. And there was enough food in the cottage to keep me going.' That last was true enough: a cupboard full of tins of salmon for Gorgonzola.

Ann-Marie looked disappointed, Roddy unconvinced.

He pushed back his chair. 'It's time to call in the police. We can use the phone in the bastar-r-rd's study.'

'No! I don't want the police involved yet. I—'

'Why the bloody hell not?' Hands on hips, he glared at me. 'The man's a dangerous lunatic. He battered you and locked you up in the cottage, for God's sake.'

'And was going to leave you to starve to death.' Ann-Marie was not going to abandon her pet theory on anyone's say-so.

'Give me a minute.' I closed my eyes, trying to work out the best course of action. The obvious thing to do was contact Gerry. It would only take a few moments to run upstairs to the phone in the study. And yet . . . if I alerted Gerry to Moran's presence, I would be ordered to keep out of things, have no further part to play. Bringing Moran to justice for the murders of the Cameron-Blaiks would be left to others. More importantly, I had the feeling some big scheme of his was about to come to fruition, a scheme that depended on him being here in Islay. What were my grounds for thinking that? When I'd recognized him, Moran had not gone immediately to ground, his usual course of action when the forces of law and order were close on his trail; then there was that urgent phone call summoning him away. Yes, if I could find out what Moran was planning, then. . . .

'Are you all right?' Roddy and Ann-Marie were looking at me anxiously.

'Yes, yes. I was just thinking that it's no use calling the police. I've no proof that Sir Thomas attacked me. It's only my word against his. And as for the Winstanley scam, he'd just produce a cask of fifty-year-old whisky with the correct number on it and accuse me of fabricating a story to blackmail him. What I want to do is get away from here. I'll get into my car and—'

Roddy sat down again. 'The ferry strike's been settled. It was on this morning's news, but you can't drive to Port Ellen in that car of yours. The colour stands out a mile. You're not thinking straight, Liz. And it's single-track road all the way to Ardbeg so there's more than a chance that bastar-r-rd Blaik might meet—'

'What about that fancy Honda bike of yours, Roddy? Liz could take that, couldn't she? Wearing a helmet and visor, her own mother wouldn't recognize her!'

To give him his due, Roddy hesitated for only a second or two before offering to trust me with what must undoubtedly be a prized possession. 'The Fireblade's a bit of a brute. Ever ridden one before?'

'Er, no,' I said.

Ann-Marie's face fell. Then, 'You can take her on the pillion, Roddy! You've a spare helmet. Two people on a bike'll be even more of a disguise.'

Operated by Ann-Marie, the gates of *Allt an Damh* swung open for us on our approach. Wearing the spare helmet, and with a leather jacket two sizes too big hiding my own one, I clung tightly to Roddy as we roared through them. Wimp or not, I'd made it clear that I wouldn't feel at all safe holding onto the grab handle behind me. Tucked in behind him, face obscured by the helmet, I was confident that even if we encountered Moran's car, he would dismiss us as tourists doing the rounds of Islay and not give us more than a passing glance. In the event, we met nobody on the single-track road and on the wider road from Ardbeg to Port Ellen, saw only a couple of cars, neither of them Moran's.

We were on the shore road near the pier when the bike slowed and came to a stop. I loosened my grip on Roddy's jacket and looked over his shoulder.

He raised his visor. 'This do? It's the nearest phone box to the ferry.'

'Can't thank you enough.' I got off the bike and unbuckled the helmet. 'I'll phone the agency to say I've resigned and left *Allt an Damh*, and then wait around somewhere out of the way till the ferry goes.' Lies, all lies. 'It's only a couple of hours. I'll be fine. You'd better get back before you're missed.'

He revved the engine a couple of times. 'Hold on to the helmet and the jacket. When they discover you've broken out of the cottage, they'll come haring down here. It's the first thing they'll think of, but they won't be looking for a biker. And don't worry about getting them back to me, they're just spares.'

Vrooooom. He roared off, arm raised, two fingers separated in a V sign.

I took a couple of steps towards the telephone box. I should phone Gerry, I really should, but . . . The Sròn Dubh distillery was only a couple of miles away, so tantalizingly close. The crisis phone call that had sent Moran hurrying off had something to do with the distillery, I was sure of it. What if I took a little scout around to get an idea of what his next move might be? Of course, if I was being really honest, I wanted to present Gerry with information that would result in a Record Drug Haul. DJ Smith, hero of the hour, and all that.

So was it to be phone call, or distillery visit? I couldn't make up my mind. It was then I saw the notice nailed to a wooden pole hammered into the strip of grass between road and beach.

Bikes for hire at Bothy Cycles, Lennox Street, Port Ellen
Why walk when wheels will take you faster
on your tour of the distilleries?
More distilleries in less time!

I followed the direction of the pointing arrow and twenty minutes later was the temporary owner of a fine mountain bike.

CHAPTER EIGHTEEN

The Sròn Dubh distillery was sited on one of the many inlets on this part of the coast. As was usual with the distilleries, a small stream brought water from a range of hills behind. To cycle in through the gates was out of the question, so taking advantage of what looked like a sheep track, I made a wide detour along the grassy hillside. When the pagoda-shaped chimneys of the distillery appeared above a clump of trees, I dismounted, hid helmet and bike as best I could, and went forward cautiously on foot.

The rear of a large, rusty corrugated iron warehouse blocked my view of the distillery. I flattened myself against the sheeting, listening for voices or any sound of activity. From out at sea drifted the harsh cries of gulls squabbling in the wake of a fishing boat; close at hand there was only the rustle of leaves stirred by the light breeze and the forlorn bleating of a lost sheep.

I lay flat on the ground and slowly edged forward till I could see round the corner of the shed. The human eye catches movement, but at ground level there was less chance of anyone seeing me. The ground at the side of the warehouse was littered with broken barrel staves, splintered and empty casks and an invasion of weeds, sad testimony to a business that was failing, and had been failing for years.

I understood now why the bona fide Sir Thomas Cameron-Blaik had fallen into temptation: faced with losing the family business, he'd resorted to the whisky cask scam. He'd thought it out carefully – it would probably be fifteen to twenty years before purchasers made a proper check on their whisky, and any awkward customer who did turn up would be shown a genuine cask with the expected number stencilled on it. A thousand pounds from each investor in a laid down cask, multiplied thousands of times by the smuggling of long-matured whisky, must have provided a nice little earner for Sir Thomas.

Mellow and relaxed after a few whiskies, he'd probably hinted at this lucrative scheme to Moran as they lounged at ease on one of the brown leather sofas of The Vaults beside the fire. And in the process signed his own death warrant. Now he was lying beneath the lichened table-stone in Kildalton churchyard sharing a grave with one of the people he'd conned.

Moran wouldn't, of course, have been interested in any long term scheme, but he had seized the opportunity to make use of Cameron-Blaik's whisky smuggling run to Ireland. The cargoless boat coming to collect the whisky would now bring in a cargo of heroin or cocaine: drugs in, whisky out. His only error had been not bothering to find out how the cask scam operated. As a result he'd been totally unprepared for Winstanley's unexpected arrival and the demand to see his cask.

The Sròn Dubh distillery building was very much like the others in Islay, but here the white cement render was cracked and large patches had fallen off. Moran's car was drawn up on the gravel in front of a closed door that, even from a distance, was blistered and peeling. There were no windows on this side of the distillery, a piece of luck, for I intended to have a look inside the warehouse. Very risky, but the whole point of coming was to gather information and I wouldn't get that by just lying here.

Speed rather than caution was what was needed. I ran down the side of the warehouse, every moment expecting a shout that would indicate I'd been spotted. At the front, I had another stroke of luck: the double door, high enough to allow entry to a heavy-goods vehicle, was wide open. I stood listening . . . there was no sound of voices or movement from within. A quick glance back at the distillery door reassured me that it remained closed. I slipped inside.

Enough daylight entered through the open doors for me to see halfway down the warehouse. Rows of casks lay on their side, kept from contact with the earth floor by wooden battens. All had a paper label bearing a year date, but only those on the first two rows were stencilled with a number. The rows of casks stretched off on either side into darkness, but at the rear a naked bulb hanging from the ceiling cast enough light to make out more barrels stacked three high in racks.

There wasn't anything here that would tell me about Moran's future plans – but this was where Winstanley had come to view his cask, and perhaps where he had met his death. To link Moran to the murder, I needed to find evidence such as bloodstains. I studied the interior of the warehouse. Would they have attacked him beside the stencilled casks where I was now standing? A bit too public, if the doors had been open as they would have been for viewing his cask.

They'd probably have lured him to the gloom at the back of the warehouse on some pretext or other. Narrow aisles separated each row of casks and a wider one ran towards the rear. Even in this dim light, blood spots on a cask might be visible. It would be worth having a quick look. After that, I'd get out of here. As it was, I was pushing my luck.

I was halfway up the broad aisle heading towards the dimly lit casks at the rear when a door banged on the other side of the yard. *Voices.* There was just time to squeeze between the nearest row of casks and wedge myself down into the dark gap under them.

'Bring the trolley up to the back, Eddie.' It was unmistakably Moran. 'We'll fling a tarpaulin over him and the two of you can take him over to the distillery and shove him in the washback.'

A voice, not Eddie's, said, 'Washback, boss?'

'The big tank of liquid mush. He won't be found till they empty the tank.'

'That should give some body to the whisky, eh. Body – get it?'

'Pretty good, Eddie.'

They all laughed.

I heard the squeak of trolley wheels passing the end of my row of casks, then, 'Can't get it any nearer, boss.' An object was dragged along the floor accompanied by grunts of effort and, 'Heavy bugger, ain't he!'

Somebody had been killed, but who? I knew what Moran meant by the washback, a big tank of barley grain and heated water stirred by rotating paddles. The perfect way to dispose of a murder victim. Not only would there be a delay in the discovery of the body, but the heated water and the injuries inflicted by the paddles would make it difficult, if not impossible, to determine the time and cause of death.

I lay there in the darkness, face pressed against the wood of a cask, breathing in damp earth and the mix of oak impregnated with sherry and maturing whisky, that slow evaporation of the cask contents known as 'the angels' share'.

The squeak of trolley wheels drew level once again with my row of casks. With awful timing, my nose prickled and twitched. Desperately I held nose between finger and thumb, pressed lips hard together. If I didn't manage to hold back that sneeze, my body would be joining that other one in the washback. When at last the urge subsided, my forehead was beaded with sweat.

Wheels scrunched on gravel as the trolley was pushed across the yard to the distillery, a door banged shut, then silence. Cautiously I raised my head and peered over the row of casks. The pale square of the open doorway was some distance away, and if I left my hiding place, there was a good chance that anyone returning to the warehouse would catch sight of me. I was stuck here till I heard Moran's car drive off, and even then I wouldn't be sure that the coast was clear. I couldn't just assume that Eddie and the other thug at the cottage, Eddie's clone, had gone with him. The man who had made the panic phone call from the distillery would probably still be here, and possibly some others. I sank down behind my cask again and waited.

Just as well. There was no warning. Suddenly from over at the doorway Moran said, 'The casks we want are marked with these numbers.' Paper rustled. 'Could be anywhere in the warehouse. MacNab would have told us exactly where the casks were. If that little mistake of yours, Rick, means we miss the boat. . . .' The threat was clear.

'I *had* to kill him.' There was fear in Rick's voice. 'He noticed that you'd changed the destination port in the bill of lading. He said that the fact your signature was on it didn't make it legal. He was going to call the Revenue buggers and the police.'

'Cut all that whining and get moving. The casks we want have been here for fifty years. They'll be discoloured and look older than the rest.'

It was impossible to see if the casks beside me were dark with age. I crouched in the shadows, heart thumping, palms sweaty.

'Lighting's crap. How do you expect—?'

'Get the flashlight from the car, you fool.'

Footsteps hurried across the gravel as Rick tried to save his skin, then the car door slammed. All too soon a powerful beam moved slowly along the rows of casks on the opposite side of the aisle. I shrank down, knowing that I was going to be discovered. It was only a matter of time.

'Start from the *back*, you clown! That's where the oldest casks'll be. If we miss the bloody boat, you'll pay for it!'

I knelt between the barrels, face resting on forearms against the damp earth. Even a glimpse of something lighter among the shadows as they passed the end of my row of casks, and they'd investigate. Shoes scuffed on the concrete floor of the aisle, approached, came level, and passed by. I realized I'd been holding my breath and let it out slowly.

Muttered curses from the back of the warehouse marked Rick's progress as he moved slowly among the casks. For all I knew Moran could be standing within yards of me. Where was he? A minute later I got the answer.

From the doorway came an irritable, 'How long is it going to take you, for shit's sake?'

After a long pause came a relieved, 'I think this is them, boss.'

Moran's light footsteps passed by the end of my row.

'Check the numbers as I read them out. . . .'

I kept a tally on my fingers. Ten casks . . . if Moran was interested in so few casks, that little lot must be worth a tidy sum.

'How about this one, boss, it looks pretty old?'

'Shut it, Rick. Get the fork-lift and have the casks at the door ready for loading on the pick-up. Eddie and Len will give you a hand when they come back. And be bloody careful. I don't want any dropped casks. Any problems' – the tone of voice made it clear that there'd better not be any – 'you'll get me at the house.'

Light footsteps again passed by my row. A car door slammed, the engine fired, wheels crunched on gravel. Any relief that I might have felt was short-lived: when he reached *Allt an Damh*, he'd find that I'd escaped.

'Bastard.' With other choice variants directed at his boss, Rick hurried past.

Even before his footsteps on the gravelled yard had died away, I heaved myself out of my cramped hiding place. I'd learned all I was going to learn and, risky as it was, if I didn't take the chance to leave now, there'd not be another opportunity till after the pick-up had departed with its valuable cargo.

Ignoring cramped and protesting muscles, I ran to the doorway and peered out. A murmur of voices came from the open door of the distillery across the gravel courtyard. An engine started up behind a low building off to the left. It was now or never. I put my head down and ran. Once round the corner of the warehouse I'd be hidden from sight and safe.

I didn't make it. With only a few yards to go, I heard an angry shout from behind. I didn't look back, just kept on running. Forced by the litter of barrel staves and splintered and broken casks to slow my pace, I ran along the side of the warehouse, trying to identify the spot among the bushes where I'd left the bike. I knew roughly where it was, but—

I should have been looking at the ground in front of my feet. My foot caught on an upturned stave. I crashed to the ground and lay sprawled there, winded, my head an inch from one of the iron-bound casks. I scrambled to my feet, but as soon as I put weight on my right foot, a sharp stab of pain shot through my ankle.

I cast a desperate glance back at the corner of the warehouse. Moran's men would round the corner at any second. The open end of the splintered cask was a couple of feet from the warehouse wall. If I could crawl inside the cask, I might have a chance. I'd be completely hidden. I took a couple of painful steps and had just curled up inside when I heard pounding feet, then a string of oaths very close by.

'Can't see the bugger. He's got away.' Len was standing right beside the barrel.

More pounding feet, then Rick panting, 'Let's call it a day, Len. He'll not come back now and we've still to load all these bloody casks onto the pick-up. Miss that boat and we'll both be joining MacNab in the washback.'

'Think I should give the boss a buzz and tell him someone's been poking around?'

More swearing. 'You're a bloodier fool than I thought you were, Len. You heard the boss. He – don't – want – problems. Do I have to spell it out to you? By not catching this guy we've messed up, and anyone who does that ends up dead. So keep your trap shut. I'm not getting on the wrong side of that bugger again.' Their voices receded.

I waited till I heard the forklift busy at work shifting the casks in the warehouse before I limped my way back to where I'd left the bike. It took a bit of locating. They'd have caught up with me long before I succeeded in finding it. Tripping over that loose stave had most probably saved my life.

Pushing down on the pedal with my good ankle made progress slow. By the time I reached the main road, I'd had time to consider my best course of action. Port Ellen and its phone boxes were much nearer than Sandy's cottage on the Oa, but the risk of encountering Moran in Port Ellen on his way back to the distillery was too great. Sandy would take me to Bowmore and I'd phone Gerry from there. Since the ferry crossing took two and a half hours, there'd be time for HMRC to organize an interception of the pick-up truck with its load of casks when it arrived at Kennacraig. Moran would almost certainly be on board keeping an eye on the whisky. So we'd get our hands on him too.

Thanks to my throbbing ankle, the hour-long detour across country by bike was more gruelling than I'd expected, and none too soon I saw the metal gate in the drystone wall near Sandy's cottage. On the way, I'd been thinking about what he would have done when I had failed to return from making that phone call. He'd have been worried. Had he thought that I'd received instructions in the phone call and gone off on some secret mission? Yes, that's what would have happened. He'd have looked at Gorgonzola snoozing on his knee and relaxed, knowing I'd come back for her. As for G, in the wily way of cats, before I'd left she had already made herself completely at home, all comforts assured.

I propped the bike against the wall, loosened the strap of the helmet, then hesitated. At the end of the tunnel formed by the beech tree branches, the grey stone gable of the cottage was slumbering in the late afternoon sunlight. A peaceful scene, but something didn't feel quite right.

By now Moran would have discovered I'd broken out of the boarded up gardener's cottage. He might have sent Eddie and Len to lie in wait for me here. I paused with my hand on the gate. If I walked down the path on that betraying carpet of brittle beech mast, would I be walking into a trap? Tiredness was making me over-react. Moran's thugs were back at the distillery loading casks. What danger could there possibly be? Nevertheless, I always take heed of a warning sixth sense that has saved my life on more than one occasion. I didn't remove the helmet, but kept it on.

CHAPTER NINETEEN

I pushed open the gate and started down the path. The trickle of smoke drifting up from the chimney showed that Sandy was at home. In a couple of minutes I'd be seated by the fire with G purring on my knee, tucking into a bowlful of rabbit stew and telling Sandy all about it – well, not quite *all*.

It turned out that the helmet hadn't been a good idea. Taking heed of that feeling of unease had been a mistake, a big mistake. I didn't hear the footsteps behind me, had no warning of the violent blow between the shoulders that hurled me to the ground. A heavy body thumped down on top of me, leaving me winded and dazed. My arms were twisted behind me and I was yanked roughly to my feet.

I'd underestimated Moran. He'd made my recapture a higher priority than the loading of the casks. While I'd been mountain-biking it across country, Eddie and Len had calculated that I would make my way back to the Singing Sands where they had found me. They would have had ample time to drive to the cottage and lie in wait.

'Who do we have here?' I couldn't see the man who was gripping me, but the voice wasn't Eddie's . . . or Len's . . . or Rick's. I'd taken for granted that Moran had only the three men working for him, those at the distillery. Assumptions again. This time fatal.

A rough hand pulled off my helmet. A man in black fatigues peered at me. 'That lump on your head and the bruise like a map of Ireland tell me that somebody's had a crack at you already, eh?'

White teeth flashed in a blackened face. 'This might be the one we're looking for, Jim. Short dark hair, female. He didn't mention the bruise and the lump, though.'

The man holding me shoved me forward. 'Tell him we've got her.'

He disappeared up the path at a run. I was frogmarched after him as

169

closely attached to my captor as a Siamese twin. The door was flung open. I was face to face with – not Louis Moran, but Gerry Burnside.

My mouth opened but no words came out. I'm not quite sure what happened next, for this time I definitely over-reacted, a combination of shock and the effects of the past twenty-four hours, I suppose. My legs gave way and I sagged in the clutch of my 'captor'. After that things are a bit hazy. I was aware of Gerry saying sharply, 'Don't just stand there. Carry her inside.'

The scent of peat smoke . . . Sandy's alarmed voice . . . a thump on the arm of the chair I was slumped in . . . a large paw patting my face. I opened my eyes to a semi-circle of concerned faces looking down at me.

'I'm all right now. Silly of me.' I tried to sit up but Gorgonzola had other ideas. She launched herself from the arm of the chair to make a heavy landing on my stomach then, purring loudly, stretched up to rub her face against mine.

'How—?'

Gerry answered my unfinished question. 'Easy. It gave us a bit of concern when you started the call but didn't finish it. We traced your last position because the mobile was still switched on. We thought we'd find your—' hastily amended to, 'that is, when there was no sign of you on the beach, we had a look in the cottage. So exactly what *did* happen?'

I stroked G's back and managed to angle her head and front paws onto my shoulder in the burp-the-baby position so that I could reply without getting a mouthful of fur.

'They jumped me on the beach and locked me up but I managed to escape.' I chose my words carefully, mindful of Sandy's presence. I looked at him. 'I hope you weren't too worried about me.'

'I was indeed, lass, but it was nothing to what I felt when this lot burst through the door. Gave me the fright of my life. They *said* they were Revenue and Customs, but they could have been from *Allt an Damh*.' He glowered at Gerry and the task force men. 'When they saw the mobile phone on the table and the cat, I was in the firing line. They put me through the third degree but I was interrogated by the enemy before they were born. I told them nothing. Only name, rank and number, that's all they're entitled to under the Geneva Convention. If they didn't believe me, they could stuff it.' Another glower. 'Now, if they'd gone about things properly, knocked politely on the door accompanied by a policeman to establish their credentials, I would have explained that you hadn't come back after going to the Singing Sands to get a signal and I'd found the phone, thanks to the cat.'

He moved away from the group surrounding me and commandeered the other armchair, a symbolic repossession of his cottage. 'That cat of yours finally convinced them I was a friend by jumping up on me and behaving as she's doing now.'

He patted his knee. Gorgonzola instantly wriggled out from under my arm and traitorously transferred her affections. She'd worked out where the next meal was coming from, and it wasn't from me. The thought of filling her empty stomach with rabbit stew obviously took precedence over welcoming back DJ Smith.

'It's just cupboard love, Sandy,' I said piqued by her desertion. 'It's the rabbit stew she's after.' Thinking about that steaming pot made me realize just how hungry I was. 'Is there enough left for the two of us?'

'No sooner said than dished up!' He jettisoned Gorgonzola. Stunned by this sudden reversal of fortune, she let out a yowl of outrage and crouched on the rug calculating her next move while he busied himself with the black pot.

Gerry mouthed the word 'debrief' and moved towards the door. I levered myself out of the depths of the armchair. Outside I brought him up to date with what had happened since the attack on me at the Singing Sands.

'So you think Moran will be on the ferry with the casks. You're probably right. He'd want to keep an eye on them since those casks of fifty-year-old whisky could be worth several million pounds.' Seeing my astonishment, he added, 'Rarity value. And certainly worth killing for. You had a *very* lucky escape, Deborah.'

I knew the signs. He was about to launch into Severe Reprimand mode. At which point I had another lucky escape in the shape of Sandy whistling *Come to the Cookhouse Door Boys*, the old army summons to eat.

I moved quickly towards the door but Gerry put out a restraining hand. 'One moment, Deborah. You have, of course, a satisfactory explanation of why you went to the distillery? I thought I'd made it very clear that as soon as you identified Moran, you were to leave the island, or go into hiding.'

'I intended to.' Even to me it sounded like a whine.

'The road to hell is paved with good intentions. Is that not the saying, Deborah?'

'But he set his thugs on me and locked—'

'I'm talking about *after* you broke out of the cottage.'

'I just thought I'd go to the distillery and—'

'Pick up some brownie points. Admit it, Deborah.'

I'd forgotten that he could read me like a book, damn him. I felt my cheeks burn.

Sandy's whistling had stopped. A yell of, 'It's on the table! The cat's already tucking in! If you don't come now, she'll have the lot!'

'Go on then,' Gerry opened the door for me to go back into the cottage, but I knew I wasn't off the hook. He hadn't finished with me yet.

Since the ferry offered Moran no means of escape, there was no longer quite the same urgency and I was allowed to finish my meal in peace while Gerry organized a police car to come and pick us up and take us to the distillery. As we left, I looked back at Gorgonzola on Sandy's lap apparently sleeping off her portion of rabbit stew. She opened one eye and slowly closed it again, sure that I'd return.

On the way to Sròn Dubh, I received the Ticking-Off, part two.

'I've radioed the task force to meet the ferry when it docks at Kennacraig. Moran should be in our hands in' – Gerry consulted his watch – 'fifty-seven minutes. So I have to congratulate you for that, Deborah. But let me come back to that little matter of disobeying orders.'

Foolishly, I tried again to justify my decision to go rummaging around in the warehouse.

He cut me short. 'Each word you utter is digging you deeper into the shit, Deborah. I advise you to stop right now.'

For the next five minutes I was treated to a discourse on Irresponsibility with a capital I, the gist of it being that if I'd been discovered hiding among the casks, I'd have been killed, and Moran would have escaped scot-free.

As I've said, he could read me like a book, and sensing my contrition and judging that I'd been made sufficiently aware of my shortcomings, he finished with, 'The one redeeming feature of your little escapade is that when the ferry docks, we'll get our hands on Moran.'

For some minutes we drove on in a rather uncomfortable silence, on my part, that is. I leant my head back against the seat and closed my eyes. I was tired, but actually I didn't want to hear any more pointed remarks about Irresponsibility. After all, I had given him the information that would lead to Moran's capture and with it the successful outcome to the mission, hadn't I? There's something utterly satisfying about a good sulk.

Gerry nudged me and pointed. 'Something's on fire over there.'

I looked for a moment at the plume of thick grey smoke drifting up into the sky on the far side of Port Ellen, then closed my eyes again, still sulking and irritated by this attempt to restore normal relations. As far as I was concerned, all was *not* forgiven, though in my heart of hearts I knew he was right. I *had* been irresponsible, but who likes admitting to mistakes?

He nudged me again. 'Can I have your attention, Deborah. This looks serious. Could it be the ferry terminal in Port Ellen?'

'That's not it,' I said, not bothering to open my eyes. 'That's about where the—' I shot upright and stared through the windscreen, knowing with a chill certainty what was on fire. 'I think it's the distillery.' My voice was barely a whisper.

He shot me a look, but restrained himself from saying anything. That was no comfort, no comfort at all. If there were any recriminations, they'd come later.

Long before we reached the distillery, the flames and smoke made it clear that there would be little left but ashes to sift through when the fire had been put out. As with any disaster, people had materialized from nowhere, as if some jungle telegraph had spread the news. We left the police driver manoeuvring the car in a multi-point turn on the narrow road and edged our way through the vehicles and onlookers to the police car and two policemen acting as a barrier 200 yards from the distillery. Gerry flashed his official card to get us past but the firemen wouldn't let us any further than the gates.

Hoses snaked from the two fire engines stationed at the entrance to the rear courtyard. Silhouetted against the red of the flames, two firemen were struggling to haul a hose across the ground. *Swooooossh* a jet of water shot out to play on the wall of fire. Even at this distance, the heat was intense, beating on our faces and forcing us to retreat after this brief view of the inferno raging where the warehouse had been. The main building, though threatened, was as yet untouched.

Just audible above the sharp crack of exploding barrels I heard Gerry mutter, 'I've got to hand it to Moran. This way, nobody will be able to tell that casks have been removed. They'll all be destroyed and there'll be no evidence that a crime has been committed.'

'Oh yes, there *will* be evidence,' I said quickly, eager to re-establish myself in his good books. 'Even if the main building catches fire, there'll be evidence, all right. The body will be protected from the flames by the water in the washback.'

'Body?' His eyes narrowed. 'What. Body. Deborah?' Each word came out slowly as if followed by a full stop. 'In the debriefing, I don't recall you telling me anything about a body. Or am I mistaken?'

Oh dear, I'd shot myself in the foot. 'I *didn't*?' I squeaked, in a pathetic and forlorn attempt to pass it off as a minor slip. But I knew it was much more serious than that.

'You most *certainly* didn't.' He gripped me by the arm and marched me back to the car.

I'll draw a veil over the unpleasantness that followed.

'. . . you have made four inexcusable errors, Deborah,' he finished. 'You failed to mention' – he ticked them off on his fingers – 'one, the fact that somebody had been murdered; two, the name of the victim; three, why he was killed; and four, who the murderer was. I'm running out of fingers, Deborah. Could there be anything else that you've omitted to tell me?'

I searched my memory of the events in the warehouse. If anything else did come to light later on . . . I shook my head.

'You know I expect *total* professionalism. Stay in the car while I have a word with the fire chief.' He marched off grim-faced.

I sat there more than a little subdued. Every bit of the dressing-down I had received had been deserved. I'd been completely focused on the object of the mission, the capture of Moran. MacNab's murder had been pushed to the back of my mind.

Gerry returned to the car. 'They think they'll be able to keep the flames from the main building thanks to its stone walls and slate roof. So it looks as if we'll still have the body in the washback as evidence. MacNab is, or rather was, the manager of the distillery.' He looked at his watch. 'The ferry will be docking any time now. In five minutes or so we should hear that Moran's been picked up.'

We waited in silence. Gerry started to doodle in his notebook, a sure sign of tension: first a square, followed by three vertical strokes – not hard to guess that these were prison bars – then hands clutching the bars and a face peering out.

At last the call sign came through on the radio. 'Operation Scotch Mist.'

Gerry's pen stopped in mid-doodle. I leant forward, heart beating faster. Moran's arrest would go a long way towards cancelling out that rap over the knuckles. At this very moment he was being handcuffed and led down the gangplank to be bundled into a police car. Blue light flashing, it would speed away, and the glory would be *mine*, DJ Smith's.

The disembodied expressionless voice said, 'Target not on board, sir.'

Gerry's pen dug a hole in the paper. After a moment he motioned to the driver to pass him the microphone.

'It's possible he may have changed his appearance from the description I issued.' He turned to me. 'We'll fly over by helicopter and see if you can identify him.' He spoke into the microphone again. 'What about the cargo we're looking for? If *it's* there, he's definitely on board.'

'Negative as to the cargo, sir.'

'*Nothing* of that description at all?'

'No, sir. Only tankers of whisky, no casks.'

A long pause, then, 'Stand down the operation. He's not on board.' His pen scored a heavy cross over the prison bars doodle.

Moran had given us the slip again. The operation had failed. And I'd just remembered something else. I sank back against the upholstery, eyes closed.

I'd forgotten to tell Gerry that the bodies of two murdered men were concealed in Kildalton churchyard. And that Sir Thomas Cameron-Blaik was one of them.

CHAPTER TWENTY

Islay fell away below the wing of the HMRC plane. In keeping with my mood, the grey haze of late evening had drained the vibrant colour from sea and fields. Only a week ago I'd come as a stranger, gazing down at a string of grey roofs and white houses, unable to identify any of the places that were now so familiar: the ferry pier, the white block of Laphroaig distillery and the ribbon of road leading to *Allt an Damh*.

I stared out of the window. I still hadn't nerved myself to tell Gerry about the bodies in Kildalton churchyard. There had, of course, been opportunity on the silent journey back to the Oa, but one look at his face and I'd chickened out. He remained in the car while I made my way to the cottage to express my thanks and collect Gorgonzola. While I was still crunching my way up the path of beech-husks, Sandy appeared in the doorway.

'Heard you coming, lass. You'll be on your way now. Mission complete, eh?'

'Seems so,' I said. 'Only a few loose ends to tidy up.' I smiled but I had a nasty feeling they'd be of the sort that would form a noose round my neck. 'Sorry about all the hassle you've had.'

'Nothing to be sorry about.' His eyes twinkled. 'Brought back the old days. A bit of adventure keeps you young.'

I followed him into the cottage and scooped up G. 'I'm not forgetting our wager and that bottle of Ardbeg.'

'Two bottles, double or quits, remember?'

Hang the expense to HMRC, he was going to get a dozen.

From our first encounter to the last, Sandy Duncan turned out to be a man of many surprises – in the brief embrace on our departure I discovered that wiry-looking beard of his was in fact most delightfully silky and soft. As the car drove off, I looked back. The ramrod-straight figure put his hand up to the brim of the battered trilby in what was unmistakably a military salute.

I brought my thoughts back to the uncomfortable present. Disappearing under the engine cowling was the white tower of the lighthouse and a tiny patch of silver that must be the Singing Sands. Just visible through the thickening haze as the plane banked and climbed, was one landmark that hadn't been there a week ago – the black smudge and thin column of smoke marking what remained of the Sròn Dubh warehouse.

Even after Islay had dropped away behind us, I stared out through the window, dreading the moment when Gerry would continue his investigation as to why the operation had failed.

'*If* I can have your attention, Deborah? Not every operation succeeds, we all know that, but it's the *reason* for failure that is important, don't you agree?'

I nodded. I had the sinking feeling that the reason for failure was because of something I'd done – or failed to do – and that Gerry was going to winkle it out. Feverishly I reviewed my actions of the last forty-eight hours, checking for anything he could seize on. I'd recognized the significance of the ring 'Sir Thomas' was wearing. But then, I'd allowed him to catch me looking up the clan badge in the library, and when his contact lenses had revealed dark irises, I'd failed to hide the shock of realization . . . and so set off a train of events that had led to my capture. But *these* errors hadn't been the reason for Moran's disappearing act: it was the distillery manager's discovery of the alteration on the bill of lading that had precipitated the removal of the casks ahead of schedule.

That had nothing to do with my actions. The only other possible thing Gerry could seize on was that instead of going straight to Sandy's cottage, I'd made that detour to the distillery. But how else would Gerry have learned that Moran had stolen the whisky casks? I relaxed. I was pretty well in the clear.

Gerry was saying, 'Let's go over again, Deborah, what Moran and his men said about shipping the casks.'

I thought back to the conversations I'd overheard in the warehouse. 'Well, as far as I can remember, Moran said that MacNab's death could mean they'd miss the ferry, because now they didn't know where to find the casks they wanted. And after he'd gone, the ferry was mentioned again. His men were in a panic that they wouldn't get the casks loaded in time to catch it.'

Gerry was silent for a moment, deep in thought. 'Their exact words, please.'

'Moran said something like this—'

'His *exact* words.'

I thought back to when I was crouched on the earth floor of the warehouse, breathing in the mixture of damp earth and oak impregnated with sherry and maturing whisky. The menace in Moran's voice brought his words back as clearly as if I was there again. I said slowly, 'If that little mistake of yours, Rick, means we miss the boat—'

The flat of Gerry's hand crashed down on the dropdown table. '*Boat*, not ferry. Think carefully, Deborah. Was the word ferry ever *actually* mentioned by anyone?'

'No-o.' It came out as a whisper almost drowned by the noise of the plane's engines. 'When I heard the word boat, I just assumed—'

I'd never seen Gerry so angry. 'Those bloody assumptions again, Deborah. The road to Hell is paved with assumptions. Due to your *assumption*, while we were sitting there like blockheads waiting for the ferry to dock, Moran was slipping away on some *boat* or other, to God knows where.'

He fell silent, allowing me to mull over the enormity of it all. It would have been better if he had ranted on about my stupidity. Overwhelmed by the gravity of my error, I could think of nothing to say in my defence. 'Sorry' was so completely inadequate that it would seem as if I was treating it lightly, laughing off the seriousness of my mistake.

'There's something that doesn't quite add up, Deborah.' He must have been picking over the finer details of my story, and homing in on anything I'd skated over. 'The wearing of coloured contact lenses is a common enough fashion, though indulged in more by women than men, wouldn't you say? I'd be interested to know why this made you come to the conclusion that Sir Thomas Cameron-Blaik was in fact Louis Moran. Was this yet another of your inspired assumptions, or was it based on something a little more concrete?'

I felt his eyes upon me. It was the moment I'd been dreading.

'Er. . . .' I said, wishing myself anywhere but here, even back in the boarded-up gardener's cottage.

'I gather there's another something you've omitted to tell me. Out with it.'

I couldn't postpone my confession any longer. 'I knew he couldn't be the real Sir Thomas because. . . .'

A dangerously calm, 'Yes?'

It all came out in a rush. 'Because . . . because the badge on the ring he was wearing was not the Cameron badge. One of the two bodies concealed in Kildalton churchyard, the one with the Cameron ring, was much more likely to be Sir Thomas. . . .' I tailed off.

He sat very still. 'I want a *detailed* report on this and anything else you've omitted to tell me. Have it on my desk by Tuesday at nine o'clock.'

For the rest of the short journey to Glasgow Airport neither of us said anything. What else was there to say?

At the Galbraiths' B&B on Portobello promenade I was welcomed back with solicitous enquiries about my bruised face, now an interesting mixture of purple and blue. I passed off this and the lump on my head as the result of tripping over Gorgonzola while visiting a friend in Islay. (It's always best to tell as much of the truth as possible, then you're not caught out by somebody saying, 'I come from there/ was there last week/ where did you stay?')

I spent most of Monday typing out the report on my laptop, making sure I left nothing out and feeling a bit like an offender listing all her crimes to be taken into consideration before sentence was passed. Gorgonzola, as ever sensitive to my mood, sat on the table and watched. The occasional sympathetic *miaow* was accompanied by well-meant consolatory pats on my arm with a sympathetic paw. Ignoring these was a mistake. The gibberish sentence *Winstanley camellooking for hiskwinec;askols* brought things to a head. I gave in, picked her up and cuddled her, which of course was exactly what she wanted.

'In the old days of typewriters and paper, you'd have ruined my work and I'd have had to retype the whole page.' I nuzzled my face into her soft fur. 'I'd have been very, *very* angry.'

G's copper eyes looked into mine. Her *purr* said, 'But I know you're not.'

'But Gerry Burnside definitely *is*,' I sighed.

I sat in front of Gerry's desk, trying in vain to decipher his expression as he read through the pages of my report. At last he tapped the pages into precise alignment and looked at me thoughtfully. He was coming to a decision.

'Your ferry botch-up, you will be relieved to hear, has not had the serious consequence I feared.'

I tried to work that one out. The whole aim of the operation had been to capture Moran. Now he was on the loose again, and if that wasn't a serious consequence, what was?

'I don't understand,' I said, 'he's—'

'Dead. The Fire Investigation Unit found a man's body near the smouldering remains of the warehouse. He seemed to have been caught in the fireball when the warehouse went up.'

'But how do we—?' I said.

'How do we know it's Moran? The body was quite badly burnt but I asked forensics to check and there were indeed traces of contact lenses.' He riffled through the neat pile of papers. 'Not conclusive, I know. But the identity of the body has now been confirmed, you'll be pleased to know, by this report of yours.' He waited, and when I failed to rise to the bait, continued, 'The man was lying on his left side, arm beneath him and so we could identify him as Moran because—?'

Aware of how much it irritated me, he was putting me through a 'brain exercise' session again. 'The left hand is the ring hand,' I gritted. 'It was protected. So identification was confirmed by the ring.'

'Correct.' He passed over a photo of the ring. Though distorted by the heat, it was the Brodie badge all right, a cluster of horizontal arrows with a motto. I didn't look too closely at anything else that might be in the photo.

He slid the photo into a manila folder.

'So what about Gabrielle Robillard? Isn't she going to face charges?'

'When a car arrived at *Allt an Damh* to bring her in for questioning, she'd packed up and gone. But there's nothing we could have held her on. It's not a criminal offence to be the girlfriend of Louis Moran. I very much doubt if she had anything to do with the murder of either of the Cameron-Blaiks – and if she did, with Moran dead we're not going to be able to prove it now. Once Moran decided to steal the identity of Sir Thomas, that signed the death warrant of Lady Cameron-Blaik. He couldn't have her deciding to visit her husband in Islay. Cameron-Blaik himself was already dead by the time Robillard arrived in Islay. As for Winstanley, your report confirms that she wasn't present when he was killed.

'So that's the operation wound up.' He gathered up my report and put it in the manila envelope with the photo. 'We'll be hushing up the involvement of Louis Moran. Wouldn't do for the newspapers to go on the rampage with banner headlines of *Master Criminal Runs Rings Round HMRC*. The bodies at the distillery can be passed off as accidental deaths. Manager overcome by fumes falls into washback, unidentified distillery worker killed in warehouse blaze, sort of thing.'

'But the bodies at Kildalton, we can't cover up those—'

'It'll be several days before that's released to the newspapers. As you know, Cameron-Blaik's body was badly decomposed. Proof of identity from dental records, DNA tests – all takes time. When it comes out, it'll be presented as a case of a serial killer loose on Islay. Nine day wonder in the press. Unsolved mystery. So all's well that ends well. Case closed.'

It was then he delivered the *coup de grâce*.

'This doesn't let *you* off the hook, however, Deborah. Until further notice I think it would be a salutary lesson if you returned to freighter surveillance at Portobello.'

I could look forward – certainly not the right turn of phrase – to unending, boring, monotonous nights of eyes glued to binoculars watching for small boats slipping ashore under cover of darkness. He didn't need to spell it out. I was on punishment detail, relegated from the first division, the equivalent of putting a promoted police officer back on the beat.

CHAPTER TWENTY-ONE

I laid down the binoculars and rubbed my eyes. Just over two weeks ago when I'd been taken off the interim surveillance duty and given the Islay assignment, I'd little thought I'd be back on it again. I should have welcomed the boring routine as a relief from the tensions of Operation Scotch Mist, but all I felt was resentment. Two long nights of staring out to sea and I had had enough. The more I thought about the situation I was in, the more I felt the injustice of it all. How long would I be condemned to this simple task, fit for the rawest of raw recruits, before Gerry decided that I'd learned my lesson and gave me a new assignment?

'I'm in Gerry's black books, in the doghouse, G,' I sighed.

She pricked up her ears. To her, a dog was a challenge, a foe to be outwitted, or, if small enough, beaten up. All night she had been sleeping soundly, curled up in the centre of my bed while I sat at the window with the binoculars. She yawned. A slow stretch of first one leg, then another, indicated that she, thank you, had had a very good night's sleep and was ready for action. Dog to be chased away? She was my girl. I picked her up, kissed her and whispered in her ear, sure of a sympathetic hearing.

'After all, G, he's treating me as if my mistake about the boat allowed Moran to escape with all that whisky because HMRC was focused on the ferry.'

My hand stopped in mid-stroke of her soft coat. Moran hadn't been on board the ferry when it docked, but neither had the pick-ups with the whisky. So what had happened to them? There'd been no mention of the burnt-out remains of two vehicles being discovered at the distillery, so the casks Moran's men had loaded on to the two pick-ups definitely hadn't gone up in flames.

Gerry's sharp mind had overlooked this crucial detail. When the ferry docked, he'd been too focused on the fact that Moran had slipped through his fingers and that his months of planning had all been for nothing.

'So, G, I'm sure that the whisky has been put on board a boat, somewhere on Islay, probably at *Allt an Damh* at the drugs-in, whisky-out bay.'

Far from being impressed by this brilliant piece of brainwork, Gorgonzola's yawn and half-hearted wriggle to escape from my arms indicated that all this chat was delaying breakfast. Since taking up residence at the B&B, G had scorned my offering of breakfast on a saucer. Instead, she favoured 'hunting' it down herself in the form of the graceful limbo under the sash of the open window, the expertly judged jump onto the roof of the extension, the sure-footed scramble down the lilac tree to the front lawn and the appetite-raising saunter round to the kitchen where her persuasive *miaow* had the Galbraiths just where she wanted them.

I raised the window and watched her go, then went down to breakfast in a more orthodox way. While I ate, I thought about the missing whisky. I shared Gerry's view that Moran would not have let the whisky out of his sight, so . . . could it be that he was not dead at all, had murdered one of his men, slipped the contact lenses in his eyes and the ring on the dead man's finger? Had the master of disguise put on the ultimate disguise, passed himself off as a corpse? That had all the hallmarks of Louis Moran. It made perfect sense.

Gerry had assumed Moran was dead: I was convinced he was not. I finished breakfast feeling a lot better that I was not the only one guilty of making an assumption.

What was I going to do about it? How do I delicately tell my boss that he's goofed up? Faced with such a situation, most bosses would fly into a rage, cut me off before I've finished, or plain refuse to listen. Gerry Burnside was not like that. He wouldn't brush aside as mere conjecture what I had to say in order to gloss over his own error. He'd give me a fair hearing, consider my theory dispassionately and if he thought I was right, act on it.

He was due to leave Edinburgh by the afternoon plane. I went up to my room, phoned his office on the secure line and asked to be put through to him.

'Tyler, here.' The voice was cold, hard and horribly familiar. Andrew

183

Tyler, known unaffectionately to his subordinates as Attila the Hun because of the brutal and unsympathetic way he swept aside anyone or anything that didn't fit with his way of thinking. Unfortunately, the dealings I'd had with him in the past had been rancorous and abrasive.

'I was hoping to speak to Gerry Burnside,' I said, resisting the urge to press the button to end the call.

'*Mr* Burnside has been called away to oversee an operation that has reached a critical stage.'

'He's my controller for Operation Scotch Mist and—'

'*Was*, Smith. The file's been closed. Not one of our more successful operations, I may add.' The accusation implicit that the blame was mine.

'It's just that – I've just had the thought—' I stuttered, caught off balance, and rendered inarticulate with rage.

'I fail to see how an afterthought can have any bearing on a closed case. I suggest you focus any thoughts on your *current* assignment. Now, *if* that's all. . . .' It wasn't a question.

A vicious jab of my finger ended the call. Petty, I know, but it afforded me a great deal of pleasure.

I was staring thoughtfully across the Forth to the hazy smudge of the Fife coast when the phone rang. It was Attila.

'Did you ring off, Smith?

'Sorry about that, Mr Tyler,' I said cravenly, 'I dropped the phone.'

A sceptical silence. 'Well, as I was saying, *if* that's all, in future I would ask you to consider carefully before wasting my valuable time.'

'But what if—'

Click. He'd terminated the call.

I flung myself on the bed and pummelled the pillow, then hurled it across the room, narrowly missing Gorgonzola who was sitting briskly licking a paw in a post-breakfast clean-up. She stared at me with narrowed eyes, leapt onto the windowsill and with a expressive wag of her bottom in my direction disappeared – no doubt to seek solace in Hilda Galbraith's kitchen. I sighed. That made twice this morning that I'd given offence.

Even thinking about that brush with Attila made me grit my teeth with rage. He'd cut me short without listening to a word I'd said, hadn't offered to take a message to pass on to Gerry. The more I thought about it, the surer I was that Moran was still alive. But with Gerry off on some assignment, I was on my own. Moran-whisky-Gabrielle. Find her, find him. But first I'd have to get a couple of hours' sleep. I set the alarm for noon and was out like a light.

I slept through the alarm and it was Gorgonzola's rough tongue licking my face that woke me. Four o'clock! I'd wasted precious time. If Gabrielle and Moran were in Edinburgh, they wouldn't be here for long. Where could I start my search? Gabrielle might make a fleeting visit to Harvey Nichols department store, and there was, of course, The Vaults. . . .

I pulled out the membership booklet for the Scotch Malt Whisky Society and flipped through looking for the phone number. Inspiration came in the form of the page *Accommodation: The Vaults. Stay overnight at one of our cosy self-catering flats* . . . With rising excitement I realized that if Moran was holed up in Edinburgh, this would be the perfect place. Only members could stay there so he'd still be Cameron-Blaik. He'd feel perfectly safe keeping that identity as there'd been nothing in the newspapers about finding Sir Thomas's body either at Sròn Dubh or at Kildalton. And he'd be confident that whoever had sent Elizabeth Dorward had been fooled into calling off the hunt, thinking that the burnt body at the distillery was Louis Moran. By the time the death of the real Sir Thomas Cameron-Blaik reached the newspapers, Moran would be gone, long gone.

Five minutes later I had my accommodation booked. For tonight and the next couple of nights I'd be sleeping in the two-bedroom Ardbeg apartment at The Vaults.

'What's Attila going to say about *that* on my expense sheet, G?' I said. But it was two bedroom or nothing, the one bedroom accommodation had already been booked to somebody else.

I jotted down the booking details and the cost for an expenses claim, pushing aside a niggle of worry. Even if all this came to nothing, Gerry would certainly authorize the expenditure as being justified. But an awful thought – if Gerry was still occupied with that other case, it would be Attilla the Hun on whose desk the claim landed for authorization.

'Am I bothered, G?' The answer, if I was honest, was a definite 'yes.'

There was also, of course, the Dereliction of Duty aspect. If I was staying overnight at The Vaults, I couldn't be scanning the Forth with my night binoculars. I talked it over with Gorgonzola.

'It'll be OK because there will be others on surveillance duty along this coastline, won't there, G? During the time we've been in Islay they've managed without my eyes watching for that little fast boat making for the shore. Three nights and I'll be back. Who will know?'

G stared back at me and said nothing. I had the distinct impression that she thought I was making the wrong decision and would undoubtedly regret it. It was certainly a gamble, and it had better come off.

In the meantime, I had a more urgent concern. Food. And I knew just the place to get it: as a reward for the night hours of boring tedium when I'd first come to Portobello, I'd drawn up a list of places I wanted to visit. Those included, on Mrs Galbraith's recommendation, The Sheep Heid Inn at Duddingston. I chose it, not for its association with Bonnie Prince Charlie and Mary Queen of Scots, but because it was only a five minute bus journey away and served good food all day.

Feeling guilty about the forthcoming desertion, leaving G behind under the care of the Galbraiths for the next three days and nights, I unzipped the rucksack. She pawed at the rucksack and attempted to climb in, plainly indicating that she was coming with me.

'This is on the strict understanding that you'll be no trouble.'

She looked at me with the innocent eyes of one not given to misdemeanours, leapt in and sank out of sight.

The Sheep Heid Inn is situated at the foot of Arthur's Seat, the volcanic plug that dominates the city of Edinburgh. In previous centuries it was within a conveniently short horseback ride of Edinburgh Castle and Holyrood Palace. For present day visitors it is conveniently close to the historic Duddingston Kirk, the Duddingston Loch bird sanctuary and one of the paths that lead up to the top of Arthur's Seat.

A board with gold lettering was strategically positioned on the corner of a narrow lane opposite Duddingston Kirk.

Sheep Heid Inn
Oldest pub in Scotland
Morning coffee
Fine selection of malts
Beer garden

The inn itself was a white, two-storey building with its name in large letters across the frontage. A shield-shaped green sign depicting a ram's head swung lazily in the breeze. The multi-paned windows on either side of the entrance door held an intriguing collection of antique bric-à-brac including an ornate Victorian cash register, a copper samovar labelled 'mulled wine' and a dusty violin and case.

Would the interior be equally intriguing? A brass plate fixed to the door augured well: 'In God we trust, customers pay cash'. I pushed open the door.

Warm amber lights, shadowy nooks and crannies. As my eyes became accustomed to the subdued lighting I could see dark brown tongue-and-groove panelling, dark ceiling beams hung with pewter tankards, dark furniture under a low red ceiling. Very little of the ochre walls above the panelling was visible under the array of objects hanging on them. Every wall had a unifying theme – of pictures, horse brasses, or clocks (each long-stopped clock showing a different time). Space had been found for jugs, plates and mugs on a shelf that ran round the walls close to the ceiling.

At this hour of the afternoon few of the tables were occupied. I took a menu from the bar and looked round for a suitably discreet corner where I could unzip the rucksack enough to allow G's head to emerge. She was a people-watcher and, as long as I offered her the occasional titbit, would sit there contentedly while I ate. I knew that if I left her closed up in the rucksack, she'd smell the food and show her resentment by bouncing about, emitting awkward-to-explain mews and yowls.

The main room of the inn was divided into 'sitting opportunities': armchairs round the Victorian fireplace – too near the bar and too public for my purpose; a cluster of little wooden tables behind a partition wall – already occupied; the very suitable wing-backed leather chairs in a dark corner by a front window – claimed just before I got there by a cheerful bunch of young men.

All that remained was through a doorway towards the rear, an area with three stained-glass skylights in the ceiling, and too brightly lit to conceal G in the rucksack. I'd just have to put her under a table, choose something from the menu that she didn't like and hope she wouldn't draw attention to herself by stroppy behaviour. But just through the doorway I made a discovery. What had once been a passageway was now a dimly lit alcove that held a tiny table and two chairs. It was a cosy little den completely hidden from the rest of the pub. I stowed the rucksack under the table, screening it with my legs from anyone who might wander past, and ordered smoked salmon and salad, something that would suit both of us.

Once the order had been brought to the table, I allowed G to poke her head out and survey the scene – not that there was much scene to survey. Our view was strictly limited to a picture and a bagatelle board hanging on the wall of the skylight-lit area, but G seemed quite content with the occasional morsel of my salmon meal passed down to her. Hunger satisfied, I sipped a lager while I read through the leaflet on the history of The Sheep Heid and the famous people who had visited it in the past.

Then I turned my thoughts to my stay at The Vaults, how I'd find out who the other residents of the self-catering accommodation might be, and what I would do if Moran was one of them. Known by sight to the staff as Sir Thomas Cameron-Blaik, he wouldn't have been able to drastically alter his appearance. One glimpse of him would be enough for me to be sure, and this time there'd be no delay, I would make that phone call right away to— I sighed, all too easily imagining Attila the Hun's reaction to my request to arrest a dead man.

I put down my hand and ruffled Gorgonzola's furry head. 'Our man would just disappear and I'd never be able to prove that I was right.'

Dejected, I slumped back in the comfortable chair and closed my eyes. I'd cancel The Vaults booking. What was the point?

From the other side of the wall a woman's voice rose above the murmur of conversation, the occasional clink of glass on table and the bursts of laughter drifting through the doorway.

'These seats are not taken. Over 'ere, darling.'

Chair legs scraped on the wooden flooring. A man's voice murmured something.

The woman called out, 'Please to bring the whisky list, *monsieur.*'

With Moran in my thoughts, the woman's French-accented English seemed uncannily like Gabrielle's. Wishful thinking. I sank once more into the depths of dejection.

'Islay whiskies?' The barman had come over with the list. 'Yes, madam. As you can see from the list, I can offer Ardbeg, Bunnahabhain, Bruichladdich, Bowmore, Caol Ila, Lagavulin and Laphroaig.'

'Eet says 'ere, "Caramel shortcake dominates this splash of ocean spray".' A trill of laughter. '*Certainement* we must 'ave the Bruichladdich.'

The thought flashed through my mind, Gabrielle and Moran. I knew

I was deluding myself, clutching at straws. I'd pay my bill and go.

I was reaching under the table for the rucksack when I heard glasses clink and a toast, 'To our time in Islay!'

It might be only one in a million chance that I was listening to Gabrielle and Moran, but if I left now I'd have to edge past their table. I'd stay here in the alcove till I heard them getting up to go, and then while their backs were turned, I'd take a look. I settled back to wait.

. . . They were asking for the bill. I reached under the table to push Gorgonzola's head gently down and close the rucksack. But in the uncanny way she had of reading my mind, she'd already sunk down and my fingers met empty space.

'What a clever girl, G,' I whispered, and pulled the zip closed.

Taking care not to make the couple I was interested in aware there was anyone on the other side of the wall, I eased back my chair and picked up the rucksack. And knew by the weight that it was empty. Far from meriting the praise I'd bestowed on her, G had been very bad indeed. Bored with her restricted view from under the table, she must have inched back the zip far enough to leap silently out and slink past my legs. Immersed in despondent thoughts, I hadn't even noticed.

Shit shit shit. Of all the times for G to go AWOL. I relaxed. Perhaps it wasn't such a big disaster. Anyone who spotted her would think she was the inn's cat and lean down to pet her. And she'd follow me out when she saw me leaving the inn. Were the couple still there? I stood listening.

Suddenly all hell broke loose.

Grrrrrufff rrufff rrufff rrufff

A woman screamed, 'Get hold of the dog! It'll kill the cat!'

The uproar and general pandemonium increased. There was no point in hurling myself into the mêlée. Nothing I could do would make any difference. I heard the crash of a table overturned . . . the smash of glass . . . cries of alarm as the artistically arranged bric-à-brac was knocked off the wall.

Rrufff rrufff rrufff. RRUFFF RRUFFF RRUFFF! The barking and crashes rose to a crescendo.

'Quick, open the door and let the buggers out!'

All at once the crashes stopped, the barking faded into the distance. Inside The Sheep Heid the hubbub of voices continued, louder if anything. I sank back onto my chair in the alcove, trying to tell myself that once outside, G would surely escape her pursuer by taking refuge

189

under a parked car, on top of a wall, up a tree.

Someone was saying loudly and defensively, 'I've been bringing Nero in here for a couple of years, and there's never been *any* trouble. Lies there quietly at my feet. Been no trouble, no trouble at all, has he, Bill?' A pause as the barman presumably confirmed this with a shake of his head. Then, 'Where did the bloody cat come from anyway? If Nero hasn't torn it to shreds, I will! Bloody cats should be—' The outer door slammed.

I lingered in the alcove, torn between rushing out to make certain that G had survived and not wanting to miss the chance of a sighting that could lead to the capture of Moran. The couple could still be somewhere in the next room, standing around discussing the carnage – only a sliver of a chance but. . . .

The sounds of clearing up died away. Conversation returned to normal levels. New voices took possession of the table on the other side of the wall. It was time to go.

The barman handed me my change. 'Sorry about the disturbance. Don't know how that cat managed to get in.'

'These things happen,' I said, studiously avoiding staring at the bare patches on the walls where bric-à-brac had been dislodged.

Outside there was no sign of Nero or his owner. No sign of Gorgonzola either. I looked up and down the narrow street. The upper windows of large houses peeped over twelve-foot walls, too high for a cat to scale. The couple of parked cars would only have provided temporary refuge. Her best bet would have been to squeeze through the vertical railings of the wrought-iron gates to that driveway.

Nobody was about. I called softly through the gates. There was a rustle from a laurel bush and Gorgonzola peered out. I called again. From the way she came swaggering down the driveway, it was plain that, far from being overcome with shame or fright, she'd actually relished the adrenaline rush of the awful episode. She sashayed through the bars and I scooped her up and pressed my face against hers.

'Where's the guilty, I-shouldn't-have-done-it look, then?' I whispered.

Her answer was a loud, self-satisfied *purrr*.

A voice behind me said, 'Hey, I've seen that effing cat before.'

I swung round. Standing a few feet away was a sallow-faced youth, cigarette clamped between fingers stained yellow with nicotine.

'Isn't that the one the dog was chasin' in there?' He jerked his head in the direction of The Sheep Heid.

'Must be. The poor cat's so frightened,' I lied. 'It's trembling like a leaf. I just had to pick it up.'

'Ach,' he spat into the gutter, 'I wouldn't bother with the likes o' that. Not exactly a beauty, is it? Looks like a stray to me. Watch you don't catch fleas.'

CHAPTER TWENTY-TWO

By the time I got back to the B&B I'd come to the decision not to cancel my booking at The Vaults. For the rest of my life I would wonder whether I'd allowed one of the world's most wanted criminals to slip through my hands. Thanks to G's unfortunately timed shenanigans, I hadn't managed to get a glimpse of the couple in The Sheep Heid, and though I had to admit it was unlikely they were Moran and Gabrielle, or indeed that I would find Moran staying in The Vaults accommodation, nevertheless, Attila the Hun or no, I was going to check. If I drew a blank tonight, I'd continue to check out The Vaults for the next two nights and by day stake out that Mecca for Gabrielle, Harvey Nicks. If I drew a blank, only then would I admit defeat.

My story to the Galbraiths was that I was spending these three days with a friend. 'My friend has a dog,' I said, 'so if it's at all possible, I'll leave Gorgonzola with you.'

As I knew they'd be, the Galbraiths were only too pleased to welcome G into their kitchen for the time I'd be away, even more so when I pointed out that if she was missing me, she was more likely to be in painting mood.

'Make sure the acrylic paints you've put out haven't dried up,' I said, picking up my small overnight holdall. 'If she sits staring at the wall, that's a good sign. She'll dab a paw in a colour and wipe it across the paper you've pinned up.' I stooped to stroke G. 'I'll be back soon.'

As I closed the door behind me, far from staring sadly after me, G was twining herself ingratiatingly round Mrs Galbraith's legs in a blatant charm offensive designed to conjure up a totally unearned snack.

*

'Enjoy your stay.' Sarah, the receptionist at The Vaults, smiled as she handed me the keys to the self-catering apartment. 'The flats are entered from the courtyard next door.'

The Ardbeg flat was tastefully themed in aubergine and cream and had a fine view of the rooftops of Leith. I'd hoped to catch a glimpse of the names in the guest registration book when I checked in, but I could only have accomplished that by wresting the book from the receptionist's hands. The best I could do was to note the drawer in which it was kept and hope there might be an opportunity to sneak a look at it.

An hour of keeping watch to see who was coming into the courtyard convinced me that this was even more boring than keeping watch from my window at the B&B in Portobello for little boats slipping in with drugs. There must be a quicker and easier way to find out who was in the other rooms than this. An artfully slanted conversation with Sarah might do the trick . . . the risk of encountering Moran was negligible, he probably wasn't here anyway.

There was nobody at the reception desk, nobody about at all. And there was no sign of the registration book. For a moment I contemplated whipping round the counter in search of it, but I heard approaching footsteps and when Sarah appeared I was thumbing through some leaflets.

'Ah,' I said, 'I was hoping to catch you. I'm really impressed with the accommodation and I know my friends visiting from London would be too. Is there any chance of them getting a room this week?'

She shook her head doubtfully. 'Rooms usually have to be booked many weeks in advance. You yourself were very lucky that we had a cancellation.' She reached into the drawer, pulled out a book and flicked through the pages. 'Yes, the other two rooms are booked, and there's nothing till after the weekend, I'm afraid.' She closed the book.

That was that then. I'd gone a few steps when she called after me.

'There is, of course, the *possibility* of a cancellation for the one bedroom Linkwood apartment. Sir Thomas Cameron-Blaik and guest are due to arrive tomorrow night, leaving on Monday. If he phones to say he's had to cancel, I'll leave a message for you.'

'I'll keep my fingers crossed.' I said.

I went through to the members' room, sat on a sofa by one of the fires and thumbed through the Outturn whisky list. *Dancing on the Rooftops* suited my mood perfectly. Smoky and from Islay, a perfect combination.

Back in my room I stared out at the rooftops of Leith. I'd promised myself in The Sheep Heid that as soon as I'd established Moran's whereabouts, I'd make that phone call to HQ, so why wasn't I reaching for the phone?

It was because I could hear the exchange with Attila the Hun as plainly as if it was taking place right now:

Me: I've discovered there's a booking at The Vaults for tomorrow night under the name of Sir Thomas Cameron-Blaik. That means Moran's not dead and will be here. That is, unless he cancels at the last minute. I've arranged for the receptionist to let me know if he does and—

The Hun: Moran is dead, Smith. He cannot cancel if he is *dead*. Unless, that is, there is a phone line to Hell.

Me: But there's a definite booking in Sir Thomas's name. I've just checked.

The Hun: And just when was that booking made? Did you check *that*?

Me: Er . . . no. I didn't think. . . .

The Hun: Exactly. You are paid to think, Smith, but it appears that I have to think for you. Moran is dead. He made the booking *before* he died.

Me: But—

The Hun: Don't waste my time, Smith. Moran is d-e-a-d, dead. *Dead*, I tell you.

And much as I hated to admit it, that booking *could* have dated from a month ago, before Moran met and killed Sir Thomas. Hadn't the receptionist said that bookings were usually made many weeks in advance? Whether Moran would turn up or not was too uncertain. No, there was no point in making that phone call yet. Tomorrow night I'd be sure.

That night I didn't sleep well, tossing and turning, waking in the midst of a half-remembered dream in which I was engaged in a Scrabble game with Attila the Hun. Every time, the word I made spelt out MORAN; every time, he triumphantly snapped down the letters D, E and D, so that the board was criss-crossed with the message

```
            M
            O
            R
        D E A D
            E   N
    M O R A N
        O   D
        R
    D E A D
        N
```

Brrr Brrr, Brrr Brrr. Attila glanced at the caller display on the phone beside the Scrabble board.

'Better answer it, Smith. It's the direct line from Hell.'

Brrr Brrr . . . The sun was shining and the phone beside the bed was ringing. Groggily I stretched out a hand and lifted the receiver. The call didn't come from Hell but from reception and the message brought me fully awake. There had been a phone call re the Cameron-Blaik booking, not to cancel it, but to confirm it. The Linkwood apartment was definitely going to be occupied tonight. That was perfect – the door was only a couple of steps away from mine, across a very small landing.

There was no excuse now to delay making that phone call to HQ. Even Attila the Hun would have to accept that he'd been wrong . . . or would he? If there was a flaw in my reasoning he'd find it and once again send me packing with a flea in my ear. I thought it over as I munched my way through the provided breakfast of fruit juice, cereal, bacon, eggs and toast. Even he couldn't deny that *somebody* was about to turn up at The Vaults claiming to be Sir Thomas Cameron-Blaik.

I spread marmalade on the toast, then paused, hand halfway to mouth. That bastard Attila would take considerable delight in pointing out that until I actually set eyes upon Moran, I really had no evidence at all to back my theory that he was still alive.

'Booked in the *name* of Cameron-Blaik, you say? I would suggest, Smith, that this is merely a *friend* of Cameron-Blaik, not the man himself.'

Much as I hated to admit it, he could be right. I'd have to wait to make that phone call till after I'd identified Moran.

Meanwhile I'd some homework to do. I pushed the breakfast things aside and spread out the map of Scotland I'd bought on my way here. On the assumption – oh dear, that word again – that Moran would not let the whisky out of his sight, he would have sailed his boat across from Islay to mainland Scotland and then ... my finger traced the route linking the West of Scotland and the North Sea – the Caledonian Canal, Loch Ness. Then he'd sail from Inverness, south past Aberdeen to arrive at the Firth of Forth and finally, Leith, Edinburgh's port. Yes, it was all quite feasible.

I brought out the map of Edinburgh and marked the position of The Vaults. Nicely close at hand was Leith Docks, but the security there would ensure any boat coming in would attract attention. Newhaven Harbour, sited next to the Docks, was so small that the size of boat he'd need to transport ten casks would attract immediate unwelcome attention, so I discounted it too. That left Granton Harbour, only a short bus journey away. I was sure I was on the right track. All that remained was for me to get a glimpse of Moran or recognize his voice. Then, and only then, I'd phone The Hun and leave the rest to him.

My bedroom window offered an oblique view of the entrance gateway to the courtyard. I pulled up a chair and screened by the Venetian blinds, sat watching the comings and goings. Time dragged, as it does when you're waiting for something to happen. 'A watched kettle never boils' as the saying goes. Though I was buoyed up with anticipation, I found it more and more of a struggle to stay awake. I can only put it down to the legacy of my disturbed night. Dreaming, I've read, takes place in real time and therefore a dream event can be as exhausting as if it had actually happened – that panic-filled attempt to outrun a pursuer, that fraught snail-pace taxi ride to the airport, and for me last night, that mentally draining Scrabble game with the Hun. That and the warmth of the sun coming through the glass was a powerful combination. . . .

The watched kettle may never boil, but the unwatched milk pan boils over the minute you take your eye off it. It was the murmur of voices outside my door that woke me. I'd nodded off for only a short time, but it had been enough to miss seeing who had entered the courtyard. All that time keeping watch had been wasted. Across the landing the door closed quietly. Moran or not? It was impossible to tell.

I eased open the door of my apartment and looked out. The door with the Linkwood nameplate gazed back, keeping its secret. I'd tiptoe across and ascertain if the voices came from inside, the thick pile of the carpet would deaden any sound I might make.

Two steps across the landing and I was listening at the door. To my horror the round handle turned slowly as someone inside prepared to come out. The door began to open.

CHAPTER TWENTY-THREE

The gap between jamb and door widened. I stared at the slowly opening door, envisaging Moran's explosive reaction when he saw me. There was no time to regain the safety of my own apartment. No time to turn and hurry down the stairs. No time to do anything before he would drag me into his room. What a stupid, stupid way to bring to an end Operation Scotch Mist. And, of course, my life. He wouldn't hesitate to attack me. No one would hear my screams: the landing door and a flight of stairs separated me from the other flat, and the members' lounge and whisky-tasting rooms were on the other side of the building.

He'd kill me, hide my body and disappear tonight. The murder hunt would be for the man known as Cameron-Blaik – who was dead. By the time HMRC got involved, Moran would have melted into thin air, whereabouts unknown. It was of little consolation that when my body was discovered, Attila the Hun would be forced to admit that he should have listened to me and given me the backing I had asked for.

A thin line of daylight was appearing along the jamb and the top edge of the door. The shadow of the person about to emerge blocked the line of light. I might just have a chance if I launched myself at the door and took Moran by surprise . . . But he must weigh twice as much as me. Charging at the door would have little effect. I'd just be throwing myself into his arms. I wouldn't go down without a fight, I'd—

From inside the room came a voice I recognized. 'There's no need to go down to reception, darling. I've found eet.' Gabrielle Robillard.

The door closed with a click and the key turned in the lock.

Back in my room I sank onto a chair, torn between elation at finding

Moran and shock at my narrow escape. I picked up my mobile and phoned Attila the Hun.

'Put me through to A—' I almost said 'Attila,' correcting it just in time to Andrew Tyler. 'Priority.'

But he wasn't in his office and I had to be content with leaving the message that I'd made a positive identification of the supposedly dead Moran. Accompanied by Gabrielle Robillard, he was staying at the Scotch Malt Whisky's premises in Edinburgh. I ended with, 'I'm convinced he has a boat carrying whisky and drugs moored in the Leith area. Awaiting instructions.'

Two hours later I was still waiting for those instructions. I'd just decided to try to contact HQ again when I heard the door on the landing open and footsteps going down the stairs.

I took up position at the window. A minute later a man and a woman emerged into the courtyard, their backs towards me as they made their way to the gate. It wasn't Moran and Gabrielle. Robillard had long jet-black hair but this woman's hair was short and blonde. But the man's walk seemed familiar. I snatched up binoculars I'd brought with me from Portobello. As the couple turned out of the arched gateway, their faces jumped into focus. The man's hair was thick and dark, greying at the temples, and expensively cut and styled . . . the bushy eyebrows . . . it was unmistakably Moran; despite the colour of her hair, the woman's full, almost pouting, lower lip was Gabrielle's. Since Cameron-Blaik's face was familiar to the staff, the best he could do was to change the hairstyle and colouring of his companion.

Tempting though it was, I didn't hurry after them. They wouldn't be going back to the boat so soon after their arrival, so it wasn't worth the risk of them catching sight of me. Tempting too, to make use of the picklocks I'd brought with me in my overnight bag to break into the Linkwood apartment. Again I resisted. A man like Moran had kept one step ahead of the law by being ultra-cautious, so he would undoubtedly have left traps for snoopers. I've done that myself on many occasions – the careful placing of a piece of thread, a hair, the precise angle of a book – anything that, if moved, would indicate someone had been searching the apartment.

While the three-night reservation might be part of the smokescreen behind which he was planning to disappear, I could count on him staying here for tonight at least. That gave some hours for Attila to get his finger out and do something.

By eight o'clock I was fuming. There'd still been no phone call from Attila, sod him. What *was* he playing at? Why hadn't there been a raid on The Vaults to arrest Moran? Well, *I* wasn't just going to sit here and let him slip through our fingers. I'd do some snooping at Granton Harbour. There'd be a harbour master there. If I'd been armed with Attila's authorization, it would be a simple matter to ask to see the list of today's arrivals. As it was, to search out the boat's details was going to be difficult and time-consuming, but vital, if Attila's lack of action allowed Moran to do another disappearing act. I took up position at the window again.

Eventually Moran and Gabrielle returned, and as soon as I heard their door close, I was on my way to Portobello. To have any hope of success in my search I'd need to enlist Gorgonzola's help.

I explained my premature return to the B&B with, 'I'm *so* missing Gorgonzola, but,' I beamed, 'my friend no longer has her dog, so she says it's quite all right to bring G to stay with me at her place.'

The Galbraiths gallantly tried to hide their disappointment. G, it seemed, had shown promising signs of an inclination to paint.

Hilda Galbraith sighed. 'This morning she sat for a long time in front of the paper we've pinned to the wall, just staring at it.'

I nodded. 'Ah, that's one of the first signs.'

'Unfortunately, *somebody*,' Tom Galbraith cast a dark look at his wife, 'somebody thought a saucer of fish would spark off some creative action.'

'Oh dear,' I said, 'I'm afraid—'

'Yes, it sparked off action, all right. Gorgonzola hoovered up the fish, then curled up on the windowsill and went to sleep.' His eyes wandered disconsolately to the pristine piece of cartridge paper.

G didn't share their disappointment at my return, and was purring loudly and rubbing herself against my legs. I scooped her into the rucksack.

'I'll be back in a couple of days. There'll be another chance then,' I consoled, though I knew there would be very little chance when I was here with her.

The breakwater stretched a protective arm round Granton Harbour. Fluorescent pink buoys bobbed on a vast sheet of water grey and dimpled like hammered pewter. In the distance beyond the harbour wall, lighted windows twinkled in multi-storey flats that reared up in a mini-New York skyline – a sharp contrast to the terrace of Victorian brick cottages peeping over the grassy embankment that hid the main road.

Earlier in the day the harbour must have been a picture-postcard scene of blue sky and white bobbing yachts. Now, at dusk, under lowering skies and with a biting east wind, it was bleak and colourless, the only sound the eerie whine of wind whistling through the rigging of yachts moored on the other side of a high metal palisade topped with barbed wire. An official notice warned, **PORT SECURITY** *Restricted Area.*

'Some security.' I muttered. There was no gatehouse, no guard and an invitingly open gate.

I stared at the other notices, variations of the order, **KEEP OUT!** *High Visibility Clothing Must Be Worn.*

I looked down at my merge-with-the-dark snooping outfit of black jacket and trousers. 'I think we'll have to disobey that, eh, G?'

Rabies Warning! No Animals allowed on Port Estate. A silhouette of a dog with the red slash of 'forbidden' reinforced the order.

'Doesn't apply to you, G. You're not a dog. That's OK, then.'

Three hundred yards of road stretched emptily behind me, and on this chilly evening there didn't seem to be anybody about on the other side of the gate either. Act confidently and you can get in anywhere. I marched through the gate as if I had all the right in the world to be there.

In spite of those shiny official notices, the area beyond the gate was rundown and neglected. A green tide of weeds and grass lapped the base of a flat-roofed derelict building. An orange lifebuoy hung on its wall, a vivid splash of colour against the stained and grimy grey of the stone. Its glassless windows were barred and netted with rusty wire, except for a ground-floor window where two of the bars were missing, wrenched off by intruders. I stood on tiptoe and peered in. The floor was thick with pigeon droppings, the walls scrawled with graffiti, a pigeon *croo crooing* on a rafter the only witness to my own intrusion.

I sat on a bollard on the quay, looking out towards the harbour over the rotting beams of an old pier. 'The boat we're looking for, G,' I said, 'has to have storage capacity for ten whisky casks. So that discounts all these small yachts and cabin cruisers, don't you think?'

A scrabbling from within the rucksack on my knees indicated that she couldn't possibly give an opinion without surveying the scene. Recalling the unfortunate incident at The Sheep Heid, I unzipped the rucksack just enough to allow her head to emerge.

'You're on probation, G. I'm not taking the chance of you leaping out and me having to chase you along the quay.'

She nudged at the zip trying to ease it open, at the same time emitting a mew conveying, 'How could you *think* such a thing?'

I sat there in the dusk listening to the metallic *ting ting ting* from the rigging of the line of yachts moored to a pontoon and the distant hum of traffic from the main road.

What kind of boat would Moran use? I was assuming – no, no, mustn't assume – I was *counting on* him having both whisky *and* drugs as his cargo. He'd had to remove the whisky from the warehouse in a hurry, and so he'd have had to make use of the boat already lined up for shipping in the next consignment of drugs.

'What kind of boat would be big enough to take those ten casks, G?'

Her whiskers twitched as they did when scenting fish.

'You're right. The answer is a fishing boat, and that's what you and I are going to look for.'

I stared across the darkening expanse of water. The problem was, there didn't seem to be any fishing boats in the harbour, or anything larger than those small yachts. I wasn't going to give up. I was convinced that Moran would moor his boat in exactly this sort of place, neglected as it was, and with no security. Out of sight of the smart yachts of the Yacht Club, nobody would notice his boat slipping in and out again.

At the end of the quay, near a modern cone-shaped brick building with its glass windows still intact, I could just make out in the gathering dusk the shapes of larger boats resting on trestles. Another part of the harbour basin must lie over there. I'd been looking in the wrong place.

I fastened on G's working collar with the radio transmitter. Wearing that collar, she would be centred on sniffing out drugs and not be led astray by the smell of fish or the nocturnal scurrying of mice. I snapped on her lead and together we walked towards the cone-shaped building.

Once we'd rounded the boats on their trestles, a whole new area of the harbour opened up. A thin black line of harbour wall, so distant it was barely visible, separated the vast expanse of water from the slate-grey bowl of the sky. But there were no boats, large or small, moored in the huge harbour basin. And yet I'd been so *sure*. . . .

Fifty yards away the silvered beams of a substantial jetty reared out of the water with two small dinghies beached on its grassy top. An ideal mooring for a larger boat, but through the criss-cross of beams there was only the glint of empty water.

A sudden movement at the far end of the jetty startled me. Heart beating fast, I shrank back into the shadows cast by the boats on their trestles. I relaxed as an arm rose in the throwing movement of a fisherman casting his line. With darkness falling and at this distance, if he noticed me at all, he'd assume that I was a local taking a small dog for a walk.

I was about to turn to go back to the main gate, but G tugged at the lead with other ideas. She hadn't had much exercise recently, so I let her have her way and we continued our walk along the quay. As I passed the end of the jetty, the fisherman was staring across the black waters of the harbour, seemingly unaware of my presence.

We walked on past more boats on trestles. Then, invisible until now below the level of the quay, nestling next to the wall, was a boat of the right size. I stood at the edge of the quay looking down. At just over sixty feet, the *Island Spirit* was chunky like a small fishing trawler but with the superstructure of a cabin cruiser, not the kind of boat that would attract attention for its sleek stylish lines.

The curtains were drawn across the horseshoe of windows. I could see no lights, hear no sound from within, only the *slap slap* of water against its sides. Had I found Moran's boat? Standing here wasn't going to tell me. I'd have to get on board.

I swooped on G and put her in the rucksack before she could protest over the sudden curtailment of her evening stroll. Then I searched round for a stone, dropped it down onto the highly polished roof of the saloon and hurried back to the shadows cast by the row of trestles.

There was no sound of a door opening, no enquiring shout, only the lapping of water. I sent another stone clattering onto the deck and, when there was no response, I moved forward to stand at the top of the ladder fixed to the quay wall. I'd have to take a chance. I wasn't going to turn back now.

I had negotiated two rungs on the ladder and was feeling with one foot for the third rung when from above a voice said, 'Recognized you right away.'

I flung back my head to look up at a tall shadowy figure silhouetted against the night sky. My foot slipped off the rung and for a precarious moment I hung there, both hands gripping the cold metal, helpless to defend myself against attack while my feet swung in space. It was a ten-foot drop to the ship's deck below. If I fell there was every chance I'd land awkwardly, twist an ankle, or topple backwards and injure Gorgonzola.

'Recognized you right away.' he'd said. It could only be Moran. *Shit shit shit*. Why hadn't I taken the elementary precaution of checking to see if anyone was following me? My head was just below the level of the quay and I couldn't release my grip to defend myself. All he had to do was kick me in the face and . . . My hands tightened on the ladder.

Now he was bending to look down at me, judging where to aim the blow. If I released one hand, swung sideways and grabbed his foot, perhaps it might be enough to unbalance him.

I scrabbled frantically for a foothold on the ladder. As first one foot then the other found the rung, I got a better look at the figure looming over me. Just in time I registered that his silhouette was almost skeletally thin. With a physique like that, whoever it was, it couldn't be Moran.

The man on the quay whispered, 'But mum's the word, S.'

S? I stared up at him. Mum's the word? That's all I needed, a drunk accosting me and causing a scene. That would end all hope of a clandestine search of the boat.

'Yes, knew it was you right away,' he hissed. 'On another secret mission, eh?' He tapped the side of his nose knowingly.

That gesture brought the memory of a previous HMRC operation flooding back. This was the man who had helped me track down my quarry at the golf championships at Muirfield in Scotland, the man who on that occasion had saved my life.

'*Adam!*'

'No names, S.'

Before I could say anything, he said, 'You're wondering how I recognized you in this bad light, aren't you? I was fishing on the jetty there when I saw you walking past.' His prominent Adam's apple bobbed up and down like a cork on the end of a fishing line. 'It's not just faces I've a memory for, it's the way people walk, things they say. Once noted, it's in *there*.' He tapped his forehead with a bony finger.

Standing like this on the ladder I would be in a vulnerable position if anybody was on board the boat below or if the owner, possibly Moran, came along. I climbed quickly back up the ladder, and playing along with the James Bond role he'd assigned me at Muirfield, I beckoned him away from the edge of the quay.

I whispered from behind my hand, 'Important mission, A, involving this boat. Do you know if there's anybody on board?'

He looked theatrically up and down the deserted quay. 'The answer's negative, S.'

A classic Delphic Oracle answer that could be interpreted two ways. While I was pondering which way to take it he said, 'Good cover that, walking the. . . .' – with exaggerated lip movements he mouthed the word – 'cat.'

'Well spotted, A. It's on a mission too.'

He pursed his lips and nodded slowly. 'Nuff said.'

'While the cat and I are investigating this boat, I need eyes and ears to warn me if anybody comes along. You fishing from the quay is perfect camouflage. Your country needs you, A. Will you accept the assignment?'

'Affirmative, S.' His Adam's apple jerked convulsively like a float when the fish has taken the bait. 'I'll get my rod. Back in a jiff.' A man on a mission, he loped off towards the jetty.

Time was precious. I climbed quickly down the ladder, my soft-soled boots making no sound as I crossed the deck. A padlock fitted as an additional lock to the saloon doors was another indicator that nobody was on board at present. I cupped my hand against the glass to cut out reflection from the sky and peered into the saloon, but thick curtaining prevented any view of the interior. While G prowled around the deck areas fore and aft, I got to work with my picklocks.

As I eased back the hasp, G joined me with a 'Nothing yet' *miaow*. Another ten seconds and I'd dealt with the lock on the sliding saloon doors.

'This is the moment of truth, G.' I slid the doors apart and shone my pencil torch on the interior of the saloon. The narrow beam played on u-shaped seating below the row of windows on the left . . . moved towards the centre of the cabin and— There, wedged side by side between the seating that lined the left and the right of the saloon were two rows of wooden casks.

'I've hit the jackpot, G. Now it's your turn.'

I pointed towards the wheelhouse at the far end of the saloon beyond the casks. It didn't take long for her to give it the once-over, find nothing, and come back to sit on a cask awaiting further instructions. I wasn't discouraged. A consignment of drugs would be transported in large packages, not hidden away in a nook or cranny in the wheelhouse.

With G at my heels I made my way over the bench seating to the far side of the casks and down the steps to the cabins below. Adam would give enough warning of anyone approaching. I switched on the light. At this level, barely above the waterline, the portholes would be fully screened by the quay wall.

A double bed on a deep base filled most of the floor space in the master cabin with storage cupboards lining the walls from floor to ceiling.

'We'll check the upper cupboards first, G.' I bent down to pick her up.

But she avoided my outstretched hands and stalked round the base of the bed, tail erect, tip twitching. From her throat came the croon that I'd been hoping for. I slid open one of the access panels to the underbed storage space. It was crammed with plastic-wrapped packages. I did some rapid calculations.

'Do you realize that this bed is worth fifty million pounds, G?'

She leapt onto the bed and paraded up and down the duvet, tail straight, tip relaxed, signifying, 'Am I not a clever girl! Without me, what would you do?'

I picked G up and hugged her. Now I could go back to Attila in triumph with a hat trick of successes: the recovery of valuable whisky, the discovery of an even more valuable quantity of drugs, and to cap it all, information that would lead to the capture of the master criminal who had tricked HMRC into believing he was dead. Oh, the sweet, sweet satisfaction of hearing Attila admit that lowly DJ Smith had been right all along!

G's head turned and her ears swivelled. Had she heard something? Then I heard it too. A faint, barely audible *tlick tlick tlick*. It seemed to be coming from the saloon above. *Tlick tlick tlick*, louder now and more urgent. Puzzled, I stood at the bottom of the steps and looked up into the saloon trying to pinpoint the origin of the sound. *Tlick tlick tlick*. It was coming from the cabin roof. My mind was still savouring Attila's humiliation and my triumph, so it took me a moment to realize that Adam was sending a warning signal.

I'd left it too late. Once I'd seen the casks I should have got the hell out of here. Stupid, stupid *stupid* of me. I grabbed G, stuffed her into the rucksack and switched off the lights. Clutching the rucksack in one hand, torch in the other, I raced up the steps to the saloon, ran half-crouched along the seating, flung myself outside and slid the doors closed. The lock clicked shut.

The float on the end of a fishing line was dangling just above the saloon roof. I stared up at Adam, a pale blob of a face and shadowy outline against a sky now darkened to violet-blue. He didn't have to say anything: I could hear voices on the quay, voices coming closer. *Island Spirit* was the only boat in this section of Granton Harbour. They were coming here and it could only be Moran or his thugs. Once up on the quay, I might have time to find cover, lose myself in the shadows.

I shrugged on the rucksack and scrambled up the ladder till my head was level with Adam's feet. The voices were louder now, more distinct: the high notes of a woman and the deeper base of a man. Gabrielle and Moran? Whoever they were they weren't yet in sight. To my dismay I could see that the only cover was the dark bulky shape of a piece of machinery more than a hundred yards along the quay.

Adam was performing a strange sort of anxiety dance, hopping from one foot to another. 'You'll have to pull something out of the bag pretty damn quick, S. Once they come past the trestles, they'll have us in their sights.'

It was then that I remembered the padlock. I'd laid it on the deck while I'd tackled the lock on the saloon doors. And it was still lying where I'd left it, the tell-tale sign that someone had broken in. In a surge of adrenalin I shot up the ladder onto the quayside.

'The cat's in here, A.' I thrust the rucksack into his hands. 'The Service is relying on you. If we don't manage to rendezvous later, contact HQ on this number, give them this, my emergency back-up code, and tell them what's happened. Then take the cat back to the Beach View B&B on the promenade in Portobello. I'll pick her up there.'

He repeated the phone number and code word. 'Got it, S.'

He'd said he had total recall of things he'd noted. I could only hope that this was true and that it hadn't been an idle boast.

There *definitely* wouldn't be time now to descend the ladder, snap the padlock onto the doors, climb back up again and make it along the quay to hide behind that piece of machinery. I'd have to hide somewhere on deck and hope they were coming merely to make a security check, and after that leave.

It took less than thirty seconds to have the padlock back in place. Then

I was running across the deck towards the small inflatable lashed on its side to the rail at the stern. I glanced up at the quay. I'd been right to rely on Adam. I could see him silhouetted against a lighter patch of sky. He'd moved clear of the boat and was standing rucksack on back, rod flicking forward into the water in a fisherman's cast. I slid between the inflatable and the rail and lay flat on its rubbery bulge.

'Hey, you!' I heard the sound of running feet: the *thud thud thud* of rubber-soled shoes and the *tap tap tap* of a woman's high-heels. 'What the hell are you doing near my boat?' It was Moran's voice.

His fist would be raised in a threatening gesture. And I was afraid. Not for myself, but for Adam. I'd been wrong to take advantage of his passion for a fantasy world of the Secret Service and 007. If Moran perceived Adam as a threat to the vast profit tied up in the boat, that would be enough. The smallest mistake now would mean Adam's death. And I would be responsible.

'I asked you what the hell you're doing here. You deaf?' Moran must be very close, standing above on the quay and a little off to the left.

Could Adam convince Moran he was harmless? What would he say? Mouth dry, I strained to hear. He didn't say anything.

For a few moments there was silence above, then I heard an alarming guttural *grunt grunt grunt*. It was the sound of someone choking. My worst fears had been realized: Adam had been strangled, or stabbed.

Even though it was too late, I couldn't just skulk here and do nothing. I tensed, preparing to fling myself out from under the inflatable.

Gabrielle was saying, 'What ees the man trying to say? I think 'e ees deaf and dumb and 'e cannot understand you.'

I sank back.

'Well, he'll understand this.' There was the sharp *crack* as something snapped, a guttural cry from Adam, and Moran's voice, low and threatening, 'Now, bugger off, damn you. And don't come back.'

I heard Adam scuttling along the quay and breathed a sigh of relief. He and Gorgonzola were safe.

'Was eet necessary to break the poor man's rod, darling?'

'Only way to make him understand.' A short laugh. 'Actions speak louder than words, as the saying goes.'

I was shaking. Feet scuffed on the ladder, followed by a thump as someone jumped onto the deck.

From the quayside came a wail of, 'Darling, the shoes, 'ow can I come

208

down the ladder wearing the *shoes*?'

A mutter of, 'Silly bitch.' Then louder, 'Take them off and throw them down on deck. We've not got much time. Hurry up, I want to be away from here.'

One shoe, then the other, clattered onto the wooden deck. I charted Gabrielle's slow progress down the ladder by the little screams and shrieks and Moran's increasingly impatient mutterings of, 'For Christ's sake.'

Keys chinked.

'The padlock's still in place, it's not been tampered with.' The saloon doors slid open.

Was Moran, as I'd hoped, just making a quick visit to check on the whisky and drugs? For the first time it occurred to me that he might be intending to leave the harbour and head out to sea. I'd be wise to take my chance to escape while they were below deck. I'd learned enough. I certainly didn't want to find myself trapped on board. I peered round the side of the inflatable, ready to slither out.

From the saloon entrance, only a few feet away, Gabrielle shrieked, '*Merde*! You drag me away from dinner and now you expect me to crawl *comme un bébé* past these disgusting barrels? Are you a madman that we come 'ere in the night? Why do you do this to me?' A foot stamped furiously on the wooden deck.

Like a tortoise into its shell, I withdrew my head into my rubbery carapace.

'Gabrielle,' Moran's soft tone was more frightening than an angry shout, 'do you want these lovely wrists of yours to wear handcuffs? Listen to me. On my way back to the apartment to collect that handbag of yours that you're always leaving down somewhere, the receptionist told me that a friend had been enquiring if I'd arrived yet. And *that*, my dear Gabrielle, means that someone knows that Sir Thomas did not die in the distillery fire. Someone has traced me to The Vaults.'

Gabrielle's shriek was cut short by a slap.

'Shut *up*. All I need is for you to have hysterics. I'm going up onto the quay to throw down the mooring ropes. Stay in the cabin.'

That ill-timed enquiry about Sir Thomas certainly hadn't come from me. It could only have been Attila. He'd got round to action at last. And it might well lead to the escape of Louis Moran – and the death of agent DJ Smith.

Vibrations in the hull told me that the engines had started up. From my hiding place behind the inflatable I saw the seaweed-green stones of the quay receding into the darkness. With no navigation lights or cabin lights all that would be visible to a watcher on shore was the dark shape of the trawler-yacht slipping out of Granton West Harbour.

CHAPTER TWENTY-FOUR

The increased motion of the waves told me we'd rounded the harbour breakwater. I tried to tell myself that it was the chill wind biting through clothing inadequate for exposure to these conditions that was causing me to shiver, but I knew it wasn't only that.

I'd had time to explore my options. And there were only three: I could jump overboard right now while there was still a slim chance of swimming to shore; I could take Moran by surprise and hope to overpower him; I could lie here wedged between the rail and the inflatable and await inevitable discovery.

If I was being realistic, I didn't think the first two options had a snowball's chance in hell of success. With every second the shore was further away, and though I was a strong swimmer, hypothermia would set in long before I could reach it. And to surprise Moran and overpower him in the wheelhouse, I'd have to negotiate the barrier of casks without making a sound or Gabrielle catching sight of me. Not much possibility of that.

My only realistic hope of rescue – and that was a slim one – was the watcher on shore. Adam knew I was on board. But what if he hadn't remembered that phone number? Even if he had, would he be able to convince Attila to act on the message? The Hun was much more likely to concentrate on establishing Adam's identity and finding out how he had come by the phone number and the emergency code. Hope died . . . and flickered into faint life again as I recalled how quick thinking and resourceful Adam had been when he'd fooled Moran into thinking that he was deaf and dumb.

Meanwhile I wasn't going to lie here, do nothing, and wait for the outcome of option three, to be killed like a rat in a trap. The lights of Fife were almost directly ahead, a sparkling amber and white necklace strung between sea and sky. The stern must therefore be facing directly towards Granton and Leith. On a dark night with clear visibility such as this, a light at sea, even a weak one, can be seen for miles. A winking light would have a very good chance of attracting attention.

I felt in my pocket for the torch and twisted round onto my side to face towards the water. Holding the torch out past the rail and pointing towards the stern, I flashed the Morse code SOS, the internationally recognized signal of distress. Once ... --- ... Twice ... --- ... Five times in total. To indicate that this was definitely a signal, after counting out sixty seconds I sent the five SOS flashes again. When muscles ached and protested, I supported the arm holding the torch with the other arm as best I could. I repeated the pattern of flashes . . . interval . . . flashes . . . interval, again and again and again.

We had just passed the lighthouse on the island of Inchkeith, giving me a rough idea of our position, when at last somebody replied to my signal – three flashes of light, then darkness for . . . I counted eighteen seconds. Was the response from the sleek, powerful Customs cutter that constantly patrolled the Firth of Forth? Heart pounding, I waited for the beat of powerful engines, the grey shape of the frigate looming up, the powerful searchlight slicing through the darkness to transfix Moran's boat in its bright beam. Nothing. Just the same constantly repeated three flashes then an interval of darkness – gradually dropping astern. I slumped back, hope draining away with the realization that the signal must be coming from one of the buoys warning shipping of the shallow waters round Inchkeith.

Time passed. The motion of the boat, the hum of the engines, the cold, all combined to numb mind and body.

The shock of icy water splashing into my face jolted me fully awake. I was still gripping the torch – but how long had it been since I'd last flashed the SOS signal? I was dismayed to realize how much effort it took to press the button. It was only a matter of time before my fingers became too cold even to hold the torch.

The minutes dragged by . . . then above the hum of the boat's engines I heard a louder roar. I turned my head to look up at the bright landing lights of an aircraft on its final approach to Edinburgh Airport. And that gave me an idea. Stiffly I pulled myself to my knees and leaned out between the rails to look ahead for the lights of the next plane.

... There it was, the distant winking red port light as an aircraft banked before it straightened to begin its approach up the Firth of Forth. I pointed the torch skywards. ... --- ... The aircrew might spot the pinpoint of light flashing SOS in the black void beneath them and radio the position to the coastguard. ... --- ...

BANG. With a horrible rending CRUNCH from the bow, the boat heeled suddenly, hurling me violently against a metal upright. My numb fingers lost their grip, the torch flew out of my hand and with barely a splash the black water swallowed it up.

The engines changed note, the propellers churned the water at the stern into a maelstrom of white water. Tortured fibreglass groaned as the boat slowly reversed away from a submerged obstacle, slowed and drifted to a stop, wallowing in the troughs of the waves.

The saloon doors crashed open as someone stumbled out. Gabrielle, judging by the terrified sobs.

'Louis, Louis, we must float the lifeboat *immédiatement*. We are going to drown.' *Thump*. Aubergine-painted fingernails clutched the bulging side of the inflatable above my head.

The inflatable shuddered as it was subjected to frantic attempts to pull it away from the rail. I pressed myself against its slatted wooden flooring and shrank back under the bulge, ready to throw myself into the sea if I was discovered. In the cold water and with no life jacket there was perhaps one per cent chance of survival, but that was a hundred per cent more than if I remained on board.

'*Leave it.*' Moran had joined her. 'If you think I am I going to abandon this boat and lose the cargo, you're out of your mind. We'll be all right, I tell you. Inchkeith harbour is only twenty-five minutes away and—'

'Twenty-five minutes!' Her voice rose to a scream. '*Imbécile!* In less than *five* minutes the boat goes down! Already water ees over the floor in the bedroom, my new shoes they are *ruined*.' Again her hands scrabbled at the side of the inflatable.

'*Quit it*, I say.' The sound of a slap accompanied the words. 'Calm down and listen to me. The bow's damaged but if I judge the speed right, the pumps will keep pace with the water coming in. There's a small private harbour on Inchkeith, not much used, and—'

'And what then, Louis? What do we do then? No one knows we are there, 'ow can they come to rescue us? Nobody finds us . . . never . . .

never. . . .' Gulping sobs made the rest unintelligible.

He slapped her again, harder than before. 'Pull yourself together, woman. For Christ's sake, let go of me or we *will* sink. When I increase speed, I need you to shout up from the cabin down below how much water's coming in.'

'*Non*, Louis, *non*. I will be trapped by the water. I'm *not* going down—'

'You bloody well are, even if I've got to drag you there by your hair.'

'No, no . . . you're hurting me, Louis. *Aahhh . . . aaaow. . . .*'

The cries continued, muffled in the interior of the saloon. Some minutes later the engine note increased, the water at the stern swirled and eddied, and the boat moved slowly ahead, turning in a wide circle to head back towards Inchkeith. The lights of Edinburgh were deceptively close, sparks of orange and yellow against the black mass of Arthur's Seat and the Lothian hills.

I tried to work out what Moran would do when – if – we eventually made it to the harbour on Inchkeith. With its outboard motor attached, he could beach the inflatable anywhere on the Fife or Edinburgh side of the Forth and disappear again, this time for good. But I didn't think that was what he had in mind. It was unlikely he'd abandon a cargo as profitable as this, worth millions of pounds, for HMRC to impound, or a criminal like himself to chance upon and make off with.

So what was he planning? When he'd hit that underwater obstruction, he must have been on his way to rendezvous with a ship somewhere at the mouth of the Firth of Forth. He'd radio that ship at the first opportunity, could even be doing so now, and arrange to transfer the cargo at Inchkeith. And there was nothing I could do to stop him.

The beam of the lighthouse flashed white, and went out. The lights of Edinburgh disappeared, blotted out by the volcanic bulk of Inchkeith, only to reappear as we slowly rounded the north of the island. I pressed the button on my watch to illuminate the dial. It was just after midnight. Moran had taken longer than he'd calculated by having to decrease speed every time Gabrielle screamed a warning that water was flooding in at a faster rate.

A half-moon had risen, lightening the sky and back-lighting the clouds. From my position lying behind the inflatable on the port side, I could make out low rocks, some barely visible above water, and behind them cliffs; then a few minutes later, the tall wall of a stone breakwater about fifty yards off. The engines slowed till they were just ticking over. We were barely moving.

Suddenly a shudder ran through the boat. The hull had touched bottom. A wave passed under us, the boat lifted off, drifted forward, scraped, then aided by another wave, nosed alongside the end of the breakwater. My plans were already made. While Moran and Gabrielle were waiting in the wheelhouse for the arrival of the ship they'd radioed, I'd slip from behind the inflatable onto the quay and find somewhere to hide.

Very slowly and carefully to avoid any betraying movement of the boat, I eased myself to my knees, ready to slide between the rails and climb up the ladder onto the quay. I had one foot through the rail when the saloon doors slid open. I froze.

Moran snapped. 'Stop snivelling, woman. Just get up there and I'll throw you the rope.'

Gabrielle whined a protest as she stumbled across the deck. The boat bumped hard against the breakwater as the swell moved under it, covering any movement I made as I ducked quickly back behind the inflatable.

'No, not there, you fool.' Moran must have been standing within inches of me. 'Pass the damned rope through that metal ring beside your foot. No, don't try to tie it. Your knots are shit. Now throw it down to me.' The rope thumped onto the deck.

'I am *not* coming back onto that boat, Louis. She ees sinking.'

'For God's sake, Gabrielle, don't start those hysterical dramatics again.'

'I tell you, that boat ees not safe. I stay up here.'

That put paid to my plan to slip ashore while they sheltered in the wheelhouse. I should have known better by now than to assume anything at all.

He muttered, 'Silly bitch,' but called out to her, 'There's nothing to be afraid of. There's only a foot of water, if that, under the boat. *I'll* go below and pass the packets up to you in the saloon ready for the transfer. Come *on*, darling. It'll take too long to do it by myself.' There was no tenderness in that 'darling', only exasperation and fury, thinly veiled.

Gabrielle wasn't fooled. 'So eet's darling now, ees eet? I'm not coming, I tell you. So, are you going to drag me down there by the 'air like the caveman treats the woman?'

He slammed his fist into the side of the inflatable. 'I'm not going to waste time arguing. If you're not on board in ten seconds, I'll cast off and anchor out there till the ship comes – and don't think I'll bother to come back for you.'

'You think I care? You are *merde*. As you say, bugger off.'

Good for you, Gabrielle, I thought. Hell hath no fury like a woman scorned.

'Right, suit yourself, damn you. Stay here till you rot. No one's going to find you.' An unpleasant laugh. 'The lighthouse is automated, so don't think you'll get any help there.'

There was a thump as he pulled the rope back on deck, followed by a violent push against the wall that sent the boat drifting away from the breakwater. I buried my face in the rubber side of the inflatable, hoping that to Gabrielle looking down from above I'd be just another shadow.

The engine note changed from a tick-over to a steady throb and we moved slowly away to drop anchor a couple of hundred yards from the harbour mouth. Over the water from the quay drifted a long drawn out, 'You are *me-e-e-r-r-de*.'

The engine note dropped back to a tick-over, enough to service the pumps. Over the next three-quarters of an hour, a series of thumps and grunts told me that Moran was bringing the packets of drugs up from the cabin and stacking them on deck.

I lay there trying to work out what I was going to do when the ship arrived to transfer the whisky casks and the large consignment of drugs. If it didn't have the draught for this anchorage, Moran would have to move out into deeper water, so it would make sense to slip over the side now when I had a chance of reaching the shore. Another advantage of leaving my hiding place was that if that ship approached on the port side its searchlight would pick me out.

I could, however, think of a very good reason for staying where I was: if the ship approached from the starboard side, I had a chance of escaping detection, and once they'd taken off the cargo and abandoned the sinking boat, I'd have no difficulty in making my way to Granton in the inflatable with the outboard motor attached.

I was still thinking it over when from the north-east I heard the powerful beat of ship's engines, faint but clear, growing louder as the minutes passed. Moran must have heard it too, for the anchor chain rattled, our engines throbbed and we moved further out into deeper water. The ship was approaching on our starboard side. That decided me. I'd stay where I was. That was better than facing hypothermia and drowning on the long swim to shore.

'Hallo-o-o. O-ver he-e-re. . . .' From the triumph and relief in Moran's voice, this was the ship he'd contacted.

The beam of a powerful searchlight shot out, pinning the trawler yacht like an insect to a specimen board.

The tinny voice of a loud-hailer boomed across the silvered expanse of water. 'Are you in trouble, *Island Spirit*?' My hopes rose. This wasn't the ship he'd expected. Moran's welcoming shouts cut off as abruptly as if a door had slammed shut.

In a bid to escape he must have rushed into the wheelhouse, for a few moments later the engines burst into life, the water at the stern foamed and the *Island Spirit* surged forward.

The loudhailer boomed again. 'Revenue and Customs. Heave to for inspection.'

The cavalry had come to the rescue in the shape of the Coastguard cutter that patrols the Firth of Forth. Had one of my torch signals attracted attention? Had the cutter picked us up on its radar, on collision course with the wreck, and come to offer assistance? It didn't matter, they were here.

The *Island Spirit*'s engines roared into full power. Facing as he did the loss of millions of pounds and, more importantly, arrest and life imprisonment, desperation was fooling Moran into thinking that he could outrun a cutter with a top speed far in excess of the *Island Spirit*'s.

I let out a cheer and clung desperately to the rail as the bow lifted and the water creamed past. Then I remembered the damaged bow and realized that water would be flooding in. My elation died. How long before the pumps couldn't cope? A jagged rock flashed by only feet away. His reckless disregard of everything except the urge to escape could only have one outcome. I tightened my hold on the rail till my knuckles whitened. If I was thrown off at this speed, my injuries would be as severe as if I'd fallen from a speeding car.

Spot-lit like a star performer on stage, the *Island Spirit* rushed on. A sudden swerve to port loosened the grip of one hand and I was only saved from being flung through the rails by an equally wild swerve to starboard which sent the stacks of plastic-wrapped packages on deck flying overboard to trail bobbing in the wake.

The engines were still roaring on full throttle, but the *Island Spirit*, now lower in the water, was slowing. Several hundred yards behind and off to starboard, the Cutter had launched a pursuit-inflatable. It zoomed towards us, rearing and bouncing across the waves.

BANG. CRACK.

It was as if the *Island Spirit* had hit a brick wall. The impact hurled me headfirst over the rail into the water and down . . . down . . . down. A lifetime elapsed before I came up gasping and choking, only to almost immediately sink back under the weight of my waterlogged jacket. I flailed to the surface, sucked in a breath and, as the water again closed over my head, tugged frantically at the zip, pulled my arms out of the sleeves and allowed the jacket to fall away.

Plastic-wrapped packages bumped my face, obstructing my view of the *Island Spirit*. Treading water, I pushed them aside. The boat was half-submerged, bow down, evidence that the collision with an underwater rock had dramatically enlarged the previous damage to the hull. As I watched, the trawler-yacht sank lower in the water till the few remaining packages on deck drifted off. I expected to see Moran burst out on deck but there was no sign of him. Water was spilling over the raised threshold and flooding through the open doors into the saloon – and still the doorway remained empty.

The casks of whisky in the saloon hadn't been visible. Now one of them was floating in full view, dislodged from the wedged rows by the impact, an indication that the *Island Spirit* was full of water and about to sink. I was too close. I turned on my back kicking out feebly and waving an arm to attract the crew of the pursuit-inflatable's attention. The roar of its engines died as it throttled back and heaved to.

I became aware of a frantic banging from the wheelhouse of the *Island Spirit*. Body and mind numb with cold, it took me some moments to realize that the noise was Moran battering at the wheelhouse window in a desperate effort to break his way out. Of course. He hadn't appeared on deck because the floating casks had blocked his exit via the saloon. He was trapped.

Bang . . . bang . . . bang. The Perspex starred. *Bang . . . bang . . . bang.* There was a sharp *crack*, and a piece fell out. His face was framed in a hole too small for escape. For an instant his eyes met mine. In them I saw, not fear, but recognition and helpless fury.

A second later, with a gurgle and a swirl of water the bows submerged, the boat slid under the waters of the Firth of Forth and the *Island Spirit* and all it contained was gone.

CHAPTER TWENTY-FIVE

My memories of being fished out of the Forth are a trifle hazy – being hauled aboard the pursuit-inflatable; lying shivering uncontrollably on the duckboards as it sped back to the cutter; attempting to tell them about Gabrielle marooned on Inchkeith in words that were slurred and mainly unintelligible even to my own ears. By the time we reached the cutter, I had difficulty in recalling what else it was that was so important to tell them, but then, it didn't really seem to matter so very much.

I'd expected to leave hospital after a cursory check up, but the diagnosis was moderate hypothermia, which solemn faces assured me could have very serious consequences – such as further cooling of core temperature, post rescue collapse, cold-induced depression of the respiratory centres, cardiac complications, ventricular fibrillation and – at that point I stopped listening. The approved treatment was 'inhalation rewarming' (or 'steam inhalation' to us laymen), but what did more for my recovery than anything else was the knowledge that Gerry was back in charge.

I lay back against the pillows and read his note. *Cat delivered safely by 007. Report to me at 10.30 tomorrow morning after your discharge from hospital.*

Good of him to try to set my mind at rest over G. But I couldn't help being a little worried about her reaction to finding herself suddenly abandoned into the hands of Adam, a stranger. I tried to tell myself she was probably being spoiled rotten by the Galbraiths in Portobello, but still the worry persisted. I'd go to the B&B before I reported to Gerry.

But best laid plans . . . an emergency delayed the doctor's round and I wasn't discharged till 10 a.m. My return to the B&B had to wait.

Frowning, Gerry Burnside slowly turned the pages of the reports on his desk. One of them was mine. The only sounds to break the silence were the rustle of paper and the loud *tick tick* of the wall clock.

I sat nervously on the edge of my chair and tried to gauge his mood. The signs were not good. Apart from, 'Sit down, please', he hadn't spoken since I came into the room assigned as his office for Scotch Mist. He looked tired. I'd heard whispers on the grapevine that things had gone badly wrong with the rescue operation that had called him away.

At last he looked up. 'I'm trying to fathom, to use a nautical metaphor, exactly how an agent on specifically *shore-based* surveillance duty can turn up in the middle of the Firth of Forth in danger of drowning and suffering from hypothermia. Perhaps you can enlighten me.'

'It's all in my report,' I said, trying to look as if I didn't understand why he'd asked that.

'I see.' Elaborately he went through the pantomime of scrutinizing each page, looking for what both he and I knew was not there and never had been. When he judged I'd squirmed enough, he looked up. 'Unfortunately, the first page appears to be missing from the copy I have on my desk. Perhaps you can tell me what's on the missing page.'

'Er. . . .' I said, thinking feverishly how to put the best slant on why I'd omitted that part from my report.

His pen sketched a cat's head. 'Perhaps it will help if I read out what I've got here. Your report starts: *Having located what might possibly be Moran's boat in Granton Harbour, I boarded it with a trained sniffer cat. . . .*' He threw down the report and doodled rays spreading out from the cat's nose. 'Now that cat of yours has already proved what a fine sensitive nose she has. Nevertheless, I find it difficult to comprehend' – a large question mark appeared above the doodled cat's nose – 'how she was able to detect drugs in the cabin of a boat situated . . . how far, would you say, from your base in Portobello?'

Damn him. He knew exactly how far it was, probably to the nearest inch. 'Er . . . not far,' I said.

'Let's agree on five miles as the crow flies or the cat sniffs, shall we?' He passed a hand wearily over his eyes. 'I'm tired. I've been up all night. Don't make me have to drag it out of you.'

'Well, it started with the, er. . . .'

'Assumption?' he supplied.

'Er . . . the *thought* that Louis Moran might not in fact be dead, and if so. . . .' And I told him how I'd tracked down Moran at The Vaults and worked out where the boat might be. 'So you see, it was *reasoning*, not assumption,' I said defensively.

For the first time he smiled. 'I think we can allow *that* kind of assumption. Congratulations, Deborah. Without your input Moran would have tricked us all and made his escape with millions of pounds' worth of drugs and whisky.'

I felt myself redden. 'I can't take all the credit, Gerry. I found Moran and his boat, but he would have got clean away if it hadn't been for the Coastguard cutter appearing on the scene. Can I, er, assume that Adam's message got through?'

'Nope. Assumption wrong. The pilot of an aircraft making its approach to Edinburgh Airport saw your SOS signal, alerted the Coastguard, and their radar picked up a small boat east of Inchkeith in the vicinity of a wreck. They tracked it, assuming *it* had sent out the SOS after holing itself on the wreck.' The corners of his mouth twitched. 'A rare and interesting example of an assumption that is both right *and* wrong.'

'But didn't Adam—?'

'Ah, yes, the resourceful 007. That reminds me that HMRC owes him a fishing rod.' He scribbled a note on a memo pad. 'His message was logged, but no immediate action was taken. Andrew Tyler, it seems, was in central Edinburgh raiding the Queen Street premises of the Scotch Whisky Society.' Gerry's pen sketched a rectangle on the pad. 'Heads will roll.' The pen slashed a line across the rectangle converting it into what looked very like a guillotine. 'Andrew rather unfortunately overlooked the fact that the Society has, not one, but two establishments – one in Queen Street, the other in Leith.'

I adopted a 'Fancy *that*! Tut tut!' expression though the Queen Street premises was news to me too. I thought back to the message I'd left for Attila: what had I *actually* said to him – that Moran was at The Vaults, or merely that he was at the Scotch Whisky Society? I stamped firmly on a twinge of guilt. Attila deserved all he got – he should have called me back to check the exact address.

I shifted uneasily on my chair. Gerry was eyeing me thoughtfully. I should have remembered that he could read me like a book. A quick change of subject was required.

'What's happening about Gabrielle Robillard?' I said, avoiding his eye by pretending to brush a cat hair off my jacket.

He looked as if he was about to say something, then smiled, sorted through the reports and picked one out. 'Ah yes, Gabrielle Robillard. She's lucky you were there. According to the captain of the cutter, you were rambling on about Inchkeith and a woman stranded there. Once they had delivered you to the medic on the cutter they took the inflatable over to investigate and found her. Now she's our guest and we're inviting her to tell us all she knows about Moran and his associates. According to your report, Moran roughed her up and abandoned her on the island, so she might very well co-operate in revenge.'

He gathered the reports into a neat pile. '007 delivered your cat to Portobello as you instructed. I suggest you go back there now and see how she's been getting on without you.' He suppressed a yawn. 'Well, I'm off to bed. Take the rest of the week off to recuperate. Thanks to you, Scotch Mist can be judged a complete success. Report next week for your next assignment.'

That was Gerry's way of telling me that all had been forgiven, if not forgotten.

I pushed open the gate of the B&B. One moment the front garden seemed deserted, the next moment the skirts of the feathery-plumed pampas grass twitched and G's face peered out at me. She made no move to come to greet me. As I'd feared, she felt betrayed. I knelt down in front of her and stroked her head.

'I'm sorry, G,' I murmured.

Five minutes of grovelling later, when I rose to my feet she emerged from the pampas grass, twined herself round my legs as a sign of forgiveness and darted up the path ahead of me.

Tom Galbraith greeted me with barely suppressed excitement. 'You'll never guess! At last we've got a Cat Artwork!' He led the way to the kitchen. 'You were right. A painting like this could hang on the walls of a gallery of modern art.'

He flung open the door and stood aside. I was looking at G's latest oeuvre: black smears and paw print-size blobs on a white background. It brought to mind a simple ink-on-paper drawing by Jackson Pollock.

It was certainly worthy of hanging on a gallery wall. There was only one slight problem: the Galbraiths were now the ecstatic owners of a cat-customized fridge door.

EPILOGUE

In the weeks that followed, I sometimes wondered about the fate of Ms Chang. Had she given Moran and Waddington the slip? Was she now enjoying a luxury life on the far side of the world, smiling as she savoured her clever double-cross of a stupid aristocrat?

I got my answer when a small newspaper cutting arrived in my pigeonhole via HMRC internal mail. Beneath it, Gerry had scrawled, 'Thought you'd be interested in this.' It was from *The Oban Times*.

The body of a woman has been found washed up at Tarbert Bay on the island of Jura. A police spokesman stated that due to the length of time in the water it has not been possible to ascertain the cause of death. The deceased was of Oriental origin and has not been identified at the time of going to press.